Praise for Amy Spalding

Ink Is Thicker Than Water

"Amy Spalding has a knack for capturing the messiness of family in a way that feels as familiar and comforting as a pair of perfectly worn jeans or favorite pair of flip flops. With Ink Is Thicker Than Water, Spalding depicts a blended family with compassion, humor, love, and pitch-perfect authenticity."

—Trish Doller, author of *Where the Stars Still Shine* and *Something Like Normal*

"A hilarious yet moving story about growing up and growing apart. You'll finish reading this book with the characters tattooed on your heart."

—Elizabeth Eulberg, author of *Revenge of the Girl with the Great Personality*

The Reece Malcolm List

"The Reece Malcolm List *is moving and funny; a terrifically satisfying read."*

—Sara Zarr, author of *How to Save a Life*

More praise for Amy Spalding

"Funny and poignant, this lively book totally charmed us."
—Heather Cocks and Jessica Morgan, authors of *Spoiled and Messy*

"Brilliant!...Unique, honest, and quite often flat-out hysterically funny. I laughed, I cried, it was way, WAY better than Cats!"
—Miriam Shor, star of *Hedwig and the Angry Inch* (Original Cast) and *Merrily We Roll Along* (Kennedy Center's Sondheim Celebration)

"Amy Spalding deftly explores family and identity in this charming, heart-warming and thoughtful debut."
—Courtney Summers, author of *Cracked up to Be and Some Girls Are*

"Heartbreaking in the best way, this book is excellent YA contemporary."
—Miranda Kenneally, author of *Catching Jordan* and *Stealing Parker*

"This book has so much warmth and charm that you'll find yourself wanting a second helping."
—CK Kelly Martin, author of *I Know It's Over* and *The Lighter Side of Life and Death*

INK IS THICKER THAN WATER

a novel

Other books by Amy Spalding

The Reece Malcolm List

a novel

AMY SPALDING

Entangled Publishing, LLC
2614 South Timberline Road
Suite 109
Fort Collins, CO 80525
Visit our website at www.entangledpublishing.com.

Edited by Stacy Abrams and Alycia Tornetta
Cover photograph and design by Jessie Weinberg
Cover tattoo design by Mike Erwin

Print ISBN   978-1-62266-040-7
Ebook ISBN   978-1-62266-041-4

Manufactured in the United States of America

First Edition December 2013

To my friend Meghan Deans

CHAPTER ONE

Where are you? I need you. (If you have time.)

I shove my phone into my pocket instead of responding to the very unlike-my-sister text Sara has just sent. My best friend is in emergency mode, and I am best-friending.

"But if what Chelsea heard was *true*, why would he be talking to *her*?" Kaitlyn stares at herself in the bathroom mirror and then spins away from her reflection. "We're not even supposed to *be here*, and if he's just going to talk to *her* all night—"

"No one cares that we're here," I say, even though I have no proof of that fact. I'm not letting Kaitlyn panic. "It's a party. People go to parties. We can be people who go to parties now. Or at least bathrooms of parties."

"Ha, ha." She gets her phone out of her purse and checks it. For what, I don't know, but whatever she's hoping for isn't there. "Seriously, Kellie, what am I supposed to do now?"

Here's the thing: I don't really know. But I will be The

Friend with The Plan. "Probably we should get out of the bathroom. And you should just go walk in his sightline."

"'Walk in his sightline'?"

"Kaitlyn," I say like this is all so obvious and I'm not just making things up as I go. "He supposedly told a bunch of people you were hot. Go be hot in front of him. He'll stop talking to Brandy about whatever popular people bond over. He will make out with you."

Kaitlyn peers even more intensely into the mirror. "You promise?"

If I'm honest, I'll admit that lately I don't exactly love gazing into mirrors where both Kaitlyn and I are reflected back. It's been years since our bodies had first gotten the memo about grown-up things like boobs and hips, but now that we're well into being sixteen, things seemed to have settled, and I guess we're just going to look like this.

That memo circulating in Kaitlyn's hormones must have used lots of references to the magazines she reads (and I don't because Mom thinks they set bad examples and expectations for teenage girls). Kaitlyn emerged from puberty with a tiny waist and the perfect bra size: not flat-chested but not so developed people make up unfounded rumors about her experience level. Meanwhile, my hormones had taken that memo very literally. Boobs, check, hips, check, two of each and all in the right places.

A renaissance painting for Kaitlyn. Artless puberty for me.

Not that I'm Ugly McUggerstein or anything. Up until very recently, it balanced out, because Kaitlyn always had very normal brown hair that just sort of hung there, the way normal hair does. I'm pretty sure my hair's texture had up until my birth only been seen on lions' manes and expensive stuffed animals, but at least Mom dyes it for me. Currently, it's flamey red and combed through with enough vanilla-scented styling product to behave. From enough of a distance, I absolutely look like I have beautiful, flowing, naturally vanilla-scented red hair.

Lately, though, Kaitlyn has been taking the Amex her parents gave her to make up for getting divorced or whatever to a fancy salon where she emerges with sleek caramel-colored hair that rests above her shoulders with a thoughtful little flip. The first time I saw the new style I told her it looked like angels had patted the ends into place with a flap of their wings. Yeah, that was a joke, but it really did look that flawless. No one prepares you for waking up to realize your best friend who grew up with you step by step and side by side is suddenly, okay, hot.

Also, I should clarify that I hate that I hate this. I am not the kind of person who's ever cared about being the hottest or coolest or most congenial or whatever girls are supposed to get hung up over. So having up my hackles because Kaitlyn now ranks above me in these categories isn't exactly a shining achievement for me.

"I promise," I say, even though I know it's dangerous making promises about another person's actions. This one's as safe a bet as you can get, though. Of course Garrett will want to make out with Kaitlyn! I start to open the bathroom door, but my phone buzzes again in my pocket.

It's another text from Sara: *K? Are you there?*

"Go!" I ignore the text, put my hands on Kaitlyn's shoulders, and steer her toward the door. "Conquer!"

"Hang on." She pulls the strap of her (black, lacy) bra

out from her shirt (also black, lacy). "You saw this, right? It's okay? Like, if we get that far?"

"Trust me. Boys will be happy to just see your underwear. I wear frigging boy shorts, and I've had no complaints." I say it so easily by now that it's basically no longer a lie. "Seriously, go do this."

Kaitlyn gives me a hug before flinging open the door of the bathroom. I follow her out, but since I'm only at this party for moral support, I now have nothing to do. I find an open spot on the couch in the living room of whoever's house this is and get my phone back out. *r u ok??* I finally text Sara. *kinda stuck at this party right now.* I don't add that Sara's never not okay because it's probably not nice to make people justify their not-being-okay-ness.

Sara texts back fast: *Sorry about that. I sounded so dramatic! I'm fine.*

This is a Cool Person party, and Kaitlyn and I are definitely not Cool People. I figured I'd be exerting a lot of energy trying to just blend in, but it doesn't actually look any different than any other party I've been to. No one's circling up to take a gulp from the golden chalice of popularity.

"Hey!" Jessie Weinberg, a girl I kind of know from my Literature of an Emerging America class, sits down next to me as I'm texting Sara to make sure she's actually fine. Ticknor Day School isn't big enough not to know everyone— if not by name, at least by face. "I just wanted to tell you that I read your piece and it was *hilarious.*"

"My English paper on Mark Twain?" It does not seem possible for a short biographical assignment to be *hilarious.*

"Oh, no, your thing for the *Ticknor Voice.* I know it's not public yet, but Jennifer couldn't shut up about how funny it was."

"Thanks," I say even though I hadn't been trying to be funny. When I saw the flyers for our school newspaper's op/ed column, it just felt *right*. I've been just fine not caring too much about anything for a long time, but that's starting to feel like it's a size too small for me now. I worked as hard as I could on my submission. But I guess if it's funny, whatever works! "Wait, does that mean I'm going to be the new op/ed writer?"

Jessie makes a face like she's thinking, *awkward!* "I probably shouldn't talk about it."

I make the *awkward!* face, too. This makes her laugh, so I guess whatever's up with the paper isn't too big of a deal. And it's so weird I care. I was convinced not caring too much about stuff kept you sane, but lately this tiny voice in my head says it wouldn't be the worst thing in the world.

…Not a literal voice, of course. I'm trying out for an extracurricular, not developing a second personality.

"Kellie." Kaitlyn runs into the room and yanks me to my feet. "We have to go."

"Hey, Kaitlyn," Jessie says.

"Hi, Jessie," Kaitlyn says, then, "Bye, Jessie," and I'm pulled out of the room and then the front door. "Let's go. Tonight's the worst. Tonight is a *disaster*."

"Okay." I don't ask anything, just get her to my car as she starts crying. We sit there for a while in the darkness, and when my phone buzzes again, I leave it and wait.

"He didn't even say hi to me," Kaitlyn says finally. "And then he started making out with Brandy. Like I wasn't even there or didn't even *matter*."

"He's an idiot, then," I say. "Brandy's pretty, but you're…

pretty. And that whole crowd is made up of idiots. You could do way better."

Now that the silence is broken, I take the opportunity to check my phone. *Yes, I'm sure I'm fine. We're at South City Diner if you want to meet us after your party.*

"Want to meet up with Sara and her friends?" I ask even though I already know the answer and am already turning on the car.

"Help me fix my makeup," she says.

"Your makeup's unfixable! Just go with the badass smeary-eyed look. It works on you."

Kaitlyn laughs and flicks me in the head—*ow*—and hopefully that means stupid Garrett Miller is forgotten for now. And also hopefully the crowd Sara's with at the diner includes her boyfriend and his friends, and Kaitlyn can find a new distraction to get her through the evening.

I drive east on Highway 44 all the way to South Grand, where it feels like I spend as much time as I do in Webster Groves, the suburb of St. Louis where we live. Parking can be crowded, especially on weekends, but I'm so used to the side streets that I zip around and slide into a spot on Hartford almost immediately. When we walk in, the diner's so packed I can't even spot Sara, but Kaitlyn does and pulls me over to the table crowded with, yes, Sara, Sara's boyfriend Dexter, and a bunch of other guys.

"Good evening, ladies," Dexter says, affecting an old-timey accent. "How is this beautiful Saturday treating you and yours?"

Sara and I tell each other almost everything, but we don't really talk about guys—who knows why—and so that was only one of the reasons I was surprised when she started going out with Dexter. Wasn't my perfect pre-prelaw sister way too serious for stuff like boys and dating when she was studying her butt off and worrying about college applications? And if I *had* been forced into describing the kind of guy Sara would end up with, I would not have said *redheaded hipster hottie*. But then all of a sudden, Dexter was a thing.

Dexter is a senior at the all-boys school Chaminade, where he wears his uniform tie slightly askew and heads up both the Young Democrats Club and the Poetry in Action Club, the latter of which he'd also founded. (No one really seems to know what Poetry in Action actually *is*. Poetry seems like a pretty passive activity. Sometimes Dexter recites Yeats really loud and in public. Is that it?)

Anyway, I guess it works because they *are* serious, about each other and about the stuff in their lives. They study together and talk nonstop about college and go to lectures and museums and foreign films. Even when Dexter's doing goofy accents or shouting poetry at the stars, Sara looks at him like it all makes sense to her. The lesson I take from this is that love is finding someone who thinks everything about you that's weird is actually hot.

"Make room for Kellie and Kaitlyn," Sara says, and the guy on her other side jumps at her command by shoving in two chairs for us. Kaitlyn's immediately eyeing the other prospects, but I stare Sara down until she notices.

"What's up with you?" she asks like she didn't send me two emergency-ish texts less than an hour ago.

"You're sure you're okay?"

"Don't I look okay?" she asks with a smile. And *of course* she does, because Sara is basically two steps shy of a supermodel. Tall and blond and the kind of cheekbones that people comment on. Four separate times people have asked Sara if they saw her in a Macy's ad. (No, but that seems like a pretty good compliment.)

"We can talk later if you want," I say even though that's the kind of thing she says to me and never vice versa. Sara's only a year older than me, but she's got it *together*.

"Sure." She turns her attention back to Dexter, who's in the midst of some elaborate story about a fight he witnessed between two stray cats. Kaitlyn's talking with the guy on her other side, so I finally glance all the way around our table.

Across from me, sitting just a few people down—like it's *normal!*—is Oliver.

Oliver! Dexter's brother. Who knows a lot about me. Who knows things I don't want anyone else knowing. Who I hoped would have found a way to text me even though I'd never given him my number and even though the thought made me a little terrified.

Oliver.

He raises his eyebrows at me and grins. And I don't know what I'm doing any more than I did back in May when everything happened—or, well, didn't happen. But I can't help it. I grin back.

CHAPTER TWO

My plans the next morning are the usual: brunch with Mom, my stepdad Russell, Sara, and Finn. Since the shop's closed on Sundays, it's Family Day, and I'm completely fine with that. I guess now plans also include replaying in my head every time Oliver grinned or raised his eyebrows at me last night (seven total, by my count).

Still, I'm looking forward to brunch. Seeing Oliver last night made me so jumpy I was afraid to eat and just stole some fries from someone else's plate. But when I walk downstairs expecting pancakes and eggs or at least bagels, what I see instead is *Dad*.

"There she is!" he says. It's the only way he ever greets me, like I'm a contestant on the game show in his mind. "Hey there, kiddo."

I figure if he's doling out normal salutation-type stuff, probably no one is dead or maimed or whatever tragic event would bring him here. "Hey, Dad."

"Hi, baby." Mom pops into the front room, right next to Dad, and I try for the ten billionth time to comprehend that they'd ever been married. Photos *and my own memories* tell me they were, but it still feels like fabricated history, a novel based on actual events and not the nonfiction it is.

It's a casual day for Dad, which means he's in shiny black dress shoes and perfectly pressed black slacks, with a gray shirt and a patterned blue tie that pops exactly how all the fashion magazines say a tie is supposed to. It's a casual day for Mom, too; she's wearing ragged jeans with a black sweater of Russell's that features a little skull and crossbones on each shoulder. Since she's inside, her feet are bare, chipped red manicure showing as well as the black line drawings of flowers tattooed across the tops of both her feet.

"How was your Saturday night?" Mom asks.

"It was fine. Is everything okay?"

"Everything's fine." Dad kisses my cheek, smelling— like always—of coffee and the spearmint gum he chews obsessively since he quit smoking when I was nine. "In fact, I'm on my way out. See you this weekend."

When I was little, I'd cling to him whenever we said good-bye, but now it's just life. "Bye, Dad."

He leaves, which is for the best because I always worry the universe will explode if he spends much time in this house. Well, the universe or Mom's brain, and I don't see myself surviving either one of those catastrophes.

"Why was Dad here?"

"It's nothing," she says as Finn barrels into the room wearing Mom's black leather jacket, which hangs past his knees, and a black ski mask covering his face.

"I'm a pirate!" he shouts.

"No, you're a ninja," I tell him. Finn always gets those confused. "Also ninjas don't shout. You have to be super sneaky."

He nods solemnly before racing up the stairs and letting out some kind of war cry. Well, I tried.

Even Mom says I'm biased, but I'm positive Finn is the cutest kid in the world. I've seen hundreds of photos of myself, and I definitely didn't hold a candle. His hair is sandy brown like Russell's, he got Mom's perfect little upturned nose (which genetics conveniently didn't give to me), and big blue eyes (I'd at least gotten those), and when he smiles he somehow looks just like Mom and Russell at once. Total cute overload.

"What happened to brunch?" I ask Mom as she sorts through the mail on the front table even though nothing new could have come today. Mom might be sort of old— she just turned forty-three—but she's the kind of lady you totally believe when you hear she'd once been a cheerleader. Still blond, still smiles all the time, still pulls off a high ponytail, still, you know...cheers for things. With Mom, no achievement is too small for hugs and congrats. (And she can still turn a pretty mean cartwheel, if you beg.)

"What? Oh, right, sure. Russell's out picking something up." She turns back to the mail like it's urgent when in reality it piles up there constantly.

I run upstairs and down the hall to Sara's room, where Finn is jumping on the bed while she's curled up on one corner of it doing homework. From here it looks like physics, but considering I'm three levels of science behind her, I'm probably not the best judge. Still. Physics on a Sunday morning.

Sara is really good with numbers. Honestly, she's good at everything, but numbers especially. Normally when people say things like that they just mean someone's good at math, but the point is that she's good at something useful. When we moved into the big house down the street from the old house, Sara knew how many boxes each room would take. It probably doesn't sound that exciting, nothing like knowing how many jelly beans are in a giant jar and then winning a prize, but way more useful.

I'm not good at many things that are useful, a fact Mom *delights* in telling me. It's not that she's disappointed—no, her parents had always told her the same thing, which she bought into for a long time. She says, "Kellie, baby, I bought into that, can you believe it?" and I actually can't. No matter how many times she tells the story, I can't believe Mom trained to be a paralegal and went to work every day in a jacket and skirt and the scary flesh-tone pantyhose with tasteful pumps, until the day she realized she was miserable. "I ripped myself free of a nylon hose existence," she likes to say, which I thought was a figurative saying until the day we were packing to move into the new house and Mom actually found the torn pair of hose. Mom hangs on to the weirdest stuff.

So, anyway, I've been carrying on family tradition. Well, *Mom* traditions, at least. Dad gets this concerned look on his face whenever he sees one of my report cards. He's a lawyer—that's how he and Mom met, one billion years ago—and he thinks grades are a window into our futures. "Kellie, you want to get into a good college, don't you?"

Good colleges all want Sara already, two months into her senior year. I remind Dad of this, that I'm only a junior and therefore who would be courting me yet? Unfortunately, he has a better memory than I do and points out that a year ago Sara was already being wooed by universities from east to west.

Obviously, Sara is Dad's favorite. And while I really should have had a shot at being Mom's favorite, she spends loads of time detailing how she loves all of us exactly the same amount. My only hope is that maybe she's lying to spare Sara's and Finn's feelings.

Oh, right, Finn. Since he's only four, we don't know if he's going to make Mom proud by being as unskilled at useful things as me. So far his big interests are zebras, kaleidoscopes, and this stupid singing fish Mom let him pick out at a garage sale, so all signs point to yes.

I haven't admitted to anyone that the more often I think about Sara away at college with her clear path in front of her, the less delight I take in feeling *useless*. When I think about how long it took Mom to shift her life into the place she actually wanted—or to even *know* what she wanted—well, I love Mom, of course, but I don't want that for me. And that's some of what I would have said if I'd answered the "Why do you want to join the *Ticknor Voice*?" essay question a little more honestly.

I sit down next to Sara. "What's up with Mom?"

She waves an arm at me like I'm a bug to shoo. Not so easy, sister. "Today or in general?"

"Today," I say. "What's up with brunch? And why was Dad here?"

"Who knows?" she says. "Do you mind taking Finn? I need some time alone."

"Come on, ninja." I catch Finn mid-jump and cart him

into the hallway instead of interrogating Sara. Anyway, it would have concerned me more if she wasn't always needing time alone. (Though, maybe Dad would be less freaked out about my grades if I occasionally did my homework without simultaneously pointing out differences between ninjas and pirates.)

I head back downstairs because if brunch is on the way, I might as well be nearby. Our house isn't that big compared to the others on our block of Summit Avenue, but the kitchen and dining room probably outsize everyone else's. When Mom and Russell bought the house, I remember Mom marching Sara and me in here with her hands on our shoulders and declaring this kitchen was going to see the best of us. Mom had been crazy-dreamy-eyed back then, between her engagement and the house purchase, but I think that actually turned out to be true. Even on cloudy days, the golden walls, packed with picture frames painted in every color imaginable holding images of our family, make everything seem sunny.

"Look, look!" Finn runs into the dining room while I'm lining up knives with spoons on the red-topped retro aluminum table. "Kellie, look!"

I finish positioning the knife and turn my head to see that Finn has placed his ski mask over the head of his favorite stuffed zebra. "Oh, awesome, Marvin's a ninja, too."

"Yeah, awesome. Can me and Marvin help?"

Helping means that most of the silverware ends up on the floor. "I'm okay, Finn, you and Marvin can just hang out with me."

Russell walks into the house with a huge bag I'm pretty sure is from his favorite vegan café in Maplewood. I honestly love eating with my family and I rarely mind getting up early, but there are days when I wish my stepdad would eat just one animal. I understand ethics and all, but animals can be so tasty.

"I got some of those scones you like," Russell tells me.

I know it's a bribe so I won't mind eating vegan, but the scones *are* delicious, so it works. And I swipe a piece of fake bacon (facon?) as Russell's putting everything onto the table—okay, also delicious—which prompts a glare from Mom. "What? It's a tiny piece."

"We eat as a family, you know that. Finn, sweetie, go get Sara."

Finn pulls his ski mask back on before bolting upstairs.

Mom walks to the refrigerator to get orange juice and milk, of the real and of the soy varieties. "How was your Saturday night?"

"You asked me that already."

"Did I?"

Finn leaps back into the room, sliding a few inches across the coppery orange tile in his monkey-print-stocking feet. "Sara's not hungry."

Whoa, that never flies. Mom and Russell totally believe that the 1950s-everyone-sitting-down-together family dinner is a cornerstone of a civilized society.

"More for us, then. Kellie, help me carry in the rest of this."

As if Dad's presence in the house wasn't weird enough. Now Sara is allowed to skip brunch like we're one of those uncaring families Mom likes to lecture us we'll turn into if we don't spend enough quality time together? "Mom? Is everything okay?"

"Everything's fine, Kell-belle. You know what we should

do soon?" Mom asks as the four of us sit down at the table. "Your hair. Yeah?"

"You have some big plan?"

"When don't I have a big plan?" Mom never has a plan. Mom just has a lot of impulse buys from the beauty supply shop down the street, where they never check to see if she actually has whatever license you're supposed to be in possession of.

"Hmm, maybe."

She ruffles my hair and grabs my face in her hands. Her rings are cold on my cheeks. "I love you, Kellie baby."

We're a pretty mushy family, but this is a lot even for us. I don't have that much more time to wonder if something is up, though, because soon Finn is yelling that he loves us, too, and I am really hungry, animal products or not.

I text Kaitlyn after we eat to see if she's surviving, post-Garrett-making-out-with-Brandy. I'm honestly not really expecting a response, since Kaitlyn likes to sleep in, but my phone beeps almost right away.

Except it's not Kaitlyn.

It's a text from *him*. I don't know how he got my number (though, I'd bet big money on Dexter, if the source of text messages was the kind of thing people gambled on), but it's the most obvious thing in the world that it's from him.

Good seeing you last night. Is the fish still singing?

It sounds dirty, but the day Oliver and I met, he'd brought up those nightmare-inducing dancing and singing Santas, which had directly led into a conversation about Finn's stupid singing fish and my burning desire to follow its orders and take it to the river. And frigging drown it.

So I know what it means, but I also don't know what it

means.

Sara's the one I go to for all advice, but I've let that stop where guys are concerned. Probably by now I should have cultivated the kind of relationship with her where we talked about sex or dating or at least guys in general, but I'm just about positive the way to start that shouldn't be, *hey, this one time I almost did your boyfriend's brother.*

And Oliver isn't just *her boyfriend's brother.* Oliver is...well, he's Oliver! He's in college, and he cares about philosophy, and he isn't flashy about things like Dexter is, but I know he got great grades in high school, too. Oliver is *somebody.* I'm still kind of hanging out hoping my somebodyness kicks in soon. So if I admit to Sara what happened all those months ago, how is she going to take that? I've had my whole life to get used to being the average to her stellar, but Sara's the one person who's never actually called that out. What if me professing my true and completely dorky feelings for Oliver finally brings that out of her? Ugh, I can't stand thinking it.

Anyway, even if we were incredibly open about guy stuff, like girls in a yogurt commercial, Sara clearly isn't in Advice-Giving mode if she is in Skipping-Brunch mode. And I might be the younger sister and I might not be the one who's got it *together*, but with big, important life stuff, I want to seem like I know what I'm doing.

Especially when I really, really don't.

So instead of begging for advice, I help Mom with laundry and watch cartoons with Finn and sort of do my homework and pretend—even if maybe something is up with my family—that Oliver's text isn't the only actual thing on my mind.

CHAPTER THREE

Ticknor Day School is not exactly an imposing institution of learning. Sara goes to a different, far more normal school across town, and of course even if I'd never been there, I do watch enough TV to know high schools generally look just a couple steps up from, I don't know, asylums. Just with fewer padded walls. Harsh lighting and bright white walls and forced school spirit.

I, on the other hand, step into a mural-covered corridor every morning. The hallways are organized by color and painted accordingly, up to and including the lockers, and spare wall space is crowded with flyers and posters and announcements galore. It is amazingly current, too. Today I notice the drama club's announcements (all right, technically the Ticknor Day Thespian Brigade) have been swapped out with bright red and white posters asking anyone over eighteen to donate blood. As I turn out of the orange wing to the blue one, where my locker resides, it looks like the Fourth of July.

Kaitlyn's waiting for me, like usual. "Sorry I didn't text you back yesterday. I just slept a lot and tried to forget all boys exist."

I lean past her into my locker. "*All* boys? Even Channing Tatum?"

"Duh, no, of course not him. He's still on my good side."

"You look fancy," I say, because she does, a skirt instead of jeans and a lacy cream-colored shirt that looks like the demure version of the top she wore to Saturday night's party. "Do you have to go somewhere after school?"

"Some of us just care about how we look, you know."

I figure that might be a comment on my jeans and faux-vintage mod symbol T-shirt, but I let it go. Really I *don't* care very much about how I look, at least at school.

For a split second, I think of asking her what I should do about Oliver's text, but in order to get that advice, I'd have to tell a bunch of truths that are pretty inconvenient. Or at least embarrassing. "Did you get anywhere with your geometry?"

"Here." She hands me her notebook. "But look at how I did the work, don't just copy."

Of course I'm just going to copy, even though I promise her otherwise. "Thanks. So I was thinking this weekend we could—"

"Hey, Kellie." My English teacher, Jennifer, walks up to us, bearing this huge grin. That's right, *Jennifer*. Our hippie school thinks forcing kids to address their teachers by prefix and last name creates an unfair power dynamic, so we're all on a first-name basis here. Jennifer's the kind of person who's always trying way too hard. No one has ever been that happy to see *anyone* unless it was someone returning to his great love post-wartime. "Do you have a few minutes before class?

I'd love to talk to you."

I assume this has something to do with the paper and my potential as their new op/ed writer. So even though I would rather spend my last minutes of morning freedom talking to Kaitlyn, I follow Jennifer farther down the blue wing to her classroom.

"Kellie, I wanted to congratulate you," she says, and I feel myself grinning even though I'd told myself not to care about this too much. "We got a lot of applications, but the editor and I thought yours was one of the most impressive."

"I'm the new op/ed writer," I say like I'm telling myself. I still have to figure out the least dorky way to do this thing, after all.

"Well...not exactly." She laughs and riffles through the stack of papers on her desk. "Your take on cafeteria selections, well, your style is perfect for us. But not for the op/ed column. We actually already chose a new op/ed writer, so we've decided we're going to add a humor column to the *Ticknor Voice*. It'll be the same kind of topics explored in the op/ed column, but with a funnier angle. And you are the perfect writer for it."

"Um, thanks." I can't believe I'm getting called something so impressive as a writer based off of a goofy piece about the quality of chicken nuggets and fruit cocktail. I also can't believe that my life is changing and I've actually achieved something, and all I could think to say was *um, thanks*. I smile just short of maniacally so Jennifer will know my feelings run deeper.

"Our next meeting's tomorrow, right after school. See you then."

"I'll actually see you in five minutes," I say. "In class. But, yeah, I'll be here tomorrow."

I duck out of the room so I can finish getting my stuff out of my locker, and when I head back into Jennifer's classroom, it hits me that I'm still smiling.

Mom texts me around lunchtime to go straight to the shop after school. According to the *Ticknor Day School Guidebook*, we aren't supposed to have our phones on at all during the day, but every time I've gotten caught, I showed whatever teacher had spotted me that every single new message was from Mom and were all like, *Please pick up Finn on your way home* or, *Can you please buy vegan hot dogs after school?* or even, *I love you, Kellie baby!!* and then whichever school official would just smile and say something cheesy about The American Family and Its Beauty, and I'd be off the hook.

So once my last class is dismissed (just like colleges, we don't believe in bells at Ticknor), I drive to South Grand. I love living in Webster, with its storybook houses and hatred of chain stores and the cute college boys bicycling everywhere who I always pray go to the university down the street and not the seminary next to it. But despite Webster's many charms, it just can't compete with South Grand.

I find parking right around the corner from the shop. The breeze shifts as I walk up to Grand Avenue, bringing with it a rush of aroma from Sara's favorite Thai place. Always dangerous to walk in this neighborhood on an empty stomach. There are restaurants and markets representing just about every country in Asia, my favorite diner in the world, and Italian so yummy you don't even mind waiting forever to be seated.

I walk past the antique shop, where one of the owners spots me through the window and gives me a wave. I wave back before letting myself in Mom and Russell's shop, The Family Ink.

"Hey, Kellie." Jimmy, who works the front desk and cleans the shop and does all of the boring work no one else wants to do, grins as I walk in. Jimmy looks like a rock god from the 1980s, with black hair that grows wild. He's always clad in T-shirts from concerts that are as old as I am. "How's eleventh grade going?"

Jimmy is always so proud he knows what grade I'm in. Like that isn't weird.

"It's fine," I say. "How's your band?"

Jimmy is, of course, in this band that covers heavy metal hits, and even Mom and Russell can't figure out if it's ironic or not.

"Going good, yeah. We got a gig next weekend, but it's twenty-one and up, so I can't put you on the list."

"It's okay. Well, Mom wanted to see me, so…" I make my way to Mom's station, where she's engrossed in inking a naked Bettie Page on a guy's bicep. "Hey."

"Hi, baby," she says without looking up. "I'm almost finished, then I thought we could walk down and get coffee."

"Crap, don't let her see this," the guy says, as if I haven't seen hundreds of naked Bettie Pages by now. She's probably the person I've seen naked the most times, next to myself.

"I don't think there's anything about a naked woman that's going to shock her." Mom sits back for a moment and smiles up at me. "How was school?"

"I'm on the school newspaper. It's a long story," I say, even though it isn't.

"I didn't know you were interested in journalism." She leans back over the nearly completed tattoo, the buzz of the machine only slightly drowning out her words as she presses it to Bettie's butt, shading to bring out her curves.

"I'm really not. It's a humor column. And, like I said, it's a long story." The guy is glancing up at me still, so I figure he didn't imagine this moment, whatever symbolism the naked pin-up girl means to him, in such a literal family way. So I give them some space and take a seat in the waiting area on the plush red sofa. Two of the front walls (painted the same sunny color as our kitchen because the leftover paint took up space in our storage shed forever) are covered with framed sheets of predesigned tattoo ideas. I can't imagine being so boring you'd just walk in and point to something on a wall that hundreds of people have already gotten. The other wall holds framed articles and awards for the shop, and a big photo of the five of us where Finn's arms are covered with temporary tattoos.

A girl who looks like she's my age at most but must be at least eighteen, considering how strict Mom and Russell are about the law, and also how savvy they are about fake IDs, sits across from me. She drums the fingers of one hand on the arm of the couch to the beat of the old-school punk playing overhead, while she grasps a piece of paper tightly.

I figure she might have a nervous breakdown if she sits here alone in her own world of fear any longer. "What are you getting?"

She holds out the paper, and I examine the hand-drawn

flowers looped together in crisp black ink. "Do you think they're stupid?" she asks.

"No, it's a good design. Did you do it?"

She nods. "Does it hurt a lot? I keep hearing that people faint."

"I don't have any," I say. "But my mom says the only people who ever faint are dudes. Women are built for childbirth and cramps, so you'll be fine. Who's doing yours?"

The girl digs through her purse for her appointment card. "Russell."

"Russell's awesome," I say, as the Bettie Page–inked guy walks out, his arm wrapped in plastic, just in front of Mom. "Good luck."

Mom and I walk outside, and she hugs me tightly and kisses my forehead. "You're always so good with our clients."

I shrug, because being friendly to other humans seems like a no-brainer. Ooh, but— "Maybe I could work the front counter, then. Jimmy probably needs some nights and weekends off to focus on his Mötley Crüe covers."

"I'm sure you'd be great, Kell-belle, but you don't need to worry about a job."

"I'm not *worried* about one, I just want one." I've been brainstorming to come up with the perfect job, one where I wouldn't have to work too hard and I'd still not only make a lot of money but meet interesting people. This will totally do. "And I'm hanging out there so much, couldn't I at least be useful to you?"

"You can't be useful without getting paid?" Mom laughs, and I know the subject—and my hopes—have been shot down.

We take off down the cracked sidewalk back the way I'd

just come. I rush to keep up with Mom, who always moves like she's in a hurry. We walk all the way to the coffee shop across from the park, which we would have done regardless, but it's nice on an October afternoon still warm enough we don't need jackets. I'm not one of those people who hates winter. What's not to love? There's crisp air and snowflakes and random days off school and Christmas. Complaining about any of that is like complaining about, I don't know, love or free money or cuddly puppies. Still, it's impossible not to love the fall.

"Are you hungry?" Mom asks as we walk inside. When I was younger, Mokabe's was totally a hole-in-the-wall kind of place, but now it's two levels to easily fit all the people sitting around doing whatever people do in coffee shops: working on their laptops, playing games, and talking. Things have only changed *so* much though, because the décor is still kind of rag-tag/whatever must have been on hand, and the space behind the register remains practically wallpapered with bumper stickers that call for peace and equality and a bunch of other concepts I think are no-brainers but I guess are radical ideas to some. "We could split the quesadillas."

"Hey, Melanie," the cashier greets Mom. "Your usual?"

Mom has a usual everywhere we go.

"Thanks, Bonnie. That, an order of quesadillas, and whatever Kellie wants."

I just want water, which I nearly drop because as Bonnie hands it to me, everything comes together: Dad at the house yesterday, Sara allowed to skip a meal, meeting Mom right after school. *Something* is going on.

"Mom?" I ask, feeling small and afraid. And I *hate* feeling either one of those things. "Is everything—"

"Let's sit down." She takes her dirty soy chai—which she claims is delicious but sounds too gross for me to even sample—and leads me through the noisy first floor to a table upstairs, alone, away from every other customer. Way to scare the crap out of me, Mom.

"You know Sara turned eighteen last month," she says, which blows me away with its obviousness.

"I know how old my own sister is, Mom."

"Eighteen is pretty significant for Sara."

"Because she can smoke and vote? Won't that be significant for me, too?"

"*Because* her adoption records are no longer sealed."

A guy brings out our quesadillas right as Mom says it, and must have been listening in because he scurries off with this guilty-he'd-heard-too-much look on his face.

"Is that bad?" I ask, because I really don't know. It was never this big deal that Sara was adopted and I wasn't. Doctors told Mom and Dad there was a one-in-a-million chance they'd have a baby the old-fashioned way (not that I want to think about that), and instead of spending lots of money to beat the odds, they called a bunch of adoption agencies and ended up with Sara. I was the one-in-a-million baby who showed up a year later.

"No, it's not bad." Mom takes a piece of the quesadillas, dips it in sour cream, makes this big show of taking a huge bite. "Heaven, huh?"

"Mom, shut up about food, this is huge." I realize I only think it's a big deal. Maybe she's just being really dramatic. "I mean, is it?"

"Sara's biological mother called Clay yesterday."

I never tell her that it bugs me, but it bugs me that Mom

calls him that when almost everyone in Dad's life goes with Clayton. Mom had valid reasons for divorcing him and starting this whole new life, but that should have meant lost privileges. Wait, why am I thinking about something so random? "Seriously? She can just do that?"

"Well, baby, he's in the phone book," she says before helping herself to another piece. "You know if you don't join in, I'm just going to eat this all on my own."

"I don't care. What did she want? Is she taking Sara back?"

"It doesn't work like that. She just wants to meet Sara, that's all."

I try to picture her, as I'd done before, but considering Sara is tall like Dad and has honey-blond hair like Mom, I can't. "Is Sara going to?"

"That's up to your sister to decide. We aren't putting pressure on her either way. I'm only telling you because, as you know, I don't believe in family secrets. So tell me everything about the school paper."

"What's there to tell? It's a school paper, what could be exciting about that?"

"Any paper with my daughter on staff is exciting." Cheerleader Mom strikes again.

"God, Mom, this Sara stuff is a big deal," I say. "I don't want to talk about the stupid *Ticknor Voice*. So would you meet her? If you were Sara?"

Mom rests her hand on my arm. "This is her business, and I'm not going to sit here speculating with you. If there's more she wants to tell you, she will."

I imagine there are families where boundaries aren't respected and gossip is encouraged, and the truth is that more than once in a while I wish we were one of them.

"I have a four thirty." Mom looks at the time displayed on her phone. "So I should get back. But I'll be home right after that, okay?"

I shrug. "Yeah, sure. Is Sara picking up Finn from daycare?"

"Russell's done after this appointment, so he'll get him on his way home. We thought Sara could use some time to herself."

Mom walks me to my car and kisses my forehead and sends me home. When I get there, Sara is on the porch swing, flipping through a flagged and Post-It-ed copy of *Crime and Punishment*. She's still wearing her school uniform, which means her long legs are hanging off the swing with only her plaid skirt keeping things modest.

Mom is really into letting us develop as our own people, so we were allowed to research and choose which high school we'd attend. We aren't Catholic, but Sara liked the discipline and the curriculum and the lack of distraction thanks to the lack of guys at Nerinx Hall. I wish I could say that I appreciated the nontraditional ideals of Ticknor, but my reasoning for choosing it had less to do with that and much more to do with Kaitlyn's parents picking it for her. And, really, I might not let my brain go completely crazy over guys, but I didn't want to spend four years without them, either.

I plunk down next to Sara, pulling my feet up and hugging my arms around my knees. Of course I want to mention her biological mother, but I manage to hold it back. "I'm joining the school newspaper."

"Doing what?" she asks.

"A humor column," I say.

"People always seem to have fun working on our paper, so I'm sure yours is the same," she says. "And you'll be really good at that. Your Mark Twain paper I proofread was *really funny*."

Wait, so that *was* possible?

"Don't tell Dad, but maybe he's right about putting something on my college applications," I say. "Ugh, that's dorky."

"If *that's* dorky, what am I?"

"Um, a hot dork. I thought you knew that already."

Sara grins. "I'll take that. So, you'll be happy. I broke down and talked to Mom and Russell after all about Parents' Night."

"About—" I catch myself before bringing up her biological mother as I realize what she's talking about. "So they're going?"

"Yes. At least it's my senior year and the last one." Sara watches me for a moment. "Don't say it."

"I'm not saying anything! I just don't think they're embarrassing."

"You don't know what it's like, with everyone staring." Sara shakes her head. "I know over at Ticknor you probably earn cred for bringing our middle-aged punk rock parents—"

I don't want to yell at Sara on a day when she's actually dealing with more than being perfect in a weirdo family. "Totally, I've got cred written all over me. Is Dad coming, too?"

"He always does."

Dad rarely goes to mine because he says they aren't a huge priority. I can't believe Sara's are vastly different, except that at Nerinx Hall I imagine teachers gush about Sara's grades and attitude and extracurriculars and therefore, make Dad feel good about himself.

"Do you think if Mom and Dad were still married that I'd even be allowed to go to Ticknor?" I ask.

"Who knows? Dad's still paying most of your tuition," Sara says. "And that's such a big *if* my brain can hardly handle it."

"Seriously." I was only six and Sara seven when Dad calmly packed a bunch of bags and took up residence in a hotel by his office in Clayton (yes, Dad worked in a city named the same thing as himself). I'd hated that Dad was gone; he'd felt so far away at first. Still it wasn't a huge trauma, probably because neither of them acted like one had gone down. Mom was happy to be free, and Dad's not really into emotions outside of victory (court cases, Sara's report cards and plaques and trophies) and disappointment (other court cases, me). I didn't even know I was supposed to be that upset until Mom sent us to therapy and the therapist brought it up.

Dad didn't change at all when it happened, except that he lived farther away. Mom, on the other hand, donated all of her old work clothes to Goodwill, signed up for a bunch of art classes, and began an apprenticeship at Iron Age, the most famous tattoo shop in the city. When we stayed with Dad, he assured us it was temporary, but back at home Mom was smiling more than ever before. By the time the tattoos began blossoming over her peaches and cream skin, I knew Dad was never moving back.

"Still," I say. "I'm glad I'm not at Nerinx. I hate uniforms, and I'd miss guys."

"It's not impossible to meet guys just because you attend

an all-girls school." Sara only says things like this because of Dexter, but I make a little note of it anyway because maybe we're only a step away from talking about Oliver after all. Today's not the day to push it, though.

Sara opens up *Crime and Punishment*. "Sorry for being antisocial again, but I really need to get through this."

"Accurate title at least." I walk inside and up to my room. When Mom and Russell had bought the house, they'd given Sara and me two options: one giant, beautiful room to share, or two smaller rooms that would never feel spacious. Even though we sometimes still fall asleep in each other's rooms, we'd picked privacy. What good is space when half of it isn't really yours?

Of course Sara's room is neat and orderly. She'd chosen tan walls and modern furniture that's all dark wood and clean lines, just like classy people on TV shows have. It's actually left over from the guestroom at the big house one town over in Kirkwood we lived in before the divorce. We'd both had big rooms then.

My New Year's Day tradition is painting my walls, which means that my room has been grass green for more than ten months now. I'm sick of it anyway, but ever since Kaitlyn informed me it's Oprah's favorite color, I've been itching to change it. Still, traditions are traditions. My room is clean, because Mom demands it, but my books aren't on my shelf alphabetically. I change what's on my walls too often to frame any of it, so the clean green space is littered with thumbtack holes. At night they look a lot like constellations.

I turn on my laptop and tell myself I'm going to do some homework, but really, I just message some people on Facebook and investigate Oliver's profile. (I feel better checking it periodically to make sure his status is still "it's complicated" with "counterculture movements.")

"Kell?" Sara leans into my room, her overnight bag on her shoulder. I slam my laptop shut at lightning speed. "I'm going to Dad's for the night. I just have a lot of studying, and once Finn's home…"

"Yeahhh. I'll let Mom and Russell know."

"Thanks." She pushes her hair back from her face, and I have to admit those cheekbones are definitely not of our genetics. "So…I was going to talk to you…"

I look up at Sara and give her my full attention.

"Mom said she was going to…tell you what was going on?"

"Yes!" I say. Whoa, self, take your reaction down a few notches. "Yeah, Mom mentioned everything to me. Just, you know…"

"'No family secrets,'" we say in unison.

"What are you going to do?" I ask. "If you want to tell me. You can keep it private if you want, of course."

She pulls a ponytail holder out of her pocket and winds it around her hair, getting it perfect and smooth on her first attempt. I need a mirror, a brush, and a comb, and still I generally look a little like an escaped lunatic until about the third try.

"I don't know," she says.

That's it?

"Are you okay?" Was this, I want to ask but don't, what made you text me on Saturday night when you never need me like that? Is this big and scary or new and exciting? Can it be all of those things at once?

"Of course. I'm fine." Sara waves. "See you soon."

I think about blurting out something about Oliver, to keep her there longer *and* to find out if there were rules for things like this. But I can feel that it's not only a scary move but right now a selfish one, so I just let her go.

Russell is home before too long, with Finn and a bunch of grocery bags. Our routine is always the same: Russell, who's six-foot-three, puts away anything that goes in the tall shelves, and I take care of everything else.

I still remember every detail of meeting Russell, how he'd joined us at the pizza place that used to be Sara and my favorite, even though there was nothing on the menu he could eat except salad without dressing. Back then the tattoos covering his skinny arms scared me, and the one on his bicep spelling out the name Chrystina particularly offended me. How was he going to be a good boyfriend for my mom if he'd committed some other lady's name to his body forever? A year or so later, when Mom told me they were getting married, I'd thrown that at her like maybe it could stop it. *If he's so good to you, why does his arm still say 'Chrystina'?* It was stupid because by then I did know he was good to her, saw how he came over and helped out with chores even though he had his own place across town, helped Sara and me with homework.

Chrystina was his daughter, Mom had said in this angry tone I'd never heard from her before or since. *She was killed in a car accident the week before her fifth birthday. And this is not a democracy, Kellie Louise Brooks. This decision is mine and mine alone.*

I was so ashamed of forcing Mom to use that voice that I'd hid in my room until the next morning. In the meantime I'd made her a homemade congratulations card. When I thought about handing it to her, though, I knew I'd remember yelling about the Chrystina tattoo, remember her yelling back, and instead of presenting the card to Mom, I ripped it into at least fifty pieces. There wouldn't be any mementos of that night.

"Baked eggplant tonight, Kellie, what do you think?" Russell asks.

Vegan cheese is pretty gross, but I act excited so that Finn will be, too. "Do you need any help?"

"Help? You should be doing your homework or calling your friends," he says. "You got enough time to have responsibilities like dinner when you grow up."

"Isn't homework responsibility?"

"Got me there. Your mom said you're joining the school paper. Sounds cool."

"It doesn't *sound cool*," I say. "If I went to accounting school, Mom would think it was cool. Mom thinks the fact that I breathe oxygen and let out carbon dioxide is — "

"Oh, yeah, tough break in life having a mom who thinks like that." He grins at me. "Congrats, really. I think it's cool, too."

"So what do you think of the whole thing with Sara?" I ask. Since Mom isn't home yet, maybe gossip is safe. Russell could go either way with it. "Do you think she's going to meet her?"

"Sara's a tough one to call," he says. "Couldn't say one way or another."

"You're no help."

He laughs his deep, booming laugh, which makes Finn giggle. Finn apparently thinks his dad's laugh is the funniest thing ever invented. Being four seems like a pretty good gig.

"This is Sara's thing," Russell says, obviously way too much under Mom's influence. "Let her figure this one out on her own."

CHAPTER FOUR

"You know what I heard people are doing?"

I slap Kaitlyn's hand away as she attempts to switch the radio station from oldies. When I'd gotten the old T-Bird from Russell's mom, Ginger had left the radio on the oldies station, and I'd realized I never really wanted to change it. There's something about old music, and old movies, too, that just suits me better. Stuff today seems so slick and assembled by marketing teams or whatever. I like things that are just what they are.

"What are people doing?" I ask. Kaitlyn's car is in the shop so I'm driving her to school today.

"Going over the river. There's some club there that doesn't check IDs." The last three words are said in this exuberant hush, like we'd entered the church of underage drinking.

"Why do you care about that?" I'm not trying to sound snotty; I just genuinely don't get it.

"What do you mean, why? It's what people do."

"What people?" I ask. "Garrett?"

"No, Josie Hayes and Lora Benning were telling me about it in French class." She shrugs a little. "I just thought it could be fun."

"Good for them," is all I say. But I sound like a jerk so I smile. "I could never get away with driving to Illinois and sneaking into some club. If my parents found out…"

Somehow it sounds better to have dorky parents than admit that the mere thought of this illicit activity has me refraining like heck from rolling my eyes. I was fine with Kaitlyn figuratively drooling all over Garrett, given that he has good hair and a great butt and always smells like an Abercrombie and Fitch store. But emulating that whole crowd is another story.

"Kellie, God, you wouldn't *ask* your parents. We just say we're going somewhere else." Kaitlyn sighs. "Sorry. I just thought you'd be into it. And everyone's been, like, *so* understanding about Garrett, you know? It'd be fun to hang out with them this weekend."

"You should go with Josie and Lora, then." I try to sound really enthusiastic about this suggestion, even though Josie and Lora are the kinds of girls who used to laugh at us — and probably still do — because even safely ensconced in the hippie-dippy walls of Ticknor, people can be terrible to one another. Hopefully, Kait will remember that before this weekend. Watching her cry over Garrett was bad enough.

"Never mind. It's really not a big deal," Kaitlyn says, thank God. Maybe her sanity has been restored.

When I get to class, Jennifer is caught up in conversation with Adelaide Johansson, one of those genius kids who seems to spend more time talking to teachers than fellow students, probably because she has the name of an ancient person, so the coast seems clear to look at Oliver's message. Again. Maybe the two-billionth reading will be illuminating.

"Kellie, phone away."

Grrrr, caught. I make a big show of turning it off (read: clicking it to silent) and tossing it into my purse. This is about the safest place to do anything against school policy; Jennifer is so eager for our approval she isn't about to turn into the bad guy.

"You remember about the meeting tonight, don't you?"

"Of course," I say even though once again my brain is too crowded with thoughts of Oliver's lips on my cheek, my neck, my mouth, and other places to have much room left for the school paper.

"I'm glad you're joining." Adelaide turns to face me from the desk in front of mine. I only sit behind her because she's five-foot-even, and so seeing notes on the board is never an issue. "I really like your style. Most people struggle with that balance of irreverent and intelligent, but you nailed it."

I sort of nod, because, okay, I'm not like Kaitlyn and ready to move closer to the world of people like Lora and Josie, but let's be real. In another universe, sure, Adelaide would definitely be in the popular crowd, and actually, back in grade school she was. She's tiny and blond with a seemingly endless supply of new clothes—qualities that, once you hit middle school, won't save you if you're also a crazy overachiever. Adelaide is always collecting signatures for petitions or raising her hand in class to answer questions with way too much knowledge or hanging posters in the hallway to stop world hunger and pollution and abuse and lots of things. Of course I'm against that stuff, too, but come on. Sure, I want to do more than I'd been doing, but if the newspaper is going to force me to associate with this brand of person, well, I might need a little more time to warm up. You probably have to become an achiever before you can be casual with overachievers.

At lunch I'm vaguely listening to the guys at my table describing whatever movie they saw last night that involved someone's face getting *punched off* when Kaitlyn drops into the chair next to me.

"I was just talking to Jessie Weinberg," Kaitlyn says. "I guess she used to be super close with Brandy, so she totally has an inside scoop. I should have talked to her on Saturday instead of running out."

"You were upset," I say. "You were fine running out. And we had more fun at the diner anyway."

Kaitlyn kind of cocks her head at me. "We had more fun watching your sister's boyfriends' friends have a toast-eating contest than I would have if I'd gotten anywhere with Garrett?"

I guess she has me there, but I still feel like just a couple of months ago a night out with Sara and crew would have ranked up there on really good nights for both of us. Of course I wanted Kaitlyn to find true love or at least a hot guy to make out with, but not at the expense of who she was. Not at the expense of who *we* were as friends.

"After school we could go hang out at Java Joint," I say. "We can fully discuss this without anyone around."

"Sure." Kaitlyn jumps up with her wallet in hand. "Want anything while I'm up?"

"No, I brought a sandwich, and crap, I actually can't go out after school today, and I can't take you home.

I have this thing I need to do." I can't admit to her in this specific moment that it's the paper, that I am going to be in the company of the overachievers it seems we've at least indirectly tried to avoid being. But luckily she shrugs and accepts *this thing I need to do* as an acceptable excuse before walking off.

"I heard you're joining the paper." My friend Mitchell chomps on the cold pizza he brings for lunch nearly every day. It makes me wonder how his girlfriend Chelsea can stand to kiss him.

"From where? That's the lamest gossip ever."

Chelsea giggles at Mitchell. For some reason, he still answers seriously. "Adelaide. She was going on and on about your submission."

"Are you on the paper?" I ask, and Mitchell nods. Maybe that makes me seem like a bad friend. Should I know everyone's extracurriculars? I guess I figured most of us didn't have any. Ticknor is a pretty safe place not to have to try too hard, if you don't want to.

"I'm the photo editor," he says. "Chels is one of the photographers. It's pretty cool, actually. You're gonna like it."

I didn't know about that, but at least I'd have people to hang out with.

"Weird," Chelsea murmurs, and I follow her sightline through our open courtyard to see Kaitlyn in line for a salad with Lora and Josie.

"Oh, Kait's friends with them now," I say like it's no big deal at all. "I guess she's expanding her circle of acquaintances to include even the most heinous among us. She's in line for the Nobel Peace Prize."

Everyone laughs, and normal conversation resumes.

Except now I don't feel much like joining in.

By the time the school day ends, I'm so ready to start my new life as A Writer, that when I walk into Jennifer's classroom, I can't even be bothered to pretend I don't see Adelaide when she starts yammering at me about new staff member initiation.

Though, really—initiation? What have I gotten myself into?

"Hey, Kell." Mitchell waves and points toward the open desk to his right, as if there are more than eight people in the room and I would have a tricky time figuring out where to sit.

"Is there really an initiation?" I ask, my voice as quiet as I can make it. Maybe it's genetics or maybe it's just growing up in a house with Mom as an example, but while most people have an indoor voice and an outdoor voice, I on the other hand have an outdoor voice and a stadium voice.

"Of course there's an initiation." Adelaide walks over from her spot at Jennifer's desk and hands me a roll of toilet paper. "Go on, take some."

What kinds of things does the newspaper staff actually do together? Suddenly I am kind of scared, and not just of becoming classified as a full-on geek. "I'd rather not."

"Adelaide, don't frighten our new members," Jennifer says as she walks into the room. "Kellie, don't look so horrified. I promise it has nothing to do with anything that's sprung to mind so far."

While that doesn't exactly settle me, I pull off a wad of toilet paper and hand the roll to Adelaide, who bounds back up to Jennifer's desk to deposit it in a drawer, her bright red skirt bouncing like a cartoon.

Being the new one in a room of kids who actually care

about being here when they all have to know I'm someone who just got lucky and normally struggles to keep up a B average is awkward enough. Now the room fills while I sit there holding a clump of Cottonelle.

"Maybe you should put that down." Mitchell gives me a wide smile I'm 90 percent sure is what made Chelsea fall for him. Despite his cold-pizza habit, Mitchell is pretty cute. "You look like you're getting ready to—"

"Shut up." But I laugh.

"Okay, now that everyone's here, I want to introduce Kellie Brooks, who's writing our new humor column," Jennifer says. "As for the toilet paper, Kellie, you have to tell us something about yourself for each square you took."

I'm a certified over-user of toilet paper, actually; one of my most humiliating memories is that, two days after Russell had moved in with us officially, everyone had been out of the house but us and I'd completely clogged the toilet. Nothing makes you and your new stepdad bond like watching him plunge the toilet in your bathroom. So I guess habit is the only way to explain why there are literally twenty-two sheets of toilet paper wadded up on my desktop.

"I don't think there are twenty-two things to say about me."

"We all had to do it," Mitchell says.

I shoot dagger-looks at Chelsea because she never warned me her boyfriend is a complete traitor.

It is probably the lamest list anyone has ever offered up, especially considering these kids are all Academic Achievers (what Ticknor calls their honor roll) and driven, and I'd landed in this slot in what Mom would have called a lark. Also I'm writing a humor column, and that's a lot of pressure. But I actually get laughter when I start with *Number one: my first name is Kellie. Number two: my middle name is Louise. Number three: my last name is Brooks. Number four: yes, the "Louise Brooks" thing was on purpose, because number five: my mom thought I'd appreciate being sort of named after one of the most glamorous women of all time in her opinion.* Jennifer takes that opportunity to pull up a picture of Louise Brooks on her computer and project it on the wall, so everyone will know what the heck I'm talking about. And kids sort of ooh at her beauty, which makes me strangely proud.

By the time I hit number eleven (*I spend a lot of time teaching my little brother the difference between pirates and ninjas*), I'm sort of enjoying this. Nobody looks annoyed with me, there is a lot of laughter (and you can tell it's that whole laughing *with* me, not *at* me thing), and the truth is I'm sort of disappointed after number twenty-two (*In five and a half years, I will be twenty-two myself*, which, let's face it, isn't even very funny) that I can't keep going. I mean, I thought I was funny all the time, but this is the first time I've subjected a roomful of people who aren't family to my big mouth. And this side of me—probably the same one that applied to newspaper in the first place—really likes it.

Adelaide is the editor-in-chief (of course), so once I'm through with basically what boiled down to an ode to myself, she marches to the front of the room with at least twelve times the authority Jennifer ever effuses. "Story ideas, who's got 'em?"

I definitely do not, so I keep my mouth shut. I sort of thought everyone else would, too, but this isn't like a typical English class. *Everyone* is yelling out stuff about scholarships and the lack of sports teams and SATs and the new green policy (I look guiltily at my stack of toilet paper sheets), until it hits me that Adelaide has written every writer's name on the board with his or her story next to it and every photographer's name next to an assignment. KELLY B just sits there alone.

"Kellie? Thoughts?"

"You spelled my name wrong," I say, which does make everyone laugh, but also makes me a big jerk. "No, sorry, I don't know. I've never done this before."

"You don't have *any* ideas?" I guess me not brimming with thoughts like she undoubtedly did constantly is to be pitied. Maybe it is, to genius kids like these, but I'm lucky to have a good one every once in a while. And I'd hoped that'd be enough to do this. "We'll talk more afterward, okay?"

I don't like the sound of that, but after she gets through the rest of business, I do hang around while most of the other writers file out. "Um, sorry I didn't—"

"Hang on." She pushes past me to lean over a guy's shoulder while he's messing around with the layout on some technical-looking computer program. "Be sure to add Kellie to the masthead, and be sure to get her name spelled right, okay?"

He grunts in agreement, and Adelaide's attention is back on me. "Why don't you spend tonight thinking about topics and drop me an email later? I'm sure you'll get better at thinking on the fly soon."

I shrug but accept the business card she takes out of her purse. Who has their own *business cards*?

"My mom says cards are great for networking," Adelaide says with—if I'm not completely off target—maybe a little eye-roll at herself.

I glance down at the card in my hand.

ADELAIDE JOHANSSON
THE TICKNOR VOICE, EDITOR-IN-CHIEF
ST. LOUIS YOUNG FEMINISTS, FOUNDER
Blogger: www.adelaide-doesnt-lament.com
Contact: adelaide@stlyoungfeminists.com or 314.555.9472

Okay, I guess there's a reason Adelaide has these. Besides networking. I still think she's an overachiever extraordinaire. The overachievers all seemed to be having fun today, though, and it was cool—well, a milder form of cool, I guess—seeing a roomful of people my own age getting real things done with barely any help or guidance from Jennifer. So considering that, and that Kaitlyn is suddenly maybe drawn to the kind of people and activities we both used to hate, right now there seem to be a lot of fates worse than overachieving.

CHAPTER FIVE

When I get home after newspaper, Sara and Finn are hanging out in the living room, reading Finn's favorite book about a friendly gang of monkeys. I'm not sure today was actually that weird, but I still feel relief at seeing such a familiar scene.

"Hey, Finn, can you read by yourself for a few minutes?" Sara asks him. He agrees, and Sara pulls me into the hallway where we can still keep an eye on him but kind of have privacy. We've had lots of conversations right here for that reason.

"What's up?" I ask.

Sara takes a deep breath. "I'm meeting her."

"Oh my God, seriously?" I ask. "I mean, obviously seriously, sorry. When?"

"Tonight. Which is crazy, I know. She asked when, and for some reason I said tonight, and she said that was fine, and... now it's happening." Sara shakes her head. "I can't believe I *talked* to her. We had this very normal conversation."

"That's good," I say. "That means meeting her will be fine."

"I hope so."

"I'll go with you," I say, which is stupid because Sara is older and braver and smarter than me. "If you want."

"Thanks, but I'll be okay."

"Do you want me to text you a few minutes after you get there? I know on TV when they do that it's on blind dates, but maybe you'd feel better? If it's super awkward, you can say I'm dying and leave."

"Okay, sure." She pats my hand, a total Mom move. "I should start getting ready. Do you mind watching Finn?"

Of course I never do, so I pick up where she left off in the monkey saga until Mom's home. Sara hasn't emerged from her room, so I head up to check on her. It's not that Sara has ever really needed me, but since I've needed her a billion times for help with homework, rides the year she could drive and I couldn't, and venting sessions about Dad, I owe her.

I knock on her door, and she leans out, still clad in her uniform. "I have no idea what I should wear. Nothing's right for this."

"You should consult a guide," I say. "*How to Impress Your—*"

"Stop being funny," she says with an edge to her voice. Of course Sara and I fight sometimes, because that's how it goes with anyone you spend a lot of forced time with, but this edge is something new. It feels cold and dangerous, like the expensive knives we're not allowed to use unless Mom or Russell's around. "Unless you have an actual suggestion, I'd rather be alone right now."

I don't have an actual suggestion, but I do want to help, edge or not. So I riffle through her closet while trying to look like I am in possession of A Plan. Mom fakes knowing what she's doing all the time, so this should be in my blood.

"Sorry for snapping," she says. "I'm just—"

Just that fast the danger is gone and the metaphorical knife is back in its metaphorical drawer. "I would be, too. It's okay."

I reach the brown dress Mom found at the vintage shop down the street from The Family Ink and just knew would look perfect on Sara. Of course Mom was right, not that it's tough dressing a tall, thin, with just enough boobs and hips to still qualify for *hourglass figure* status girl.

Sara slips into the dress and surveys herself in her mirror for only a moment before taking her brown flats out of their place in her shoe cubby. "Yeah? This is good?"

"You look great."

"You always think I look great; you don't count." But she smiles, just slightly, enough to catch from her reflection in her mirror. "Who knows what she's going to think?"

"She'll think you're awesome," I say, because how couldn't she?

Sara hugs me, and then we both laugh because Mom's the mushy one, never us. "I'll see you later, Kell."

"Don't forget, I'll text you."

She's out of her room and into the hallway already. "Sure." She races down the stairs and sort of sidesteps Mom, who is waiting in the front room. "I have to go now. If there's traffic—"

"I just wanted to wish you good luck, sweetie." Mom kisses Sara's forehead, no mean feat given that Sara is four inches taller than both Mom and me. "I'm so proud of you."

"Mom," Sara says in a strained voice. "Don't be proud for this. See you later."

Sara lets herself out, and I try to pretend I haven't been spying on them. The jig is up when Finn runs into the room wearing a Superman cape with a Spider-Man mask and barrels right at me.

"You are one confused superhero," I say.

"I'm hungry."

"Me, too," I say with a look to Mom.

"Let's just order pizza," she says. "Kell-belle, call for the regular, would you?"

I do, one supreme and one veggie-no-cheese-vegan-crust, and sit down at the kitchen table with my homework. Mostly I think about Sara and her biological mother as well as a possible topic for my newspaper piece. Of course the former is endlessly more interesting than the latter. I can't believe that before today I didn't spend more time thinking about this woman who'd given my sister life. Your family is who you come home to, sure, but does that mean it isn't anyone else, either?

A few minutes later, I remember my promise to text Sara and send it right away (*here's ur excuse if u need it! i have the plague! also consumption!*). That's bad because there I am, worrying on my sister's behalf and stressing out on my own, and holding the phone with Oliver's message. By now I've probably read *Good seeing you Friday. Is the fish still singing?* three hundred times. And so that's my excuse for how it happens. I can't be held accountable for hitting reply, typing, *unfortunately it is. i'd put a hit out on it, but i can't break my brother's heart.* I almost hit send, but stop. Not to delete (would have probably been the smart move) but to add, *how r u??* (Definitely the dumb move.)

And send.

"I forgot to ask." Mom takes the chair across from me. "How was your first newspaper meeting?"

"I don't know if I'm smart enough to be there."

"Kellie, baby—"

"Well, not *smart enough*, exactly. Like the right kind of smart, I guess is what I mean. Mom, seriously, you should see how fast these other kids think. They've got millions of ideas, and I just wrote this goofy paper my teacher liked. I figured I'd be okay not fitting in with all the overachievers, but ugh, now I actually sort of want to be there, and I'm afraid they'll fire me."

"They take self-esteem really seriously at Ticknor," Mom says with a smile. Our smiles are exactly the same; I've always liked that. Why didn't I realize sooner that maybe Sara wanted to see her smile somewhere else, too? "Even if they want to, they won't fire you."

"Shut up." But I laugh as my phone beeps. "It's probably Sara. I did the whole thing where I texted her so if it's awkward she can say it's an emergency and leave."

"I don't know how you could ever doubt that you're smart enough when you come up with good plans like that all the time."

I roll my eyes and then totally drop my phone when I see that the message isn't from Sara at all, but Oliver. *Good, classes are killer. You should call me.*

Call him? That's a big step. I'm barely out of texting territory with anyone. I could just *call him*? Hear his voice over the phone? And he *wants that*? Am I ready for this? Is this another thing I want to be ready for but I'm not? Why am I asking myself so many questions?

"Is she all right?" Mom's voice is immediately in Good Mom Mode. She picks up my phone, since I'd flung it in her direction, and I can't move quickly enough to stop her. "Who's Oliver?"

I literally leap across the table, getting a salt shaker to the hip, and grab it from her. "No one."

Mom gives me this grin that's new to be directed at me as she carefully sweeps up the spilled salt with her hands. I've seen it before, though, always in the context of Sara and Dexter. "Oliver McAuley?"

"I have homework. Call me down when the pizza gets here." I shove my phone in my pocket and run up to my room, taking the steps two at a time. Instead of following instinct number one and texting Sara again to make sure she was okay or following instinct number two and replying to Oliver—or even *calling him*—I get out my computer and stare at a blank Word document. There has to be at least one idea in me, doesn't there?

The blank page is still glaring at me when Mom calls me for dinner, and I say a little prayer as I run downstairs that she won't bring up Oliver in front of Russell and Finn. Or, really, at all.

"How did your newspaper meeting go?" Russell asks as I sit down.

"I'm not sure I'm right for it, no matter what she says," I reply with a look to Mom that I hope will ward off her knee-jerk defenses of me.

"Don't say things like that, Kellie." Mom cuts some of the vegan pizza into smaller slices for Finn. Poor kid being brought up to think it is perfectly acceptable for pizza to lack cheese.

"Buddy, I think you should take that off before you try to eat," Russell says to Finn, but none of us can wrestle the mask off his face, which means within minutes the Spider-Man mask is covered with pizza sauce. Before Finn was born, a lot of stuff grossed me out, but having a little kid around means you get immune to all sorts of grossness at the dinner table and elsewhere.

I sort of figure by the time we're cleaning up from dinner (Mom and I take the kitchen duties while Russell takes Finn upstairs for a bath), Sara would be home. From the way Mom keeps peeking through the red curtains framing the window above the kitchen sink, I guess she does, too. "What do you think it'll be like? For Sara?"

Mom sort of shrugs as she goes on with loading the dishwasher. "Your sister's one of the bravest people I know. If anyone could get through this without trauma…"

"It's true. But does it hurt your feelings?"

Mom looks over her shoulder at me. "Why would it, Kell-belle?"

"I don't know…you're her mom. Maybe it would feel weird that she has…not another mom, exactly, just…"

"I love that you're always looking out for all of us," Mom tells me. "But, no. I've always felt so grateful I was given this opportunity to be Sara's mom. Don't get me wrong, I feel that way about you and Finn, too, though it's slightly different. Obviously, I've always known she and Sara might reach out to each other at some point, and I wanted that for Sara if she did, too."

"You're a good mom," I say without really thinking. Of

course she gets all teary-eyed and hugs me, and I tell her she can experiment with my hair because it's the only thing I can think to do for her.

"I forgot to check my phone," I say as Mom uses a little brush to paint streaks in my hair. "What if Sara texted back?" *What if Oliver texted again? What if he called and his voice is on my voice mail?*

"Want me to get it for you, sweetie?"

I do, but there aren't any messages when Mom brings it to me. "I hope she's okay," I say.

"I'm sure she is." Mom dabs on a bit more color before stepping back and studying me. "Let it sit for a half-hour, then rinse, then tell me what you think."

"I'll set a timer," I say. "I should try to work on my newspaper thing. Or some of my other homework."

"Good girl." She kisses my cheek and pushes me to the doorway. "I'll clean up here. Let me see your hair when it's dry, okay?"

I get through most of my homework (though I'll have to request help from Sara on my Fundamentals of Geometry) while texting Chelsea and Mitchell, before rinsing my hair. For once Mom's lack of planning leads to something pretty amazing. She's deepened my natural blond hair but made it lighten toward the ends. It makes me look less like one of those girls who's trying really hard to be different and more like I maybe just am.

Unfortunately, even with awesome hair and a backpackful of (mostly) completed homework, I still am at a loss for a column idea. I take my laptop and Adelaide's business card to bed with me to type up a fast email.

TO: adelaide@stlyoungfeminists.com
FROM: kellbelle@familyink.com
SUBJECT: sorry

Adelaide,
I've been brainstorming all of tonight and can't think of ANYTHING to write about. Can you just run my cafeteria paper this week?
Kellie Brooks

After hitting send I decide to check Oliver's profile just to verify that his status is still silly and pretentious and adorable (it is), and I am about to turn off my computer when a reply pops up in my inbox from Adelaide.

TO: kellbelle@familyink.com
FROM: adelaide@stlyoungfeminists.com
SUBJECT: RE: sorry

Kellie,
There's no need for melodramatics. Let's spend some time brainstorming together tomorrow. I have volunteering right after school, but I'll be free by seven. Can you meet me then at Mokabe's for coffee? Bring your laptop (if you have one, notepad will do if you don't) and AN OPEN MIND.
AMJ

I don't like any of this, from spending my evening basically doing schoolwork with someone I really don't want to be seen in public with—even if that makes me a little bit of a jerk—to that scary command. But I do want to get better at this part. So I respond with a yes before turning off my computer and setting it on the floor next to my bed.

My eyes are only shut for a few minutes when a light tapping sounds at my door. I try ignoring it. Mom will just be happy I'm asleep at a reasonable hour.

"Kellie?"

"Sara." I bolt straight up. "You're home?"

She creeps into my room. "Yes, I'm home, dork. Move over."

I scoot to one side of my bed as she gets under the covers on the other side. "Are you okay?"

"She's *amazing*." Sara's eyes are big in this way that doesn't happen often to people who are so smart. It's tough awing them. "She's *a physicist*, Kellie."

"Like a doctor?"

"No, not a physician. She's a scientist."

"'We are not children here,'" I quote. "'We are scientists!'"

"Are you finished?"

I feel like a jerk for being unable to keep any moment truly serious. "Sorry. And of course she's a genius like you. Do you look alike?"

"A little. She's not as tall, and her hair's darker, but you can see the resemblance. Definitely. She showed me a picture of my...my biological father. He's really tall and blond, so that makes sense." She elbows me. "And I'm not a genius."

"Mmm hmmm, genius, sure. So is she young? Like a lot younger than Mom and Russell and Dad?"

"She isn't really that much younger than Mom. She was twenty-one when I was born. But she was a senior in college and already was accepted into grad school, so it wasn't a time for her to have a baby."

"Right," I say. "Is she still with your...him?"

"They broke up before I was born, but they're still friends. He lives in San Francisco now; he founded a digital startup. Camille—Camille's her name—gave me his email address so I can talk to him. If I want."

"Are you going to?"

"I think so. Yeah."

"Was it scary?"

Sara's silent for a few minutes but in that way where I can tell her brain is working, so I stay silent, too. "I guess so. A little."

"Did you—"

"If it's okay, I don't know how much I want to talk about right now," she says. "You know how sometimes, right after something happens, it's like it's so new you don't have words for it yet?"

I want to say no, but the truth is I've never spoken one real word about Oliver to anyone. And obviously that whole thing is different from what's going on with Sara, but I could connect it enough not to push her. "Yeah."

Sara watches me for a moment before turning on the lamp on my nightstand. "Did Mom do your hair?"

"Yup, another Melanie Stone slightly sketchy creation." I wait to hear how I should start going to a professional salon, which perhaps is true.

"It looks really good. I guess Mom's got a backup plan if she ever gets sick of tattooing," she says. "Well, I should probably get some sleep."

"I know it's late, but…could you help me with geometry?"

Sara sighs a big, dramatic sigh, which is how she always leads up to agreeing. "Of course. You should have said something earlier."

"Earlier you were getting ready for your life to change! I couldn't bug you with stupid theorems."

"You can always bug me with theorems."

We get out my textbook, and Sara guides me through the assigned problems. If Barry, my geometry teacher, explained things so well, I wouldn't need Sara. But there's something I love about sitting up with my sister at midnight.

Even if it's for frigging *math*.

After we get through the whole assignment, Sara switches my light back off and walks to the door. "I should get some rest."

"I'm really glad it went so well for you, Sara."

Even in the darkness I see her beam at me. "Thanks, Kell. Me, too."

Chapter Six

I spend the next day at school on full alert for any Kaitlyn changes. When she gets up at lunch to buy her usual salad, Chelsea and I watch her like hawks, if hawks were creepy little stalkers. But nothing's out of the ordinary. If Lora and Josie are pulling her into their gravitational field, it's not happening when I'm orbiting, or whatever correctly completes that scientific metaphor.

"What are we doing this weekend?" Kaitlyn asks when I get to my car after school. Her Jetta's still in the shop, so I'm still her chauffeur.

"It's only Wednesday," I say. "Can we think about the weekend when the weekend is actually happening?"

She laughs and messes with the radio station dial. "Don't hit me. Can we have just one time in your car without a sixties invasion?"

"Fine, fine." I pull out of the parking lot and down the street toward Kaitlyn's house. I start to tell her something about Oliver, since now that we're texting, it feels like maybe something more is going to happen, but I just can't get the words out of my mouth or the image of her talking excitedly with girls I've seen be *so mean* for no reason at all out of my head.

And, anyway, I like having thoughts of Oliver basically all to myself. (I'll pretend the only other person who knows something's going on isn't *my mother*, since that kind of ruins it being some kind of sexy secret.)

"Your hair looks amazing, I meant to mention earlier," Kaitlyn says. "Your mom?"

"Yeah, and thanks. She did better than usual this time."

"Imagine how cute you'd look if you wore a shirt without a hole in it," she says, and I start to get offended, but the truth is that I bought this T-shirt from a vintage shop in University City, and it does have a tiny hole where the right sleeve connects to the rest of the shirt.

After dropping Kaitlyn off, I head to The Family Ink, since I need to be in the neighborhood anyway. The shop is pretty slow, so I do my homework while sitting with Mom as she works on designs. She lets Jimmy go home early, so I keep an eye on the door like if I seem attentive enough, I still have a chance at getting a job here. The next time the door opens, I jump up and walk to the front desk. It isn't a customer, though; it's Adelaide.

"What time is it? Am I late?"

"I'm early, and I figured I could find you here."

"Hi, there." Mom jumps up and smiles at Adelaide. "We've met, haven't we?"

"You did my boyfriend's tattoo," Adelaide says. "The passage from *The Fellowship of the Ring*, if you remember."

"Oh man." Russell grins up at her. "I wanted to do that one so bad, love those books. Mel's better at text, though, couldn't steal it from her."

"It still looks great," Adelaide says. "Byron loves it so much."

"I loved doing it," Mom says. "Kellie, have a good time, baby. Be home by ten, okay?"

I'm allotted three full hours with Adelaide *plus* time to get home? "Fine."

I get my laptop bag and my backpack from the back room and follow Adelaide outside and down the sidewalk. Her black Mary Jane heels click the entire way; it sounds like some invisible grown-up is chasing us.

"How did you know I'd be at the shop?" I ask, the first thing I can think to say. For as all-powerful as Adelaide is during classes or newspaper, she's almost annoyingly quiet now. I really doubt, despite our theoretical differences in social status at school (am I really *that* less geeky than Adelaide?), that she wants anything more to do with me than I do with her.

"I assumed you would be. You mentioned the other day you spent a lot of time at your mom's shop, and I figured out from your email address what the shop was."

"Oh. So your boyfriend got a tattoo from my mom?" It's an even dumber question than the first. Clearly this matter has already been cleared up.

"It's in her portfolio, so I'm sure you've seen it."

"Mom's done a lot of text work," I say. "Maybe."

"It's the only quote from *Fellowship of the Ring*, I'm sure."

I decide not to mention that I don't read nerd. "Then I

guess I've seen it. Where does your boyfriend go to school?"

"Wash U," she says, which is the nickname for Washington University, the most smarty-pants school in town. Of course she dates someone from there. "Do you want coffee? My treat. My parents give me tons of cash for no reason."

Coffee feels like a thing I'm not mature enough for yet, but I let her buy me a hot cocoa. She orders one of those crazy drinks, a two-percent Tahitian-vanilla half-caf four-shot bone-dry cappuccino. I could never work at a coffee shop because orders like that make me roll my eyes more than a little.

"So this shouldn't be too hard," Adelaide says once we've collected our drinks and settled in a booth upstairs. "Let's come up with five to ten things you've been thinking about Ticknor lately, and—"

"Listen, I'm not like you. I know you're really passionate about all this stuff, but that's just not me. This whole thing was a mistake, Jennifer shouldn't have—"

"So were you 'really passionate'—" Oh my God she is actually using air quotes—"about cafeteria food? Or the Mark Twain paper Jennifer let me read? Or did you just write good pieces?"

Okay, so she has me there. But I'm kind of sick of talking about it already. "So where were you volunteering tonight?"

"Planned Parenthood," she says. "Five to ten things, Kellie."

"Maybe this comes easy for you, but I haven't been working on a paper. I don't just think in lists."

"Fair." Adelaide takes out her computer. "You want to do this, though, right?"

"Definitely." It's weird saying it out loud to her, for different reasons than I've avoided telling everyone else. I'm not worried Adelaide will think it's weird I suddenly care about stuff; I'm worried Adelaide thinks my wanting to do this isn't the greatest of ideas. "I thought it could be fun, but I'm just not sure I can be good at it."

"You just have to get used to thinking in a different way."

"Hey, Kellie," says a very familiar voice.

I look up with a start and promptly knock my hot cocoa all over my laptop. Adelaide and Oliver spring into Laptop Protection Mode, Oliver hoisting it into the air and Adelaide producing a bunch of napkins with which to contain the spill. How did I go five months without seeing Oliver at all and then randomly run into him twice in less than a week?

"Looks like it's okay." He takes a napkin from Adelaide and dabs at the keys. "Mine's survived worse."

"Hi," Adelaide says to him. "We met at the protest downtown the other week, remember?"

"Yeah, my friend sent me a link to your story on it, too, nicely done." He isn't watching Adelaide, though; he is watching me. "You look busy."

"We're brainstorming," Adelaide says.

Is this what qualifies as a cock-block?

"I wouldn't dare interrupt that," he says. "But I'll be here for a while; stop by my table if you finish up. Cool?"

I nod, wondering what the rules are for someone you once completely rejected in such a stupid, embarrassing way. Can you still kiss him? Five months later?

Adelaide watches me as Oliver walks back to the table he's sharing with a few guys and girls. "What's up with you guys?"

"Nothing."

"Right," she says. "Okay, back to work."

"Five ideas and I'm talking to him."

Adelaide agrees, and it's sad what a motivator that is. But maybe it's more than that, because by the time I mention the new No Laptops Policy, I also think about the dress code changes, the unending rumors of school uniforms (even though obviously none of the administration at Ticknor will ever squash our individuality or self-esteem that way), my suspicion that the focus on a supportive, noncompetitive environment will land us all in college with too many hippie ideals and not enough real-world skills, and the whole fertilizer situation. I probably could have thought of even more ideas, unbelievably, but I've technically fulfilled my obligations for the night. Time to stop by Oliver's table.

"This is a good start," Adelaide says. It's nice to hear. "See you tomorrow."

"See you." I pack up my laptop and hesitate for only a moment. Oliver watches me as I make my way over, but unlike the day we met, when his intentions were so clear and readable, I have no idea what he's feeling right now. "Hey."

"Hey." He gets up, waves to his group. "See you guys later."

I didn't mean for him to leave his friends or for us to leave completely, but I sort of tag along with him until we're outside. "Do you come here a lot?"

"Are you hitting on me?" He laughs, to my horror. "'Come here often?' 'What's a nice boy like you doing in a place like this?'"

Oh, we're joking around. "'Your place or mine?'" That is really the first thing that flies out of my mouth? What is *wrong* with me?

"I thought about calling you." He shoves his hands in his pockets, leans back against the brick building. Lanky guys leaning is something I don't really get sick of looking at. "But I didn't know how you'd feel about—"

"I was in a weird place that night," I say, not because I actually had been, but it seems like the kind of thing normal mature people in relationships say. I probably got it from some premium-cable show. "I'm sorry if I—"

"*I'm* sorry if I…" He looks up from the ground, grins as he runs a hand through his slightly shaggy red hair. Even though he and Dexter look nearly like twins, their smiles aren't alike at all. Dexter's is often too broad or too mischievous to be genuine, but Oliver's radiates nothing but. His brown eyes are calm as if nothing could shake him, and when I look into them, I feel like their calming power extends to me. Whether or not it's a good thing, I find it hard not to trust him. "We should hang out again. I actually was about to head out, got a paper due tomorrow and I'm still a few hundred words short. You need a ride?"

I shake my head. "I'm parked just down there." Jerk my thumb back to indicate. Oliver takes it as a hint, and maybe subconsciously it was one, so he walks me over, and right before I'm about to get in, he's right there. He leans in, his breath warm on my face in the cool evening, and I know we're going to kiss again.

It's weird to me how it's natural and not at all at once. My feet automatically go into tiptoe mode (Oliver must be over six feet tall), and my body leans into him, but also his chin bumps my face and our hands knock into each other's as we try to cling or grope or whatever is going to happen right here in the tiny not-dark-enough parking lot behind The Family Ink. *The ocean,* I think. Gentle, warm, pulling me in, dragging me under. *Kissing him is still like the ocean.*

"I'll call you." He sort of ushers me into my car. "Your stepdad's got a really clear view of us right now."

"Oh, crap." I buckle in and wait for him to step back so I can slam the door. Russell is indeed at the back window, probably about to lock up for the night, and he's grinning and laughing, and all of a sudden I wish for nothing more than for him to never, ever sway from Mom's no-gossip rules.

Way back in May, on Memorial Day, Dexter and Oliver's parents threw this huge barbecue for what seemed like their entire subdivision, and—probably to Sara's horror—they'd invited all of us, not just her. Sara's not a jerk in any way, but her image doesn't really line up with her tattoo artist mother and stepfather chasing after a screaming kid dressed up in swim trunks and a Batman mask/cape combo. Maybe it's some genetic default or either too much or not enough therapy, but I've just never been able to get embarrassed about my weirdo family.

I'd been helping hold Finn down so Mom could slather him with sunscreen when I noticed that this lanky red-haired guy—I knew he had to be Dexter's brother—was definitely noticing me. I didn't actually have much experience with guys, but I knew this guy was into me just from the way his gaze lingered.

Once Finn was safe from harmful UV rays, I'd walked

over to the guy and made some dumb joke about pool parties being inappropriate for the true spirit of Memorial Day except for maybe the Navy. He'd laughed, while I accepted that this tall, cute, laughing guy was interested.

I'd found out he was indeed Dexter's brother, was one year older than Dexter (and therefore two years older than me), and was about to start his freshman year at St. Louis University as a philosophy major. We hadn't spent the whole day together, just kept finding reasons to run into each other again and again. When Mom and Russell were ready to go, I convinced them I was hanging out with Sara and Dexter and would just catch a ride home with them later.

Luckily in the crowd Sara hadn't noticed I'd stayed or that Oliver found me yet again and led me inside to his room. We actually talked for a long time—school, music, our siblings' shared brand of perfection—before he kissed me, this really perfect heart-stopping kiss. And it just kind of continued; one kiss became the next, and—I mean, we were in his room, there was a bed there!—before long we were out of our clothes, and it hit me that it was going to happen: I was going to have sex with this guy I barely knew at a frigging Memorial Day barbecue. I started thinking of all these weird things—like that maybe Sara and Dexter would walk in, or that he had these really crisp, clean sheets and was I going to bleed on them or something? —and I wasn't exactly old-fashioned but didn't I want to wait to do this with someone who was my boyfriend or I'd at least met before?

And this is the thing. Oliver isn't one of those guys you hear about who is pushy—it was as much me as him. So I knew I could have just told him I wanted to cool off, and he would have understood. But I also kept thinking of how I'd never found the thought of sex scary, and I never understood those people who held out because of fear or morals or whatever else, and I felt like a big, stupid hypocrite. I didn't want to be nervous about this. I didn't want to want to stop. So I shut my mouth, and I helped Oliver scour the room for a condom, hoping we wouldn't find one. I mean, rooms weren't just automatically stocked with condoms, were they? But he did find one, and I wondered: if someone just has condoms on hand, does that mean he does this a lot?

I didn't say anything, though, and Oliver climbed on top of me and it happened.

No, not sex.

"Um," I said, my voice this mangled, hysterical, crazy sound.

"Yeah?"

I didn't just burst into tears. It was a volcano of tears. Sobbing, shaking, more of the crazy, hysterical sound.

"Are you okay?" he asked.

I should have just said *no*. I should have just said the truth, which was something like, *This all went too fast, and I need to back up, and I'm not ready to lose my virginity to a guy I don't really know, and you're so nice so can we just kiss some more and also I've talked about sex a ton, and I was positive when it happened for me I'd be ready, and I hate that I guess I'm not as brave as I think I am.*

But I'd said nothing. For awhile. And then, finally, "I have to—I have to go."

"Okay...?" He'd gotten up so I could get up, and stood there, totally naked, while I'd scrambled around the room reconstructing my outfit. "Listen, I'm sorry if—"

This was when I should have told him how it wasn't his

fault and how he was such a great kisser and maybe if we ramped up to this, I'd like to have sex with him at some other time. But, again, none of what mattered came out.

"I have to go," I'd said again. "If Sara finds out I was here—"

"Do you want a ride?"

I'd thought of my other options: finding Sara and making a lame excuse, calling Kaitlyn and making a lame excuse, calling Mom and making a lame excuse. "Is that okay?"

"Yeah, let's go."

We were completely quiet in his car, the only sound the album on the stereo, The Beatles' *Revolver*, which had made me want to cry even more because it was my favorite album by my favorite band. I had just run away from sex with a guy who was currently listening to my favorite album.

Since it happened—or, technically, not happened—I'd gone back and forth on whether or not I ever wanted to see him again. On one hand, there was a guy I really liked who actually seemed to like me back. On the other lay disaster and humiliation. Maybe it was best the decision got made for me last week in the diner. Now that I'd seen him again, I didn't want to go back, and it was funny how already I just knew he didn't, either.

Sara is walking into the house as I am, and I have this weird panic that she'd been with Dexter and he somehow knew about Oliver. Though, A) how? and B) at this point would that really matter?

"Hey. You're out late," I say. "Were you hanging out with Dexter?"

She eyes me strangely, which she should, because I'd blurted out those few sentences in a crazy tone. "Are you okay?"

"I was kissing this guy." Even if I'm not ready for her to know it's her boyfriend's *brother*, I'm ready for her to know something. Guys don't have to be the one topic we never really cover. I won't require her to give me Dexter details, but I should probably not be working through this alone.

"It's sort of complicated," I add, even though it's a sentence I probably picked up from frigging Facebook and not from my own feelings at all.

"Is it someone you don't want to be kissing?" Sara flips through the mail on the front table. There are always at least four pieces of correspondence from various universities awaiting her. "Or *shouldn't* be kissing?"

"What do you mean, 'shouldn't be'?"

"Someone who's otherwise attached? I don't know, Kell, you're the one who said it was complicated."

"I mean, when you started going out with Dexter, was it just like some normal thing?" As far as I knew, Sara and Dexter were suddenly *together* with no apparent stressing or awkwardness beforehand.

"I don't really know what you mean." She walks into the kitchen, and I follow her while she gets a glass of water. "Seriously, Kell, you look a little freaked out."

I hate that I can't find the right words, and for once she doesn't exactly seem anxious to help me. "Never mind."

"If you're not completely falling apart, I have to go to my room," she says. "I have so much homework to finish, and I should have been asleep ten minutes ago. I'm sorry."

"Since when do you stay out so late with Dexter on school nights?" I try to affect some goofy, grown-up tone. Why knowing something isn't funny is never enough to keep me from saying it is quite the mystery.

"I wasn't out with Dexter," she says. "I met with Camille again."

"Oh." I wonder if that's weird or not. I guess not. "Cool. Did you have fun?"

"Yeah," she says. "I did. See you tomorrow."

"Sara?"

She stops but doesn't turn. "What is it? *Are* you completely falling apart? It's all right if you are, you know. You can tell me."

I try really hard to shove all of this stuff I'm feeling into words that make sense and don't implicate Oliver in any way, but I can barely manage to come up with topics for a school newspaper humor column. My brain can't handle this.

Sara starts back toward her room. "I have to get this homework finished. We can talk tomorrow if you want."

I let her go, though not just because I'm not sure I could stop her. Of course I don't really know what I'm doing with Oliver, but there are way worse things to obsess over alone than thoughts of tonight's kisses, over and over and over.

CHAPTER SEVEN

Kaitlyn's car is still in the shop the next morning, so I pick her up again. The oldies station is really on a roll today, and I've got a Hollies song blasting as she gets into the car.

"Hey." She points to the radio. "Is this a protest because I made you listen to music from this century yesterday?"

"'Bus Stop' is one of the greatest pop songs ever recorded," I tell her. "Also, *yes*."

"You're such a nerd."

Kaitlyn has been calling me a nerd for ages, particularly about my devotion to music from before even my parents were born, but today it feels different. Today Kaitlyn's someone who talks to a whole new class of people and thinks sneaking into underage clubs would be cool.

"Thanks for the ride," she says. "I don't know what's up with my car."

"That's what you get for trusting German engineering," I say in what is a pretty great impression of Kaitlyn's dad.

"We're running early, should we get coffee?" Of course by coffee I mean *hot chocolate,* but it doesn't roll off the tongue as well.

"Definitely, I could use the caffeine."

The only coffee shop on the way to school from Kaitlyn's is a Starbucks, but unlike Mom, I don't think Starbucks is going to bring on the end of local businesses forever, so I pull right up and park.

"I can't believe you still get those," Kaitlyn says inside when I order my hot cocoa. "You're not a five-year-old."

"Five-year-olds can't drive themselves to school," I say. "Or their friends who have shoddy German cars."

"Ha, ha," Kaitlyn says. It's just like a flash, this thing where she's maybe judgmental of me, just like the other day with my slightly holey shirt, and then she just looks like herself again.

My phone beeps, and I check it to see that, like I hoped, it's a text from Oliver. *POP QUIZ: We should hang out this weekend: TRUE or FALSE.* I'm texting back my response when Kaitlyn cranes her neck down. "Who is that from?"

"This guy." I hit send and throw the phone into my purse. "The college guy. The thing I told you about."

"I thought you said that was just a one-time thing," she says with her eyebrows way raised like she painted them on wrong.

"I thought it was, but maybe it's not."

"Why are you talking so fast?"

"Aaahhh, I don't know, sorry." Of *course* I know why. Of course I know I'm simultaneously terrified and also thinking of little but more opportunities to kiss Oliver. And also I'm terrified of admitting I'm terrified. I frigging hate being terrified! I never planned on being terrified of anything. It's a drag. Why can't I be brave like I feel like I am?

My phone beeps again, from the cavern of my bag, and even though I am trying to play this whole thing cool in front of Kaitlyn, that part of my brain that *likes* him won't let me wait until I get to school to check the response. *Cool, instructions and directions will be forthcoming.*

"Is he, like, your boyfriend now?" Kaitlyn asks.

"It's way more casual than that." I pray Kaitlyn doesn't ask me to get more specific, because even though Oliver is basically the only image flashing in my brain right now, revealing any more wouldn't exactly make this seem *casual*.

But the barista calls out our drinks, and it's time to get to school. And my brain can get right back to thinking only about Oliver and his lips. These are great, great subjects.

Adelaide intercepts me in the hallway the moment I separate from Kaitlyn. I feel like a jerk for my relief at the timing. Kaitlyn's befriending our school's royalty, or at least talking to them casually, while I'm banding with the people who treat stories about new seats in the auditorium like serious journalism. Probably best Kaitlyn doesn't really know this yet.

"Are you busy on Friday night? Kellie." Adelaide says my name in the same tone Mom does when I'm in semi-serious trouble. "With so many locally owned coffee shops around here, you actually go to Starbucks?"

"Their beans are free trade." I don't know what that means, but they have tons of booklets and signs up about it, and it sounds good. "And at least they're providing local employment for the people who work there." I pull that completely out of my ass as I'm saying it, but it sounds pretty good.

"Well." She eyes me for a moment. "That's true. So a bunch of us are going out on Friday night, seeing *The Apple* at the Tivoli at midnight. You should come with us."

"I've never even heard of that. Is it new this week?"

"Oh. My. God." She shakes her head slowly, sadly. "*The Apple* is only one of the worst films of all time. It's so bad it comes back around to being awesome. You haven't lived until you've seen it, and I can't allow myself to let you go on with life if you don't."

"I might have plans on Friday," I say, which isn't a lie.

"You can invite Oliver. In fact, please *do* invite Oliver. He'll have a blast, I'm sure."

"I'm not inviting Oliver to some weird bad movie," I say.

"Your loss," she says. "And his. See you in Jennifer's."

I stop off at my locker to get my stuff, but of course also check my phone. There's nothing new from Oliver, but I reread all his previous texts anyway. He got up this morning and thought about me—you have to think about a person to text her, after all—and I was thinking about him, and that whole thing seems kind of magical.

Okay, *magical*, self? I can't believe a guy is turning my brain so cheesy. Previously, it was normal, and now it's made of cheddar and Gorgonzola.

When I walk into Jennifer's classroom, I drop into the desk next to Adelaide without really thinking about it. She holds up this weird picture of a guy with one devil horn, and I burst out laughing.

"See?" Adelaide's tone is triumphant. "*That*'s from the movie. Don't you want to go now?"

"I don't know when I'm going out with Oliver," I say.

"But if it's a different night, okay."

I immediately feel bad because I know Kaitlyn wants us to do something cool this weekend—and I'm 100 percent positive *something cool* wouldn't include seeing a bad movie on purpose with the newspaper staff—but I'll figure that out later.

Kaitlyn's late getting to lunch, so I quietly eat my sad cafeteria burrito while vaguely listening to the table's conversation about potential Halloween plans later this month. This is basically the same group we've sat with since freshman year, and we all get along, but honestly, when I think about friends at school I think about Kait. It's not that I never hang out with anyone else, but she's the one I share everything with. (The stuff I want to share, at least.)

"Hey." Kaitlyn plunks down beside me with a huge salad. "Sorry, I got caught in the longest conversation ever. Also, Jessie Weinberg told me you're on the newspaper now."

Unfortunately, I'm midbite, so I just shrug. Shrugging with a burrito in your mouth is not attractive, but there are no other available options.

"You joined the paper and didn't tell me?" She wrinkles her nose a little, since I am eating the way a velociraptor would approach a bean burrito. "You barely even like being in school when you have to, and now you're doing extracurriculars?"

"One extracurricular," I say, "not extracurriculars, plural."

"Remember when I was going to join French club and you said that seemed dumb?"

"That doesn't sound like me," I say even though of course it does, and also, French club does sound dumb! I don't need to join a group of Ticknor students to eat croissants and talk about *Les Miserables* or whatever they do. "If you really wanted to join, you could have, you know."

"I *know*. I'm just saying, Kell."

I feel like such a dork even *thinking* about how I used to be a really big believer in just sitting back and letting life happen. In tiny waves it started washing over me that there were things I wanted and maybe going after them wouldn't be awful. But no way I'm saying aloud what sounds like a motivational poster.

"The French club is actually really fun," Chelsea says. "Last week we learned to make crepes."

"It seems like it's just cooking club," I say, and she shrugs.

"All the food's really good."

"It's true," Mitchell says. "She gave me some of the leftover crepes."

"Okay, maybe you *should* join the French club," I tell Kaitlyn, but her attention's on her phone. Hopefully, this at least means the topic of the newspaper and me are behind us. Oh, except— "So I can't take you home tonight. I'm sorry. I have a thing."

"What thing?" she asks while still texting. "Newspaper?"

"Yeah, sorry. Can you get another ride?"

"I'm good, don't worry about it," Kaitlyn says, still all eyes on the phone. "Also, Kell, sorry for bugging you about the weekend. I'm good there, too."

"You weren't bugging me," I say, even though maybe the whole sneaking into a club thing was bugging me, a little. God, it suddenly feels like everything I say to Kait has some unspoken second half.

I'm positive it didn't used to be like that.

At today's newspaper meeting, I realize that people are turning in the articles they just talked about on Tuesday.

What the heck! It feels like one of those nightmares where you find yourself in a class you didn't know you signed up for and the final's that very moment. Except this is all real.

"I don't think I understood the deadline," I tell Adelaide as she stacks printouts of articles on her desktop. "I haven't even started any of those ideas yet."

"I know, Brooks, we just talked about them last night. Look at the whiteboard." She barely gestures to the board hanging at the back of the room. I see that all the assignments chosen two days ago have been transferred there, and also that I'm still listed as KELLY B. The good, non-nightmarish news is that my assignment is just listed as "something funny" and the due date is next week. "And if you're still nervous, we can run your cafeteria piece. Calm down. See if anyone needs your help."

I don't really know how to help anyone, but Jessie asks me to check her article for typos (and I find one, so I feel like a superhero), and then Mitchell lets me cast my vote for the best photo to pair with a story about autumn. (I'm not sure how that's an actual story topic, but whatever, at least I don't have to write it.)

Editors all have to stay late to make sure the paper's ready to go to press, but the rest of us get to go once everything's copyedited and all photos have captions. Scott Garcia suggests hanging out at the Java Joint, and since tonight I have no responsibilities, I agree to go.

"Is it true your parents own a tattoo parlor?" Jessie asks me as our whole group is crowded around a tiny table meant for two or three. I guess technically she's in a much cooler group than the rest of us, but she doesn't seem out of place in this crowd, either. People can be so many more things than you expect.

"My mom and stepdad, yeah," I say. "Also, just to be helpful, no one really calls it *a parlor*. It's just a shop."

"Do you have any tattoos?" Paul Bowen, one of the photographers, asks, and I swear he's staring at my butt even though I'm sitting down and clearly wearing multiple layers of clothing. Guys can be *really obvious*.

"Nope."

"Not even somewhere people can't see?" he asks, and now he is clearly staring at my butt.

"*No*. My mom's really hung up on the whole *not-until-you're-eighteen* thing. I'm convinced I'll wear her down, though."

"What's the weirdest tattoo you saw anyone get?" Chelsea asks.

"Someone got a corndog on their bicep," I say. "With a halo, like it was saintly. And someone got a portrait of Dr. Phil."

My phone buzzes as everyone starts chiming in with what they want to get tattooed on themselves someday, and I grin when I see the text is from Oliver. *Saturday night?* So I tune out instead of contributing my future tattoo ideas and respond an affirmative to him. I've heard that you shouldn't always be so available when guys contact you, but I don't feel like pretending I'm not into Oliver. *Meet up at Moke's at 7 and go from there?*

"Why are you blushing, Kellie?" Chelsea asks me, and then Mitchell tries to read my phone's screen, but I hide it in time—and it's not like it says something pervy anyway—but everyone knows I'm up to something. And I kind of don't even care. Oliver McAuley, who is tall and smart and a very good kisser, wants to go out with me on Saturday night.

I've put it off long enough, so that night while I'm helping Mom with dishes and getting texts from Oliver (him: *Haunted houses, cool or lame or so lame they're cool?* me: *depends. last year we went to one we heard was super scary, but it was just a church showing stuff like kids reading* harry potter *and burning in hell*), I bring it up like I haven't been obsessing over how to ask her. "Oh, Mom? Don't make a big deal of this or whatever, but is it okay if I go on a date on Saturday?"

"With Oliver McAuley?"

"Does it matter with who?"

"No, of course it doesn't, I was just—Well, a little! One of your teachers, someone my age, it would matter."

"It *is* with Oliver," I say. "But please don't make it a thing. Sara doesn't know, and I feel weird about her knowing. Can she not know?"

Mom directs a sly grin at me. "And you make fun of your dad for *his* secret relationship."

Having a secret relationship sounds like maybe there's one cool thing—or at least a mysterious thing—about my dad. But, no.

Dad is actually under the impression Sara and I have no idea he has a girlfriend, even though occasionally we run into them around town on days we aren't staying with him. Jayne works at a nonprofit cat rescue organization and is sort of like Mom in that she smiles a lot—well, the few times I've seen her she's been smiling—and she apparently really loves her job. I don't know what he's so afraid will happen if we're flat-out told of her significance in his life...and as if their time together doesn't already tell us that much anyway. But when we've asked Dad about her, it's like he's trying to do a Jedi mind trick on us. *"What girlfriend?"*

"I am *not* like Dad. If this was like A Relationship, it wouldn't be secret, but I'm still figuring out what it is, and I don't want to do that while Sara knows about it. Just, please?"

"You know I think honesty is—"

"The best policy?" I smirk at her.

"Hush." I can tell from Mom's strained, serious face that she's trying desperately not to laugh. "But—yes. Still, dating's tough enough. If you need some time to figure it out, I'm not going to announce it to your sister."

"You're the best mom," I say, because she really is. If I'm ever a mom and good at it, I hope my kids tell me.

I'm Googling stuff for my Cornerstones of American History homework that night when a message pings on my Facebook. I'm hoping it's Oliver even though we aren't official friends yet, but instead it's someone just a week ago I thought I'd never be talking to.

Adelaide Johansson: Greetings.

Kellie Brooks: i still haven't started on my article yet, sorry.

Adelaide Johansson: Jeez, touchy. I was merely saying hi.

Kellie Brooks: hi.

Adelaide Johansson: How's Oliver?

Kellie Brooks: we're going out saturday.

I type and retype the next thing a million times, finally deleting it all. But, seriously, this is *Adelaide*. Adelaide is not someone I should worry about looking like a freak in front of, and I really don't know who else to talk to.

Kellie Brooks: if you almost have sex with a guy once, and then a while later you have a date, does he think you'll have sex with him then?

Adelaide Johansson: Oh I have good advice here!

Adelaide Johansson: JUST TALK TO HIM, KELLIE.

Adelaide Johansson: Guys are not some foreign species who don't know our language. They're just PEOPLE, and if you have concerns about your sex life as it relates to Oliver, you shouldn't be talking to me.

Adelaide Johansson: And definitely don't talk to Kaitlyn Hamilton. She'll read you some article from Cosmo.

Kellie Brooks: kaitlyn's my best friend, you know.

Adelaide Johansson: That advice still stands.

I feel bad laughing, since it's not Kaitlyn's fault I haven't asked her for advice, but I do anyway. Maybe Adelaide isn't one billion percent wrong. (Honestly, it seems impossible for Adelaide to be wrong about anything.) It wasn't that long ago when I knew exactly who I was, but right now in this moment, messaging a person I never thought I'd even speak to except out of necessity, I don't really care anymore that I'm not so sure.

CHAPTER EIGHT

Friday at school is completely normal except that during lunch I get a text from Adelaide that the paper has been sent to press, so I guess that's a thing that'll happen weekly now. I had absolutely nothing to do with this issue except typo-catching and autumn-photo-selecting, but I'm still really glad everything is on schedule.

On Fridays we usually go to Dad's, even though it's a prime weekend night and Dad's place isn't really a prime weekend spot. He lives way out off Highway 44 in Wildwood, where houses are sprawling and the size of yards guarantees you don't have to see your neighbors if you don't want to. It takes twenty minutes to get there, which is good when I need an excuse to see him less, but pretty annoying the rest of the time.

His house is bigger than Mom and Russell's, and while it used to be entirely decorated in that modern style Sara loves, he recently switched it up to something he calls Japanese Pole

House. I'm not even kidding. It's nice, really, lots of screens and bamboo, and all the living room chairs and sofas are this beautiful jade green. The closest Dad's been to Japan, though, is logging a lot of hours at the sushi joint near his office. Sara and I assume Jayne is to thank (or blame) for the décor shift.

"Hey," Sara greets me as I walk inside. We try to stick together scheduling our time at Dad's because he's a lot for one of us to take at a time. "Do you have plans tonight? Dad wants to take us out for dinner, but I have something scheduled already. It'll be easier if we're both busy."

"Yeah, I do have plans, and I'd cover for you even if I didn't. You know that."

Sara smiles as she pours herself a glass of water. "I'd be a bad sister to drag you into a life of dishonesty."

"I don't know, it sounds cool to get corrupted." I leave my backpack and overnight bag on the floor and walk into the living room, where Dad's working on his laptop. It's nice, I guess, that if he can, he leaves work early when we're coming over, but it's not like he actually stops being a lawyer. "Hey, I'm here."

"There she is. How was school?"

"It was fine. How's the law?"

"Very funny. Don't report cards come out soon?"

"I don't know, like in three or four weeks."

He glances over at me. "Do you need some money to go shopping, kiddo? Those jeans look pretty old."

"Dad, they're faded on purpose. I'm fine." I sit down in the stiff chair opposite him, nervous even though one of my main reasons for submitting my cafeteria piece in the first place was Dad. "So I joined the newspaper staff."

"Since when do you write?" he asks. "Didn't you get a B in English last year?"

"I don't know, I don't memorize my grades, and also, English lit was really hard, all that stupid *Beowulf* stuff. I know a lot of people who got Bs."

"Your sister hasn't gotten a B in her life," he says as Sara walks into the room. "And a classic like *Beowulf* isn't 'stupid.'"

"Yes, I have, Dad, in P.E. and in art, and I've also wondered why modern English curriculums still skew toward certain titles without incorporating newer ideas," she says, and I wish I was that good at just shutting him down. "I talked to Kell, and she's got plans tonight, too, so can we go out to dinner next time? Sorry, Fridays can be hard for us."

"Yeah, of course, girls," he says, eyes back on the computer. Sara heads upstairs, but I stay in the chair, waiting for our conversation to start back up again. Regardless of my understanding of Ye Olde English, he must be happy I'm doing more with my life and joining up with a bunch of overachievers, right? He's silent for what feels like forever, so I guess not. Finally I go upstairs, too, until it's time to head out.

When I get to Adelaide's, I still can't believe I'm there at all, much less on this very prime weekend night. But here is the thing: in less than a week, Adelaide has somehow become not a dorky girl I avoid but just a girl I know who seems really good at everything she does.

"Come in." Adelaide yanks me inside and slams the door. "Mom says moths fly into the house if the door's open for longer than forty-five seconds. And then they might eat our good sweaters."

"That's weird," I say, like suddenly I'm one to judge about Mom Weirdness Levels. "Is everyone else meeting us here?"

"No, everyone's meeting us at Racanelli's." Adelaide ushers me right back out of the house, clearly really upholding that forty-five-second moth-flying rule.

Adelaide drives north to University City, which despite its name, doesn't have any more colleges than our town does. Its coolest section—called The Loop—does, however, have almost everything necessary to qualify it as cool: an amazing music store, dozens of ethnic restaurants, boutiques with ridiculously overpriced clothes I sometimes can't help wanting even though I'm truly happy for the most part in my jeans and vintage T-shirts, vintage stores where I purchased some of said shirts, and the movie theater we're headed to later that shows indie and cult movies.

The only thing I don't like about U City is that everyone else figured out it was cool long ago. It gets *crowded*.

The small group of who I assume are Adelaide's boyfriend and his friends from school is already crowded around one of the tables outside of Racanelli's (they make the best pizza in town, and even though there's one in Webster, the U City location is always worth visiting). A guy who has shaggy dark hair and a T-shirt calling for world peace and let's face it, is gorgeous, jumps up to hug Adelaide.

Whoa. Adelaide Johansson has an objectively hot boyfriend, and my mind is therefore blown.

"Hey." The guy who has to be Byron points to me. "Your mom did my tattoo. Check it out."

Before I can say anything, he whips off his shirt and turns away from me. I do recognize the tiny, crisp text inked on his back from Mom's portfolio. Also: yowza. "Oh. Cool."

"Put your shirt on, Byron," Adelaide says.

(*Nooooooo, don't!* I think.)

"Kells, yo."

Even though I can't think of anyone else in the world who would ever greet me that way, I'm still surprised to see Dexter walking toward me. "What are you doing here?"

"O'Shea asked me." He jabs an arm at Byron. "Why's your shirt off, good sir?"

"You guys know each other?" I ask, even though that's clearly a pointless question.

"Dexter was a year behind me at Chaminade," Byron explains.

"Hmmm," I accidentally say aloud, because another person Dexter is a year behind at Chaminade is Oliver. If Byron is friends with one McAuley Brother, is he friends with both? I guess it doesn't really matter, plus I don't know how to ask without seeming like a weirdo. So instead of sticking around to make my *hmmm* seem normal, I head inside.

"So." Dexter walks in and gets in line behind me. "What's Sara up to tonight?"

It hits me that Sara's plans aren't with Dexter if he's here with us. "Oh, actually I have no idea. I guess hanging out with Nadia and Cass."

"Cool." Dexter hooks his thumbs in his jean pockets. "So what's up with you?"

"What do you mean what's up with me? Like specifically? Or in general?"

"Either or, Kells. It's not a trick question."

"I don't know," I say, worrying we're treading near

dangerous Oliver waters here. Does Dexter even know anything's up with Oliver and me? I don't know what guys talk about, and even if I did, maybe brothers have different rules. But considering I'm still nervous just to *think* about Oliver, I am certainly not ready to discuss my status with him with his brother...who also happens to be my sister's boyfriend. Way too much overlap here. "The same stuff. The usual. I don't know."

Adelaide jumps right into line beside me, bumps against me like we've been friends forever. I think of Kaitlyn and how she'd always giggle a little when doing things like that, but also how she would probably hate everything about this night, except that Byron is hot and we all got to see his chest. Maybe I should feel guilty that I didn't even try to make time for Kaitlyn this weekend, but I guess she didn't really try to make time for me, either. Other than when one of us was out of town, I can't remember the last time that happened. Maybe we can hang out Sunday after brunch.

The movie is as bad as promised, but amazingly so: two stupid kids from Moosejaw, Canada, who have the worst music act in the world somehow getting an offer to basically sell their souls to the devil. The devil forces the whole nation to listen to their crappy disco rock, but then a hippie leader saves everyone by driving them into heaven in his flying Cadillac. Even though—unlike Adelaide and Byron—I can't sing along, I laugh at the jokes people shout aloud, I laugh at the terrifying new wave costumes, and I even shout out responses to the bad dialogue a few times like I'm an old pro at this sort of thing.

And on the drive back to Adelaide's, I have this warm feeling like this is the kind of night I should be having more.

It wasn't a weird night filled with dorky overachievers. Everyone is just *a person,* and no one (as long as you don't count Adelaide or Byron or Dexter, of course) seems that much more achieving than me.

Sara and Dad are already in the kitchen when I head downstairs the next morning. He usually takes us out for breakfast on Saturdays, even when we were both out late the night before.

"...just a lot to deal with," I hear Sara say as I walk into the room. Her voice is a little shaky, a quality I rarely hear from her. "The timing—"

"Something about timing," Dad says. "It's rarely good. Trust me."

My foot accidentally collides with the open dishwasher door, which is loud enough as it is without the sound of me yelping.

"Hey, there she is," Dad says. "If I make it up to you, kiddo, would you mind a rain check on breakfast? Sara and I just have a lot to talk about, uh, with college, you know."

"Dad, we can talk about college in front of Kellie," Sara says. "It's boring but not private."

"We should keep your sister's feelings in mind," he says. "She's just not going to have the opportunities you do, with her grades and all."

"I'm fine staying in," I say, even though I do mind, in that part of my brain that understands just how disappointed Dad is that I'm not more like Sara and less like myself. I'm too old to act like it, though, and at least Sara shoots me an apologetic look, so I wave them off.

Just as I'm ready to settle with a bowl of cereal on the chocolate-brown living room rug (I get too nervous about spilled milk, literally, to sit on that jade furniture) and the start of an *America's Next Top Model* marathon, my phone rings.

"Hey, baby, did I wake you?"

"No, I'm up. What's going on?" I try to sound calm, even though Mom rarely interrupts Dad days. "Is everyone okay?"

"Yeah, baby, everyone's fine. Do you have plans this morning? Jimmy just called out sick for the day. If you're still interested, Russell and I thought you could stop by, learn the ropes, help out a little."

"I can have the job?"

She pauses, which I know in Mom Language means she's holding back from saying what she really means. Which is likely *no*. "How about a trial basis?"

Obviously, within thirty-five minutes, I'm walking inside The Family Ink.

"Kell-belle." Mom beams up at me from her workstation, where she's sketching out the city skyline. "I'm so glad you could make it. I know it sounds like a lot of work to be the only one making appointments and getting the phone, but I know you can handle it."

"You're the one who didn't want me to have the job. I also know I can handle it." I walk into the tiny back room just long enough to dump my purse on the floor and help myself to a jelly-filled donut. "Where's Russell?" I walk back into the main shop area after having shoved the donut into my mouth in two and a half bites. Disgusting but impressive.

"Doesn't he have appointments?"

"He'll be back soon," Mom says. "Did you do anything fun last night?"

I lick the tips of my fingers, still coated with sugar, and wait for Mom to scream about cleanliness and respect for the work environment. She does, I wash my hands at the sink, and I mention the movie like maybe my whole social circle didn't just shift.

Russell is there within a few minutes, with coffee for him and Mom and hot cocoa for me. Hopefully it's just my imagination, but Russell's expression is kind of downturned today.

"Full beverage service!" I announce, and he laughs and claps me on the back.

Russell's first appointment is a lady around Mom's age and a total mom type with a nice little helmet of highlighted hair and a sweater featuring three embroidered autumn leaves, who is getting a totally clichéd butterfly on her back. I take her deposit and copy her ID and get her to fill out her paperwork like I've done this a million times before. As far as jobs go, I haven't hit the proverbial jackpot or anything, but it's still a pretty swank gig. Mom and Russell don't care if I kill time on the computer as long as I'm attentive when there are actually people who need my help.

"You're free until noon." I walk over to Mom's station after checking the appointment book. Her station is decorated mostly with pictures of all of us, but also some of the designs she's working on (currently a flaming cup of coffee and a quote about a mortal coil I'm pretty sure is Shakespeare). "You know what you could do? If you've got extra time to tattoo...?"

"No," she says firmly, taking down the coffee design and erasing the top section of flames before redrawing them. When Russell draws, his movements are slow, methodical, but Mom's pencil just flies across the paper.

"Well, *I* have an idea," I say like I didn't hear or understand her. "You could give *me* a tattoo. You can even take it out of my first paycheck."

"First of all, Kellie, your first paycheck isn't going to cover my rates. Secondly, you know how I feel about this. It isn't happening."

"Why not?"

"What tattoo do you want?"

I shrug. "Something cool, maybe on my ankle, even though I know that's totally a sorority girl place, only slightly better than your lower back—"

"If you aren't one hundred percent sure, baby, I'm not doing it."

"It isn't fair. Don't millions of people come in here and just pick out something crappy off the wall? Do you question all of them?"

Russell looks up from the butterfly that was picked out from the designs on the wall and mouths *we don't insult the flash customers*, which is one of his big policies. Flash is what all the ready-made designs are called. Since Mom and Russell prefer to do their own designs, it's cool of them to make boring people feel at home, too.

Still, I am making a point.

"Kellie Louise, the difference is that I'm not any of those people's mothers. When you're eighteen, you can go to anyone and get something on the spur of the moment, but I won't be the one to do that for you. When I ink you someday, it'll be for something you know you'll want forever."

The thing is, even though I don't want to admit it, Mom is right. Not long ago I thought it would be cool to put a line from my favorite Beatles song around my wrist, and then after sitting in Oliver's car after our awkward non-sex, I'm pretty sure I'd hate to look at those words every single day.

"It's so cute your whole family runs this shop," says the woman mid-butterfly. "I just love family businesses, don't you?"

"They're my favorite." Mom tacks up the coffee cup sketch before getting out a fresh piece of paper and pulling down a book of fonts from her reference shelf. I've pointed out only twenty-seven million times she could be using a computer for stuff like that, but she swears it's better this way. "I count my blessings all the time that Russell and I made this place work."

Mom says that a lot. It's even quoted in the article from the *Riverfront Times* that's framed here and also at home, "The Family that Inks Together Stays Together," which features a huge picture of Mom and Russell at work in the shop, as well as them with all of us at Tower Grove Park, down the street.

The article had unintentionally stirred up tons of drama, considering none of us knew Dad had kept pretty quiet about the subject of his divorce. It made it tricky for him to explain why his supposedly current wife was in the pages of the local alternative weekly next to his daughters, another man, and a punk rock toddler who wasn't his.

Mom is in the midst of telling Her Story to the butterfly woman, something else I've heard millions of times by now. "I'd just left my paralegal position because I couldn't imagine doing that a minute longer. I was still sorting out my life, looking for my *raison d'être*, you know. One afternoon after I had lunch with my sister at a café off Delmar, I was walking around, passed this tattoo shop, and just found myself going in."

At this point Mom always pulls back the left shoulder of her shirt, shows off the bluebird in flight inked in exuberant blues. I've asked Mom about the meanings of a lot of her tattoos (which is how I found out the snowflake on her forearm is for me, both because of my January birthday and apparently, my uniqueness, and the owl on her bicep is for Sara: wise and beautiful, I figure) but I never needed to with this one. *Freedom*.

"By the time my artist"—Mom and Russell share a smile here—"had finished, I'd sorted it out." Mom knew what she wanted in life: both the job and Russell.

One part of the story she always leaves out was that she was still Melanie Brooks then, had still been Dad's wife, had only been gone a day from the law firm where she and Dad had met. At home she'd prepared dinner like it was any other day.

I can't blame her for editing; the story is much sweeter her way.

Russell jumps in right where he always does. "I had ten years of experience on her, but no one's a natural like Mel. Most talented artist I ever worked with."

That's actually my favorite part of the story. If Mom hadn't known her real talent until she was over thirty, maybe there's hope for me, too.

"And you fell for her!" exclaims the butterfly woman, like this is the best love story she's ever heard. Lady, see more movies.

"How could I not?"

I roll my eyes, because even though of course it's the sweetest thing in the world, I understand the part I play at the shop. And teenagers are supposed to roll their eyes upon such utterances.

After he puts the finishing touches on the butterfly, Russell and I walk down the street to pick up lunch. Even though it may not be my business, I decide to ask about the sadness that I swear has settled on him again.

"Thanks for asking, Kell," he says. "It's good of you to take notice. Don't know if you remember about Chrystina…"

"Of course, yeah."

"Today's her birthday," he says. "*Would* have been her birthday. My ex and I, we always visit her grave, say a few prayers. Makes for a rough day."

"I'm sorry," I say. "I wouldn't have asked if—"

"I don't mind talking about it," he says. "Just rough. She'd be twenty-one today."

I think about that, how many years of her life Russell has missed out on. Also, I wonder what she'd be like if she were here. I could use someone who's twenty-one, who'd been through things with high school and guys from local colleges. Maybe Chrystina would know how to handle the Oliver situation.

Okay, wait. Have I really somehow found a way to make the subject of Russell's dead daughter all about *me*?

My cell phone rings as we walk back, loaded down with bags of Vietnamese food, and we juggle until Russell has all the bags, and my hands are free to retrieve my phone from my bag. Dad. Crap. "Hello?"

"Kellie, where are you?"

"Working," I say, like I've had a job for a million years already and he's well aware of my schedule.

"Working? We haven't discussed you getting a job."

"It's just with Mom and Russell at the shop."

"I don't feel great about you working in that part of town in that kind of environment," he says. "All those roughnecks coming in and—"

I laugh so hard my eyes tear up, and Russell joins in without even knowing what I'm laughing at. "'Roughnecks'? Dad, what are you talking about? Russell's last client was this forty-four-year-old lady. Mom's working on some frat boy right now."

"Your mother and I will have to discuss this," he says. "Will I see you tonight?"

"I have plans, so, probably not. Some night next week, okay?"

Dad agrees, and even though he snubbed me from my own frigging family breakfast this morning, I still feel bad I'm not there. He just makes it really easy for me not to be.

 CHAPTER NINE

Sara's at the house when I get there after work. She's wearing jeans and a blue sweater I've never seen before. Since she's in her school uniform so much, I always notice what she's wearing when she isn't.

"Did you guys go shopping today?" I ask.

"Just for a few things, yeah," she says. "I'm so sorry for how he was earlier."

"I know. It's not your fault anyway. And I'm fine."

"Dad wanted to buy you pants because he said yours were 'ragged,' but I talked him out of it."

"Thanks," I say, even though I probably could use some new pants. It's super nice of Sara to keep Dad from acting like everything about me needs to be upgraded. "You know I don't blame you for how he is. You shouldn't have to feel bad for being so perfect."

"One, I'm not perfect, two, I don't feel bad about *myself*, and three, I do still feel bad. I just don't know how to fix it."

"No one can fix Dad." Standing in front of Sara, I feel stupid that I've been so secretive about Oliver. There's nothing to really even be secretive *about*. True, Sara and I don't really talk *generally* about guys, and I guess there are lots of *specific* reasons I don't want to talk about Oliver. Again, he's Dexter's brother, so is that weird? Again, he's smart and at a good college, and I'm sure everyone expected if I started going out with anyone he'd be a goof-off like me. And…okay, actually, I guess I still feel better being secretive.

"Anyway, I should go get ready." I'm glad Sara isn't the kind of person who'll make me say what I'm getting ready for. "Talk to you later? Are you going out?"

"Well, I'm hanging out with Dexter while he and his friends play something on his PS3. Does that count?"

"Hmmm, maybe not. Is that like a thing you have to do as a girlfriend?"

"Generally speaking, who knows? Specifically speaking, yes, for me it is. See you later, Kell."

I'm in front of my closet before it hits me I don't know what I should wear for this. Luckily, Adelaide answers as soon as I call her. "Go."

"What? Oh, hi. It's Kellie. What am I supposed to wear tonight?"

"Brooks, what have we been discussing?"

"Guys are just people and stressing too much about clothes and other superficial items is pointless?"

"Exactly." She pauses. "But jeans and your purple shirt, if I had to pick. Have fun. Report back tomorrow."

Oliver is already at the coffee shop when I get there. In my opinion, he's much cuter than Dexter, though I guess having the same red hair and brown eyes and being approximately the same height means it's probably a pretty close race. Still, there is something in Dexter's eyes that gives away that he is trying so hard all the time. Oliver's eyes just *are*.

I guess I like a lot of things about Oliver: how his hands are big but smooth, how even when he isn't smiling, his eyes look like he is, and how his top lip is a little fuller than his bottom one. When we talk, and it's me who's saying something—even something stupid—he listens like at that very moment my dumb jokes are more important than anything else. I mean, I tell a lot of dumb jokes all the time; no one else really leaves the rest of the world behind to hear them.

He hugs me as soon as he spots me, which is nice, and kisses me as soon as we're outside, which is even nicer.

"I got a little worried about the haunted house thing when I got your text," he says. "What do you think?"

"I can't believe I'll be told two years in a row my soul will end up in hell, right?"

"Seems doubtful." He grabs my hand as we walk to his car, which is also nice. "That's a yes?"

"That's a yes." In his car we kiss again, this time with his hands on my face. And it should have reminded me of that day in his room—and, okay, honestly it does—but it isn't like it's replaying itself out now. That was a long time ago. This is now.

We get to the haunted house in only a few minutes, and I'm thrilled we're greeted by zombies and not ministers. "You picked a good one."

"That's a relief." Oliver grins, this way of looking at me like I'm someone more. I guess to him I *am*. "Hate to sentence you to hell tonight."

I lead him toward the entrance and pay for my admission. Listen, I'm not the kind of person who wants to blog about the whole world being sexist—I'll let Adelaide keep that job—but I don't want to kick off, well, whatever we're doing, with Oliver paying for everything just because he happened to be born a guy.

I climb up the creaky, dark stairs first, pulling Oliver behind me, and he yells out the very second we pass a large and very fake spider hanging over us. "Are you okay?"

"I just hate spiders, sorry," he says, getting a little closer to me. "I know it's not manly. Everything else about me is manly, I promise."

"Yeah, I remember," I say, even though *what am I doing?* Why can I talk like this when I'm not at all ready for any of that? Not *all* of that at least.

I poke at the spider, hoping to change the subject with arachnophobia. "Seriously, though, even rubber ones?"

"It doesn't look rubber from here."

I laugh and pretend to take aim at the spider. "Taken care of."

He gives me that grin again, and it hits me even more that Oliver *likes* me. Despite May. Despite that I'm kind of a weirdo. It is just this real, genuine, true thing. All for me.

I walk along right in front of him while getting growled at by surprisingly realistic werewolves, threatened with bites from vampires (I dare one guy to do it, and he laughs and breaks character—a minor victory), and held up at gunpoint by totally normal dudes with also surprisingly realistic fake guns. Oliver's not scared of anything except the fake spiders, but being brave for him just becomes a thing I'm doing, and the harder he laughs, the more I just keep wanting to do it.

After we're out of the haunted house, we go to dinner, a vegetarian place I've gone to a million times with my family, of course, but Oliver gets so excited when we drive past, I act like we weren't there just a couple weeks earlier.

"Sorry that was kind of lame," he says, while we look over our menus.

"I didn't think it was lame. And I like it when you scream." Oh my God, way to take fake spiders and make it sound like I'm one of those people on HBO skilled at double entendres. I wonder how my subconscious got so much more *experienced* than me.

"Yeah, do you?"

Oh, Oliver, seriously, you should know from that day how not skilled I am at even single entendres; please don't give me that look. Now I'm definitely back in May in my head, back in Oliver's room without my clothes or any sense of what I want.

Luckily, a waiter shows up right then, and by the time Oliver orders a veggie burger and I order plantain tacos, I can pretend that moment has passed. I'm thinking a lot about what Adelaide said, though, and if this feels weird because of the almost-sex, then maybe I should just say something.

"I didn't mean that how it sounded."

He laughs. "Yeah, Kellie, I know. I wasn't passing it up, though."

I have to agree with that, but still. I'm ready for a new topic. "Are you a vegetarian or something?"

"No way, I love meat too much. I thought you were, though."

"Why would you think that?" I ask. "Meat's delicious."

"Back on Memorial Day, your stepdad brought all those veggie burgers and hot dogs. Not to sound like a stalker, but I noticed you were eating them."

"I just felt bad for Russell," I say. "I didn't want him to take home this huge plate of crap no one else wanted."

He smiles and shakes his head. "Good thing I like this place anyway. My ex was a vegetarian, so we went here a lot."

I guess it's dumb to think I'm the first girl Oliver has messed around with, has taken on a date, has kissed like it's the sweetest moment occurring in the entire universe. I guess it's even dumber to care, so I set a goal to stop.

After we eat—with no more mentions of the ex but at least four of fake spiders—we walk around a little outside. There's an alcove behind the building, a space where the bricks sort of cut away, and it smells like the Dumpsters lurking nearby. Still, Oliver pushes me back there and starts kissing me like we're in complete privacy.

"I'm glad I ran into you," he says sort of breathlessly, raising his head just far enough from mine to speak not directly into my mouth. His voice is extra husky. "I kept thinking of texting you before but—"

"I'm glad, too," I say, hands on his face, pulling him back to me.

I hear a door open, and some cook from the restaurant yells out at us, so we laugh and make a run for Oliver's car, where we get back to business. Well, kissing. Obviously, I know there's more to it than this, and not just because we'd already gotten there. Almost there, at least.

"You want to get coffee?" he asks finally, while I fish some lip balm out of my purse. People don't say things like "making out is a killer on your lip health," but they should. That's the kind of sex advice I actually need.

"I don't know." Instead, we could be somewhere alone that isn't a car, where we could do almost as much as we had in May. I hope it's allowable to put up limitations like that. According to Adelaide and all the websites she endorses, it is. "This is pretty good, right?"

"Oh," he says, and I can tell he's running options through his head. Hopefully, they aren't ways to nicely tell me he's done making out with me for the night. "I think my roommate's out."

Success.

Actually Oliver is totally wrong. When we get to his dorm room, there is some nerdy kid doing homework and listening to crappy jam rock, but he volunteers to go to the library before we have to ask.

"I'm not going to have sex tonight," I tell Oliver as he pulls me down with him on his mattress. I hadn't known him last time, but this time I can recognize that the sheets and pillows smell like him. "Just so you know."

"You're weird," he says with a smile. "And that's fine."

"Oh, you have no idea." I kiss him a few times, trying out a few things with my lips I'd read about (props to Adelaide and some helpful links she'd sent me). He's letting out little sounds of what I take as approval, so the research has clearly been worth the effort. "I just didn't want you getting the wrong idea about—"

"I didn't," he says, really quickly. "Stuff happens, Kellie. I didn't think just because we got ahead of ourselves that we were going to pick up right there again."

It's exactly what he should have said, but it isn't what I

wanted to hear. The person I want to be would have had sex with him last time, or at least been more honest about why she hadn't. And that's who I want Oliver to see me as right now.

So I lie. "I meant that I freaked. It's not like that's my reaction to sex."

He kisses my cheek, then my neck. "Listen, I didn't think it was."

Right then I'm in two places at once, because while I'm doing dumb things like lying to Oliver, I'm also sort of floating above myself screaming, *Shut up, shut up, shut up, just* frigging do him *already if this is the alternative.*

Also, I hate both of those parts of me, so I guess I'm in a third place, too, harshly judging both of them.

"I believe you, okay?" Oliver covers my lips with his, probably kissing me to shut me up more than anything else. And the me that is floating above, cheering me on, wins out, at least a little. I mean, I don't *frigging do him,* but I get back to making out with him *sans* conversation at least.

"I should probably go," I say, finally, catching sight of his clock out of the corner of my eye. "I don't really have a curfew, but Mom knows I'm out with you so—"

He follows my line of sight and nods. "Yeah, it's late, and I don't want to piss off your family. Eventually, I'm gonna want a tattoo, and I'm sure your mom could exact revenge with ink if she wanted."

"For sure." I feel really good with this night ending in jokes and not tears. "Sorry you have to drive me back."

"I don't mind." He smooths my hair, leans in, and kisses me a little more. "I wish you could stay longer. That's my only complaint right now."

"Mine, too." I put my shoes back on and stand in front of his mirror for a moment to adjust my shirt, even though Mom isn't dumb and doesn't think I go on chaste 1950s dates or whatever.

Of course, Oliver and I kiss for a while when we get back to his car, and then when we get back to mine, and it's definitely later than planned when I finally arrive home. Mom is in the living room, reading some novel probably about a hardheaded, down-and-out woman who somehow beat the odds.

"Hey, sorry I'm late," I say.

"You're not too late." She marks her place. "Have fun?"

"I did."

Mom stands up, gives me a hug, and kisses my cheek. "I should get to bed. What are you doing tomorrow? After brunch I thought Finn and Russell could hang out, and you and Sara and I could do a little shopping. What do you say?"

"Sounds great." I curl up in the spot she just vacated on the sofa. Even though I'm exhausted—and even though I'd lied to Oliver a little—the night was too sweet to say good-bye to yet.

CHAPTER TEN

Something is definitely up the next morning, because Mom's concerned voice is making all sorts of noise in the hallway and my alarm clock reads only 6:12. We're morning people, sure, but we're not crazy.

I get out of bed and open my door just enough to suddenly be eye-to-eye with Mom. We both yell out in surprise before she waves me back into my room. She walks in as I'm crawling back to bed. "Baby, do you know if Sara went out with Dexter last night?"

"I'm not some sudden Dexter expert because of Oliver," I say. "But, yes. She went over to his house to watch him and his friends play video games. Why?"

Mom sighs loudly. "She didn't come home last night, and she's not at your dad's."

"Why don't you just call her cell?" It's way too early to deal with Sara's sudden descent into wild child or whatever this is. Later, I'll marvel over that. (And maybe get up the nerve to ask for details.)

"Of course I tried that. It went straight to voice mail."

"Did you call Dexter?"

"I guess I have to, huh?"

I think I've won out and will get to go back to sleep, but Mom dials him right then and there. Who knows why she has Dexter's number saved on her phone? Is that a mom thing? Will Oliver's get programmed in next?

"Hi, Dexter, I'm sorry to wake you. It's Melanie Stone, Sara's—Right, of course you know that. I'm not trying to get anyone in trouble, but Sara didn't come home last night and—Oh? Thanks, I appreciate it."

Mom clicks off her phone and walks out of the room. By now, I am A) wide awake and B) whatever the extreme version of curious is. So I follow. "Is she there?"

"No, you're right that they had plans, but she canceled at the last minute so—"

"Maybe she's at Camille's," I say without even really thinking about it. But, you know, maybe she is.

"Hmmmm," is all Mom says before walking into her and Russell's bedroom. I take a shower, get dressed, and settle in the living room with a bowl of cereal.

"Why are you eating?" Mom walks into the room, also showered and dressed now, like me in jeans and one of Russell's shirts (I swiped a bowling shirt and Mom has on the skull and crossbones sweater again). "Sundays are brunch days."

"Just like in the Bible. But with Sara—"

"Sara spent the night at Camille's and will be back later. There's no reason that has to throw off our whole day."

Once Russell and Finn are up, we drive into the city and

sit outside at Mokabe's, where the brunch is both meat- and vegan-friendly. I feel sort of loopy and giggly when I think about the fact that only several hours ago, I'd stood just a few feet away and kissed Oliver. It's a funny sensation, thoughts like this running through me like they know the pathways already even though it is all brand new.

I like finding out I'm capable of something new.

Back at the house, I settle in with my computer to check my email, but Mom leans into my room almost immediately. "Baby, still want to go shopping?"

I don't, not as much as yesterday, now that it's just us with no Sara. But I could probably use a few more things if I'm going to be dating—or whatever—Oliver. Plus, Mom already has one daughter who didn't come home; I'm not going to disappoint her further.

We make the trek across town to the Galleria, where I normally don't go because I think it's snooty (that's right, and my tattooed mom doesn't). I guess today she isn't too concerned about local businesses because right away she drops a huge amount at GapKids for Finn. After that Mom pushes me into Macy's and toward nicer stuff than I generally wear. Not fancier, really, just better quality or something.

"You never let me splurge on you for clothes, Kell-belle," Mom says.

I pick out a couple of knit shirts, then a little green jacket, but shrug and put them back. "You shouldn't splurge on me. I'm really fine."

"You know how proud I am of you, baby. You've earned a little spoiling."

I haven't, but I still pick the shirts and jacket back up

and try on whatever else Mom selects for me. This new Kellie looks back at me from the fitting room mirror in the new jeans and the jacket over a new shirt, and she definitely doesn't look like some underachieving weird girl who is good for very little. If I told you she has a newspaper column and a college boy who wants to kiss her and a new friend who is all about saving the world, you'd totally believe me.

"Thanks for doing this," I tell Mom while we wait in line to pay. "I guess I needed some new stuff."

"We all do sometimes, right?" She ruffles my hair, and I'm glad she doesn't say anything goofy about me growing up or whatever I'm doing these days. Embarrassing! "When does the paper come out? I can't wait to read your first article."

"Please don't get too excited about it—it's sort of dorky," I say. "And my first article won't come out until the week after this. But I'll bring a copy home for you then, I promise."

We stay awhile longer at the mall, though we only end up with a few more purchases (a new lip gloss for me— obviously a kissing-related purchase—a sweater for Mom, and some jeans for Russell). At home I attempt starting my column, but really I message Adelaide about the date going well and make a playlist to send Oliver because he'd mentioned last night that he wished he knew more about 1960s music. (He said it in his room with the lights out in a pause from making out, so he may not have actually meant it and just gotten carried away by kissing me, but I figure I can still be nice.) Sara's not home yet, but I decide not to worry about it.

I remember that I'd planned on using today to finally catch up with Kaitlyn, so I send her a quick text. *hey! good wkend? wanna get coffee now?* She doesn't respond right away, which isn't her style, but at least I feel a little less guilty about forgetting her.

Sara leans into my room. "Hi, I'm home. Sorry if I scared everyone this morning. I just ended up falling asleep, and…I know, it was completely irresponsible of me. I feel awful, and I already talked to Mom, and I explained how it was my fault and not Camille's. Mom understands, and things are fine."

"Are you just having a whole conversation with yourself?"

She laughs and leans out of the room. "Shut up."

I turn back to my computer, which is good timing because Oliver's requested my friendship on Facebook, and that feels nice and official. I lose plenty of time looking at all his photos and checking out the kinds of people he's friends with, but there aren't any scary surprises. There aren't any surprises at all. Oliver is exactly what he seems like.

But once I've finished my online Oliver profiling, there are surprises, and I guess you could call them scary. A bunch of photos Kaitlyn's tagged in start popping up. She's posing for the camera with Josie and Lora and the other girls they hang out with, and it's clear these were taken at some club they snuck into, just like Kaitlyn wanted. I didn't think she'd actually been *serious* about the whole club thing. She's dressed in something sparkly and wearing more makeup than usual, and honestly, she looks great but even less like the girl I'm best friends with.

I know she talked about us doing this like we could aspire to no greater fun, but I really did think she meant *us*. Sure, I'd left her out of seeing *The Apple*, but it was only because I knew it wasn't her thing. Seeing her captured in images looking so happy and cool, well, someone might as well have punched me in the face.

I click back to Oliver because I can't look at Kaitlyn another minute longer.

At school the next morning, I hope Kaitlyn will be at my locker. I hope she'll have a hilarious story about going out with those girls, and I'll have a killer punch line, and everything will be normal again.

But she's not there, so I hang out with Mitchell and Chelsea and discuss our favorite parts of *The Apple* (flying Cadillac wins, hands-down!) before class. It's way better than hanging out alone (or, ugh, showing up to class way early), but considering I have actual, no-need-to-lie details about my date with Oliver and it's-kind-of-weird-Sara-canceled-on-Dexter-and-stayed-out-all-night-with-her-biological-mom details to mull over, I hate that Kaitlyn's nowhere to be found. Everyone here is great, but I don't know any of them enough to say what's in my brain. I stick with flying cars.

The latest issue of the *Ticknor Voice* is out at lunchtime, and even though nothing of mine is in it, I still take it to my table instead of food. For the first time ever, I pore over the masthead. *The Ticknor Ticker: Kellie Brooks*. I grab my phone and text Adelaide, who I've realized spends her lunches in Jennifer's room, doing newspaper and yearbook stuff. *what the heck is the ticknor ticker???* Her response is almost immediate: *Sorry, that's what Jennifer wants to call your column. I did all I could.*

"Jennifer's calling my column the 'Ticknor Ticker,'"

I say to the rest of the table. "Doesn't that sound like what they call someone's heart when they have high cholesterol or something?" It hits me, as everyone agrees, that Kaitlyn hasn't shown up, even to drop off her stuff and get in line. My purse is dropped in the chair next to me, saved for her, as the first one of us to arrive always does.

"Where's Kaitlyn?" Chelsea asks as she catches me staring at the empty-except-for-my-purse chair.

I shrug, even though I guess I know and just don't want to. "No clue."

But we both crane our necks over to check out the section of tables for the Chosen Ones. My gaze catches on something familiar, a bright green shirt I'd bought for myself the other month at Kaitlyn's urging and then given to her after a few failed attempts at wearing it. It's just there, in between Lora's red shirt and Josie's white shirt.

Lora and Josie are talking, a lot, which means Kaitlyn isn't, but she is smiling. They're all smiling. How is this actually happening? Kids—not me, other kids—dream every day about suddenly conquering that table, but it doesn't just *happen*.

But of course it's not really the sudden and nearly unprecedented climb to the social top that I can't handle. It's that the climber is Kaitlyn. The climber is my best friend who didn't say anything to me.

Before I can make myself turn away, Kaitlyn catches me looking, and she looks right back. There is a lot I want to get out of that look, like apology or guilt or an explanation or *something* that would make me feel better.

But I get nothing.

Chelsea notices, too, but we don't say anything, just go

back to eating. (I also, of course, get out my phone to text Oliver, since lunch is pretty safe for breaking that rule. *hope u haven't seen any spiders today!!* He responds almost immediately: *Don't even joke, Kellie. Spiders are serious business.* And then, *Thanks for the playlist. Listening right now. You're right about The Hollies song.*) Mitchell asks about Kaitlyn, but instead of just pointing to her and explaining how she's surpassed us in the Hierarchy of High School, I shrug and change the subject to the autumnal photo that was finally settled on (leaves, which is clichéd but a good shot).

And, of course, I text Oliver as much as I can squeeze in before lunch is up. It's good to have one person who seems to care about me. Besides my family. They're required to, after all.

Kaitlyn sits next to me in geometry like always. I keep thinking of ways to address it, but I've read too many books forced on me by Mom. Saying things like, *Could you not find your way to the table?* or, *In case you thought my purse deserved its own seat, that was actually reserved for you* aren't actually helpful but passive-aggressive. And I'm not perfect, but I'm not that.

"You want to do something after school?" I ask her on our way out of class, even though it's my night to pick up Finn from daycare. Sara will understand if I ask for a switch. Retaining my best friend is high priority.

"Probably not," she says without real eye contact. "See you later."

"Kaitlyn—"

She walks past me like we've ended our conversation, but my mouth is literally still open, so I can't believe she honestly thinks we did. I'd cry except that I never cry at school, and it's also like my brain has too much to do to focus on just one thing like *crying*. Instead, I run to my car and blast the radio and speed off to get Finn. It's hard being in a bad mood when Finn's around.

Sara's already home when we get there. Finn challenges us to Candyland, and we both accept. Sure, it's not exactly a challenging game, but unlike the ones Sara really enjoys where you have to be smart with words or history or knowing what crappy pop groups somehow earned Grammy Awards, we all have a fair shot. The only bad thing about it is it always makes me hungry, so after the game is over (Sara wins, regardless), I offer to drive them both down the street so we can load up on sugar while Mom isn't home.

"Everything okay with you?" she asks me as we watch Finn decide between flavors of taffy.

"I don't know. Kaitlyn..." I shrug because I'm not even sure what to call it. "It feels like she maybe doesn't want to be my friend anymore, out of *nowhere*, and I don't even know why I care."

"Why *wouldn't* you care?" Sara leans over and helps Finn reach the blue raspberry taffy he's pawing toward. "You two have been friends forever."

"I know, but...she's been into different stuff lately." I feel no need to add that I guess I'm into different stuff, too. "She's maybe not the same person I became friends with. Maybe it shouldn't be such a big deal."

"You're allowed to *feel things*, Kell."

"I feel things!"

"Besides bravery and coolness," she says, which sounds nuts but also nice, so I don't fight her. "I'm sorry about

Kaitlyn."

"I don't know what I'm supposed to do," I say. "I don't even know if I *am* supposed to do something."

Sara reaches out and squeezes my hand. "Sometimes it just takes awhile when people change."

"Takes awhile to what? Realize you shouldn't be in their lives anymore, or figure out how you still can be?"

She's quiet for a little bit, still holding my hand. "Both."

CHAPTER ELEVEN

Tuesday isn't as bad as Monday, I guess, because the shock's worn off. Still, I hate this whole thing where Kaitlyn will walk by and stare right through me, and I have to act like that's fine. I have newspaper after school, which I'm realizing I don't mind at all. By now I have an idea about the outdoor cafeteria tables, and Adelaide and Jennifer approve it and write it next to my name on the board. Also, miraculously, my name is now spelled correctly! I'm like a real living and breathing member of the *Ticknor Voice*, and even the "Ticknor Ticker" is growing on me.

My phone is out during our meeting, in case Oliver texts (or maybe Kaitlyn with a huge and appropriate apology/explanation), but Jennifer doesn't seem to care that it rings (MOM CALLING) or that I duck into the hallway and answer it.

"Hi, baby. We're all going to have dinner tonight with Camille—"

"Like, Camille, Camille?"

Mom laughs. "Camille, Camille, yes. Your dad made reservations, and we need to leave the house by six thirty. I just wanted to make sure you didn't have plans after your newspaper meeting."

"I don't. See you then, Mom."

"See you, baby. Have a great rest of the day at school."

"I'll get right on that. Bye." I click off my phone and think about this piece of news while I listen to the rest of the staff's submissions. Yeah, by now I have a pretty good picture in my head of Camille, an older version of Sara who is smarter than anyone I've ever known, a scientist but totally not a geek.

To be honest, I'm getting a little nervous about Camille, because Camille is not going to be a weirdo. Camille is not going to be Dad with his secret girlfriend and his playing favorites, and she definitely isn't going to be Mom with her billion tattoos and free-love approach to life.

I mean, Sara *has* to like her more, deep down.

"We're all going to The Beanery," Paul tells me as the meeting's winding down. He makes really direct eye contact with me, which is about as subtle as all the butt-staring he did the last time we all hung out. "Need a ride?"

"I have family stuff," I say. "Next time."

"Come anyway!" Jessie says, and I actually feel bad that I can't, even though obviously the Camille dinner is a thing not to be missed. So I say good-bye and head outside with Mitchell and Chelsea, who I assume are off to make out instead of consorting with the other newspaper people.

Mitchell extends his hand to me as we walk through the parking lot.

"What? Are you requiring payment for your friendship

services now?" I ask, even though *services* sounds dirty once I say it.

"I need to get back that iPod I loaned you the other week. Kyle says he needs it to run."

I dig it out of my purse and hand it over, even though I haven't had a chance to steal any of its music yet. Mitchell's chemistry lab partner has surprisingly decent taste. "There's no way that kid runs. We had Fitness and Recreation together freshman year, and he got winded when we did those short relays."

Mitch laughs, shoving the iPod into his pocket. "Oh, man, I know."

Chelsea's eyes light up. "Didn't he run in, like, loafers?"

Mitch is practically giggling as we reach our cars. "Who even *owns* loafers?"

"My dad, that's it." I think about mentioning the impending Dinner with Camille, but even though I've known Mitchell since high school began, and Chelsea since last year when they started going out, they've never been people I talked to about serious stuff. "See you tomorrow. That was pretty fun."

"Newspaper?" He grins as Chelsea gets into her car. "So you're, like, really into it."

"I am definitely *not*," I say without even considering that maybe I am. "Ugh, sorry, I guess I am. You never told me it was fun. You never even told me you were on it."

"Kellie thinks something's fun!" he singsongs.

"I think lots of things are fun," I say, even though I'm not dumb enough not to know what he means. It used to matter so much that I seemed like I wasn't trying too hard at anything.

But everyone on the *Ticknor Voice* tries hard, and that turns into this tangible thing. Okay, it's just a paper lots of people barely glance at before throwing away, but it's still something real that I'm now a part of.

At home I try my best to look nice, borrowing this moss-green wrap dress from Mom that always makes me feel sophisticated or whatever and jamming my hair through the flat iron I rarely take out of the bathroom drawer. It's always a fascinating process, taming my haphazard waves. I know Mom goes through this most mornings that her hair isn't in a ponytail (and even some of those so her blond locks will hang just so), but if I'm ever the kind of lady who won't leave the house without x amount of makeup and y minutes spent on my hair, I'll kill myself.

I wear my nice boots that I'm pretty sure Jayne picked out for Dad to give me for my birthday last year, but I wear them over fishnets, because I saw a photo of some actress on some blog who was dressed really nice but with fishnets, and I sort of want that to be my thing someday. I say "someday" because even though I bought the fishnets right away after I saw that picture, whenever I wear them I feel like I'm in costume as who I want to be, or maybe even will be eventually. Tonight though, I'm in Mom's dress with controlled hair and without any chipped nail polish, I've gone out on an actual date with an actual college guy, and there is no Kaitlyn in my life, so maybe it is okay after all to be a new Kellie.

Sara is meeting us there, as is Dad, so it's just Mom and me in her car on the way to Brentwood, which is the next town over from Dad's office and where Dad tends to meet us on Mom nights when we have plans with him for any reason. The reservations are at a restaurant Dad is really into, the kind of place that is really proud of itself for serving expensive entrées and forcing any men who want to dine there to put on a jacket. I've never paid for an expensive meal in my life, but if I was putting up that kind of money, I think I should get to wear whatever I want.

"Why isn't Russell coming?" I almost ask about Finn, too, but if a guy has to put on a jacket to walk into a restaurant, he probably is also forced to take off his mask and cape.

"We thought we'd just keep it to the four of us," Mom says. "Well, the four of us plus Camille, of course."

"Why's Sara at Dad's?" I ask. Normally, we have mirror schedules, after all.

"You two are welcome to go to your dad's whenever you want, baby," she says, which doesn't answer my question at all.

I get out my phone and check to see if I missed any texts. (I did.) And it isn't one from Kaitlyn (sadly, my dream scenario #1) or Sara (I guess at this moment my dream scenario #2, for some kind of explanation or prep info about Camille so I feel less nervous about meeting her), but it is from dream scenario #3 at least. *Hang out soon? This week?* I respond right away: *yes!!* It sounds really eager, I know, but Oliver sounds eager, too. I'm not worrying about any of that dumb dating stuff. We like each other. This can be great and easy. Right now I'm so glad to have something great and easy.

Dad and Sara are already at the restaurant when we walk in, and Dad holds his finger to his watch as we walk up to them outside the restaurant's front door. He's always so eager to be the only prompt one in any situation that involves Mom or me.

"It's six till, Clay," Mom says. "We're all on time. Sara, you look gorgeous."

She does, too, in a deep blue dress and these patterned heels that contain the same blue that's in the dress. When I try things like that, I end up looking like the "before" photo in a makeover article, but on Sara it works.

"She's here," Sara says instead of *thank you*, and the three of us follow her line of vision to a metallic gray Audi. Camille looks almost exactly like I thought she would, from combining what's in my head with what Sara has told me. She's nearly as tall as Sara, with darker blond hair, and of course she has Sara's cheekbones. I did figure she'd be in a suit or something, but she's wearing a tailored brown leather jacket over a deep blue sweater, brown pants cut like jeans, and boots that put mine to shame. Fashionable is even scarier than super professional.

"Hi," she says to Sara. "I'm Camille Jarvis," she says to Mom and Dad.

Mom and Dad shake her hand, while I feel about Finn's age for getting overlooked.

"This is Kellie," Mom says.

Camille shakes my hand. "Hi, Kellie."

I follow everyone inside. The restaurant isn't like a lot of Dad's usuals—dark and straight out of a business-deal scene from a movie—but brighter and more open. If this place is straight out of a movie, it at least isn't a mob one.

That's vaguely comforting.

The maître d' takes us to a table right in the center of everything and hands us menus. To him I'm sure this looks like a very normal meal and not one of the weirdest of our lives.

Camille asks Dad a few polite questions about his law firm before it happens. "And you're a paralegal, Melanie?"

Mom is midsip on a glass of red wine, and I can tell just how close all of us come to getting doused in it. "Oh, wow, no, I haven't been a paralegal since the girls were little, way back when Clay and I were still married."

When I see the way Sara's eyes widen, then shut, I know in some ways she's no better than Dad with his secret divorce and then secret girlfriend. This is not the kind of thing I want to learn about my sister, that she thinks our family has to be edited and polished before anyone hears about us.

"You're divorced?" Camille asks, then turns to Sara. "You didn't tell me that."

"I didn't think it was important," Sara says, which makes both Mom's and Dad's eyebrows shoot way, way up. "In the context of telling you about me. We're all well-adjusted and—"

"The agency gave me a short profile," Camille says, directed at Mom. "That's how I knew you'd been a paralegal. Sara hadn't said anything to—"

"I think we're all well aware Sara doesn't lie," Mom says with a smile. "To answer your original question, sort of, my husband and I run a tattoo shop on South Grand, The Family Ink. It's our dream and the most fun I've ever had in my life."

Mom can't talk to someone for longer than ten minutes without saying something goofy like that.

"You're remarried," Camille says, piecing it together. "Do you have other children?"

"Russell and I have a four-year-old boy," Mom says, still

smiling, now with that glazed look she sometimes gets when telling someone how fantastic her life is.

"What about you, Kellie?" Camille asks.

"I don't have any children," I say. "Though I do have my own law firm. We're Dad's biggest competition."

Only Mom laughs at that, and I'm sure it's only to encourage my self-esteem.

"Do you attend Nerinx Hall as well?"

"No, Mom and Dad let us pick where we went, so I go to Ticknor Day School."

"I've heard Ticknor's a very good school," she says.

"If she applied herself, she'd get a lot out of it." It's the kind of thing Dad says a lot, but it really never stops feeling like having a bucket of cold water thrown on me.

"Kellie's on the school newspaper staff." Mom squeezes my hand under the table because she isn't big into calling Dad out on his shit, not since the divorce at least. Before the divorce I was too little to pick up on the intricacies of their relationship; also, it was tough being truly disappointed in someone under the age of six, so I'd had it easier then.

"Oh," Camille says. "Are you a writer?"

I make sort of a *psssh* noise and fidget with my salad fork. Everyone seems content to let it stand at that, but it hits me that I wish I would have said *yes*. For maybe the first time it sounds good to be anything other than nothing, and not just because of Dad.

Mom and Dad ask Camille a bunch of questions about her work, while I zone out and dip bread into olive oil. Camille's mystique alone isn't enough to make me suddenly care about physics.

"I did hope to talk to the two of you," Camille is saying

by the time our salads are being delivered by our extremely hot waiter who is built tall and lean like Oliver. I guess that means I have A Type. Anyway, since conversation seems to have left science behind, I tune back in. "Next weekend I'm attending a conference in the Bay area, where—as I think you know—Sara's biological father lives. The two of them are really looking forward to meeting, and my work will pay for Sara's plane ticket and hotel room."

"It should be fine," Mom says, because isn't everything okay with Mom? Hi, Mom, I'm joining a cult! I'm going to clown school! I'm experimenting with drugs and alcohol! All probably fine in the name of letting us be us, right? "But we'll have to discuss it first, of course."

Dad makes a face that I bet he makes a lot regarding Mom's decision making. "Right, we'll have to discuss it, Camille."

"If you could just let me know within a few days," Camille says. "I hate to put a rush on it, but considering there are travel arrangements to be made…"

"Oh, I understand," Mom says. "We'll let you know as soon as we can."

After dinner with Camille, Sara is forced to ride home with Mom and me because she forgot to take her laptop to Dad's. It is a very silent car ride.

Home, though? Another story.

I chase Sara into her room. "You're worse than Dad!"

"I am not, and you wouldn't understand."

It stops me like a force field because Sara doesn't say things like that, even though in reality of course there are so many things I wouldn't understand. I've never gotten straight As or been Dad's pride and joy or effortlessly looked like an easy-breezy Cover Girl ad.

"I know I haven't gone through this," I say. "But I'd never *lie* about my family."

"Do you have any idea how hard it was for her?" Sara asks, and for some dumb reason, I think she means Mom. "She didn't want to give me up, but she had to. And she'd picked Mom and Dad from all the profiles she'd read because she liked that they were professionals who worked together and had this great marriage. Her parents were divorced when she was little, and she didn't want that for me."

"But...we didn't go through any angst or drama over the divorce. And Mom's so happy with Russell—and we wouldn't even have Finn otherwise!—and I guess Dad's happy enough with Jayne. If Mom and Dad were still married, we'd probably all be miserable."

"That isn't the point," she says.

"I don't know how that can *not* be the point."

Mom leans into the room. "Kellie, can I have a minute with your sister?"

"Fine." I retreat to my room, where I change my new-Kellie outfit for an old-Kellie one, pajama pants and a Woodstock T-shirt, with my lip gloss blotted off and my hair in a messy ponytail. Though who knows how classic Kellie that actually is? I guess it wasn't very long ago I didn't think about how I looked at all. Now I care at least a little.

I get through my homework, as well as chatting with

Adelaide, Mitchell, and Chelsea, and am thinking about sending Oliver a text when Mom knocks on my door.

"Hey, baby." She sits down on my bed, and even though Mom isn't a nosy type, I still close my laptop, knowing the current message on the screen is from Adelaide with a link to some sex-education site she swears will simplify my life. "Just so you're in the loop, Sara's going with Camille to San Francisco next weekend."

"After she lied about us? Like us weirdos are something to be ashamed of?"

"You know that isn't why she did it, baby," Mom says. "And of course she's going. It's what Sara wants."

"Okay," I say, even though I have ten billion more questions for Mom.

"Thank you for being so understanding, Kell-belle."

"So what did everyone think about my trial run at the shop?" I ask. I'm not above using nice moments for personal gain. "I didn't mess anything up, and all the customers seemed to like me. So I was thinking—"

"Just don't let your grades slip," she says. "Or your newspaper responsibilities. And you should still go out with your friends and have fun whenever you can. And—"

"I get it, Mom. That means I'm hired, right?" I hug her again, triumphant this time. "Be happy, now you're my boss *and* my mom."

"I'm always your boss!" she says, which makes me laugh because that isn't exactly the parenting manual Mom follows. "And I *am* happy. You earned this. I hope you're happy, too."

I want to be, and I beam at her like I really am. But all I can think of is Sara, on a plane, flying away from us.

CHAPTER TWELVE

I go to Dad's after school on Wednesday, since it's a night Sara and I had already agreed on. I'm hoping we can have a normal, non-snappy conversation, but when she gets there, she just waves to me before shutting herself in her room. Luckily, after I get a bunch done on my first newspaper column and while I'm struggling through geometry on my own, Oliver calls. I pause the TiVo and click on my phone. "Hey."

"Hey, what's going on?"

In general I'm a texter not a caller, so I rarely come up with good answers to questions like that. "Just homework. Nothing exciting. You?"

"Same here. Listen, my friend's band is doing a set on campus tonight, you want to come? I think you'd really like them."

I trust Oliver about music, plus meeting him at school means there is a likely chance we can go to his room and make out again, so I let him know I'll ask Dad as soon as he's home.

If having a boyfriend is mainly about going to concerts and haunted houses and dinners, followed up with lots of making out, I am very much onboard.

Dad is home at his usual time, and I greet him while still trying to look *casual*.

"There she is. What sounds good for dinner, kiddo? I can make something, or we can go out, your choice."

"Actually, if it's okay, I thought I might go to this presentation at SLU tonight." I'm thrilled with my own quick thinking. I'm not sure if Dad would be okay with me going out with a guy, and I don't feel like finding out right now. "Is that okay?"

"Presentation on what?"

"Modern music." Nicely done, self.

"I don't see anything wrong with that," he says. "Is Sara going?"

"Just me. I won't be out too late." *Success.* I duck into my room to call Oliver, who tells me I can come over right away.

It's kind of weird, walking into his dorm room and feeling this warmth in my gut, like a good panic attack, if that is even possible. Only a few days since I saw him, and seeing him again is a very good thing.

"I have a lot of homework," someone says, and I realize his roommate is in there, practically hidden behind stacks of textbooks and his laptop.

"We're going anyway." Oliver walks me into the hallway. "That guy makes me crazy."

"I probably wouldn't like getting kicked out of my own room so people could make out," I say. "To be fair and all."

"If you can't handle that, don't go to college." Oliver laughs and leans in to kiss me, and it literally takes my breath away. We are getting really good at this. "It's great seeing you."

"You, too." I kiss him back, and before long we're the kind of obnoxious people I hate, making out in the hallway like suddenly that isn't tacky. "We should probably…"

"Yeah." He takes my hand and leads me through campus on tree-lined paths until we reach a tiny stage haphazardly set up outside. A few totally nondescript dudes with longish hair and ironic T-shirts are setting up their equipment with a very descript girl with platinum-blond hair and perfect black eyeliner (how do people do that, anyway?) and a patterned blue-and-black dress that the new Kellie would kill for. I really never get jealous of girls like that; I just wonder what it's like to be them.

"Which one's your friend?" I ask, like I can even tell the dudes apart.

"I know them all," he says. "And Sophie's my ex, but we're still cool and everything."

Oh, *hell* no. "Your vegetarian ex?"

"My vegetarian ex, yeah." He laughs. "I'm not into her anymore or anything. I just think you'll like their music."

I *do* like their music, jangly guitars and pop melodies and all that other stuff that is probably why I listen to the oldies station nearly exclusively. Oliver is wonderful to know this is exactly what I needed, and I decide to be mature and not jealous of The Amazing Sophie.

After they play, I tag along while Oliver says hi to all of the guys. Apparently, he and Sophie aren't *cool and everything* enough to actually speak to each other. She catches my eye while Oliver and the drummer are talking about some professor they hate, and I find myself turning to face her.

"You guys are really good."

"Aw, thanks," she says, and I think maybe she's pulling some *aw, shucks* faux-modesty crap. But then she grins like the sincerest creature to ever accept a compliment. "You're Oliver's new girlfriend?"

"I guess I am," I say, because he can't hear me from where he's standing, and because it might be true. "And you're the old one?"

She laughs as she winds up a cable that had connected her guitar and amp. "You might say that. I'm glad Oliver met someone. He—"

"Sophie, I'm going to bring the van around," the drummer tells her.

"Oh, great." She turns back to me, slipping the cable over her arm like a purse strap. "He does better when he's with someone. Good to meet you, thanks for coming."

I step back, rejoin Oliver, and we walk through campus in the direction of his dorm, though we stop a few buildings over where there is a little bench. We sit down, and I stretch my feet across him so they dangle off the edge. It's fun being cozy even with what The Amazing Sophie said on my mind.

"How'd you know I'd like the band?" I ask.

"Well, they sound a little sixties," he says with a grin. "And since I don't think there's one band listed in your favorites on your profile that still plays shows…"

"Not true. The living members of The Who still tour sometimes." I laugh. "You have a point. Do you think it's weird?"

He shrugs, circling one of his hands around one of my ankles, rubbing it just a little under my jeans. Why the heck that feels so good—I mean, it's my frigging *ankle*—I don't know. "Maybe. Weird's not bad."

"Truer words were never spoken." I lean forward, and he follows my lead and kisses me. "Do you want to read my first newspaper column?"

"Right now?"

I laugh and shake my head. "I can email it to you. If you want."

"Definitely. I'd send you that Kant paper I've been working on, but I don't think you'd find it very interesting. I definitely don't."

"What part of philosophy *is* interesting, then?" I ask. "I figure you like it or you wouldn't major in it. It's not like people make millions off philosophy."

"Yeah, suddenly you sound like my dad." He grins at me. "I just like thinking about life, reasoning it out, putting order to things. Does that make any sense?"

"I guess so." I shiver a little and wind my striped scarf (knitted by Russell's mom) more tightly around my neck. Fall is really here. "I have no idea what I'll major in. Dad says I need to figure that out this year."

"You really don't. You're only a junior, and you could be undeclared for a while anyway. Your dad seems a little…"

"Assholey?"

"I was gonna say 'intense,'" he says. "I know Sara feels like a hard act to follow."

"'Feels like'? So it's not my imagination." I feel bitchy all of a sudden. "Sorry, I—"

"Trust me, I get it." He leans over to kiss me again. Late at night his chin is scratchy with stubble. "Like I've said, Dexter's younger, and it still feels the same way sometimes.

One day he'll be running the country and I'll be—"

"Philosophizing?"

We both laugh really hard at that. It's funny; whenever I'd thought about meeting a guy or having a boyfriend or whatever, I'd thought about the making out and the possibility of sex, but I hadn't counted on knowing a guy who'd just *get me* like Oliver does. Get me and *care*. A good combo.

"What about writing?" he asks. "You're on the newspaper and all."

It's nice he finds me capable of things. "I don't know, it's new. Maybe I won't be that good at it."

"I dunno, Kellie, you seem like you've got a lot to say. My money's on you being more than good."

If there was ever a moment I just sort of wanted to gaze adoringly at a guy, this is it. "Thank you."

"You should probably go." Oliver checks his watch. "It's close to eleven."

I appreciate that he keeps an eye on my curfew versus acting like I'm a dork for even having one. "Yeah, I'm at Dad's tonight, I definitely should."

Of course we get into the backseat of my car. By now I'm not worried about The Amazing Sophie's words or my total fail at honesty the other night or anything else. Maybe I'm not stellar at this relationship stuff, but as long as we get to go places and talk and make out—and let me state that the making out going on right here in the backseat of my car is some of the best stuff that has ever happened to me—I can only welcome this.

Kaitlyn is waiting by my locker the next morning, a fact that causes me to spill my pile of books onto the floor.

"God, Kell."

"You've lost your right to be personally offended that I'm a klutz," I say. "What?"

"I found this at my house." She shoves a T-shirt at me, my worn-in, comfy Family Ink shirt from the batch made when the shop first opened. "It's not like I want it."

"Also it's not like it's yours." I open my locker and toss it inside. "Kaitlyn, you can't just *do* this."

"Do what?" she asks so innocently it's easy to forget she's blown me off for days now.

"Act like nothing's going on when something's going on."

"I don't know what you're talking about," she says, like having a sweet tone makes her a sweet person.

"Kellie." Adelaide barrels in between us and hands me a cardboard coffee cup. "It's vanilla cocoa, don't worry. I'm bribing you because I need your help."

Kaitlyn rolls her eyes and starts to walk off. I lean out around Adelaide, whose hair today makes her taller than usual.

"Kaitlyn—"

I'm positive she hears me—she's not deaf, after all—but she just keeps walking. And I don't know why I'm surprised.

"Ugh," I say aloud, and then I remember I'm holding hot cocoa. "Oh my God, this is so good."

"I told you to support local businesses. Back to the point, I got assigned this paper on bodily integrity, and I spent all of last night racking my brain for a good angle, and it hit me this morning that I want to discuss body modifications. So obviously I need to interview your parents."

I take another sip of the divine hot cocoa. "You didn't have to bribe me for that. Mom loves talking about herself."

"Fantastic. Class?"

"I'll meet you there." I'm not quite ready to leave the hallway and therefore admit the school day has officially started, a lot like never wanting to fall asleep on Sunday nights because doing so is accepting the weekend is over.

I catch up with Mitchell, Chelsea, and a few more newspaper peeps as they walk by. Of course I wish I could have just talked to Kaitlyn. I have Oliver details to share. I have Sara stuff to talk out. I have so frigging much going on right now, but she's giving me stuff back like we'll never speak again. Our best friendship feels like something I made up instead of our real and shared history.

"Thanks, seriously, for this cocoa," I tell Adelaide as I take my seat behind her in class. "It's the best ever."

"Normally, I'd say that's a bit hyperbolic, but I'll let it go," she says. "Ugh, Kaitlyn's heinous. I tried to save you."

"So you're not really writing a paper about body modification?"

"No, of course I am. Still, I was trying to get you out of there."

I pass her my notebook containing the essay I'd jotted down last night. "Can you look at this?"

"Kellie, I'm so proud. Getting this in before deadline!"

I shrug even though I am kind of proud of myself, too. Maybe Oliver is right because it seems possible I might be good at this whole writing thing. Maybe I even could do something real with it someday, not to hate on the *Ticknor Voice,* but let's be real. Is this what it's like to be Adelaide or Sara, ambitions and a possible future and all of that?

"It's not really in," I say. "Just a rough draft, I guess. I wanted to see what you thought."

Adelaide has edits for me by lunchtime, so I hang out in Jennifer's classroom to type up the essay on one of the newspaper computers. And, okay, avoid having to see Kaitlyn gushing all over the Cool Kids about their Cool Exploits over the Cool Weekend. Somehow Adelaide completely left the school grounds because she has Chinese takeout for all of us who are using lunch period to work. I guess when you're Adelaide, you get away with a lot.

"Fascinating picture?" I ask Mitchell, who's staring at a shot of the auditorium.

"I'm writing captions." His eyes never leave the photo. "It's harder than it looks. And I'm missing eating with Chels."

"'Auditorium Remodeled, Theatre Geeks Happy'?"

"Hey." Adelaide perches on the desk next to me. "Kellie, stop helping. Mitch, we all appreciate your caption-writing sacrifices. So you and Oliver are official, I hear."

"Official what?" I ask, as Mitchell asks, "Who's Oliver?" but Adelaide ignores him, takes over my computer, and pulls up Oliver's online profile stating he is now—"In a relationship?"

"I know, no longer *it's complicated* with— Are you okay?"

I stare at the words. *Relationship* seems so grown-up. "Yeah, I'm okay. I'm good. I'm apparently *in a relationship.*"

Adelaide cocks her head at me. "You guys have been on two dates. Sounds to me like someone jumped the gun."

"No way, there's been no gun-jumping," I say. "Wait, so you think it's weird? Is it weird?"

"Just talk to him, Kellie." If Adelaide ever wrote a relationship self-help book, it would definitely be called *Just Talk to Him*.

Instead I log into my own account. I have the relationship confirmation request from Oliver with a message. *Cheesy, yeah, but be Facebook official? Big step taking it to the Internet, I know.*

"He's being cute," I say to Adelaide, swiveling the computer monitor in her direction. "See?"

"Hmmm," she says, and she's already back to her own computer. "Do whatever you want, Brooks."

Should he have talked to me? Am I bad at boyfriend stuff? Do I even know enough to be bad? I hover my cursor over *Confirm*, but all I can hear in my brain is *just talk to him*, so I log out and decide that my wanting to do so is mature and not the opposite.

CHAPTER THIRTEEN

Sara texts me as I'm leaving school the next afternoon. *Mom has Finn; meet me at Barnes & Noble in Ladue?* Even though I'm not really over her lying to Camille or semi-ditching us over the weekend, I text back an affirmative and speed over. Being actually mad at Sara is not a thing my brain knows how to do.

I spot her right away in the literature section. "Gross, Hemingway? Doesn't he hate women or something?"

Sara laughs really loudly, for her. "I guess he can be misogynistic on occasion. I'm working on my English paper, though; the topic wasn't up to me."

"You should just go to the library," I say. "Books are free there."

I always tell her that, and she always responds the same way. "The library doesn't really take kindly to all the highlighting I do. This shouldn't take long. Then we can get drinks and talk, okay?"

I sort of frown, because for all the time we spend hanging out, we never need to formally request it with *get drinks and talk*. We just, you know, do. "You're not dying, are you?"

"Not yet." Her focus is already back on the books. "I'll find you in a few, if you want to look around."

I do, and not just because watching someone else shop for books is insanely boring. For once I have extra cash, thanks to my job, so I prowl around for a while and even check out some stuff on essay writing, until Sara walks over with an armful of books.

"Ready?"

I turn away from the section. "Yeah, let's go."

We walk to the café where Sara orders hot cocoa for both of us and hands over her books. I watch her pay with a credit card and don't ask about it until we sit down at the back corner table with our drinks.

"It's nothing," she says. "Dad just thought it would be easier, since I spend so much money on things for school."

That is definitely true, but it's one more thing Dad would never do for me.

"Don't," she says really quickly. "Whatever you're thinking. Dad's just—"

"Easy for you to say." I pick up a copy of some crappy tabloid from the next table and leaf through it.

"I know," she says. "But you know how Dad is."

"Oh, yes," I say. "I definitely do."

"Kell, this isn't a thing. I'd be on your side if it was, but it's only a credit card, and I'm not getting anything fun with it at all." She smiles at me in the way that means I'm supposed to forgive her for being Dad's favorite when she can't help being inherently better-suited for that job. And of course I always do. "Except our drinks. Which was my first breaking of that rule."

I roll my eyes, but I shouldn't get annoyed with her when it is Dad who's behind this. Also, for anyone else cocoa would hardly be seen as a badass move, but for Sara it actually is. "You're such a rebel."

"Anyway." She folds her hands on top of the table. Serious Sara again. "I texted you because I saw — well, maybe it's a joke, considering he used to have that thing about it being complicated with counterculture movements but — "

Oh, crap. I hadn't accepted his request yet, but people had commented and he'd mentioned me.

"Are you and Oliver going out?"

"Why, would that be a problem?" I ask.

"Is that a yes?" she asks in a tone that indicates it very much would be.

"Um, yeah," I say. "I guess we are."

"How do you even know each other? I didn't think you two even spoke the other week at the City Diner."

"It's sort of a long story," I say instead of, *Well, Sara, back on Memorial Day we sort of almost had sex, and we didn't talk for months, but ever since running into each other, something kind of clicked, and he's funny and smart and he's interested in my life, and when he kisses me, I feel a little explodey inside.*

"Hmm," is all she says in her very Sara way.

"I know what you're thinking." I'm desperate to cut her off before she can say what I've been dreading this whole time. Okay, yeah, it isn't like I don't ever worry this smart college guy needs someone more on Sara's level, intellectually or whatever. Weirdly enough, though, we make a lot of sense, at least to me. Oliver laughs so much at the goofy things I say, things I could never imagine Sara coming up with. And Sara would never understand how Oliver feels compared to Dexter, considering it's the way I sometimes feel compared to Sara.

Of course that doesn't mean anyone else would understand us, though.

"Kell, I was just surprised—"

"Is it that shocking that someone who isn't perfect like you could still have someone interested?"

Sara blinks a bunch of times. "What? I didn't say anything like—Why would you—"

"Then what *are* you saying?" I don't like being mad at Sara, beyond dumb stuff like hogging the bathroom or occasionally conveniently having plans on nights she was supposed to watch Finn. But I hog the bathroom and have convenient plans sometimes, too. Stuff like lying to Camille and thinking Oliver is too good for me...this is all new. It's like Sara isn't safe anymore. Sara's as big and unknown as the rest of the world.

"I just don't know if it's a good idea or—"

"It's not up to you." I very calmly stand and grab my purse from the floor. "I'm going home. See you later."

"You really don't have to—"

I slide into my green corduroy jacket and loop my scarf around my neck. "I really think I do." I head out the little side door so I can walk straight to my car. Of course I text Oliver right away, but he's too busy with homework to hang out, a fact I can't hold against him but one that still disappoints me. I'm so used to texting Kaitlyn when I'm annoyed with Sara that I start the message before realizing how royally dumb that is.

Even though she is probably walking pit bulls or handing out condoms or blogging about any number of things, I decide to text Adelaide. She responds right away: *Come over if you want. I'm just stuffing envelopes.*

I laugh aloud at that and take off for Adelaide's house. She opens the front door, and I—remembering the forty-five-second rule—hurry inside. "Hey."

"Hey." She holds out a hand to take my jacket and scarf. "Can you help me with these envelopes?"

"Sure. Is it weird I texted? I mean, we haven't hung out much."

Adelaide shrugs, bounding up the giant staircase in her living room and down a hallway to her room. It's easily twice as big as mine, though painted a similar green and wallpapered with posters (of course hers are mainly of the saving the world variety whereas mine are only capable of saving the world through good music). Her bookcases are jam-packed, just like Sara's, and a retro-looking avocado green desk takes up almost an entire wall.

"I like your room," I say. Good rooms deserve props.

"Thanks." She points to a pile of fliers and envelopes on the floor. "Start stuffing."

I sit down and study a flier. "It seems kind of oxymoronic to send out a bunch of fliers about saving the earth."

"It's recycled paper," she says. "But *I know.*"

I try to fold the paper into neat thirds, like Adelaide is doing, but it takes me a few attempts. She waves an envelope in my direction. "There's a machine that seals everything, so don't worry about that."

That's a relief; this glue isn't exactly tasty. "So my sister thinks I'm an idiot."

"I doubt that." Adelaide folds a few papers in succession like a miniature assembly line. It isn't the response I want at all; Kaitlyn would have helped me bitch about Sara as long as I needed to. "What are you writing about for next week's column?"

"I have no idea." I really doubt my afternoon would have been any worse if I'd just gone home instead of deducing the best methods for folding recycled paper in perfect thirds. "Do you think I'm an idiot?"

Adelaide looks up from her mailings. "What are we even talking about? No, Brooks, you're not an idiot, but you know that. And so does your sister, I'm sure."

Considering that Adelaide doesn't seem to be very good at telling anything but the very direct truth, I force myself to accept all of that and move on. I stay just long enough to get all the papers into envelopes. Adelaide's mom arrives home and invites me to stay to eat, but I'd just gotten a text from Mom that dinner was *one of [my] favorites!!* so I figure I should head home.

Mom insists she doesn't need any help in the kitchen, and Finn is hard at work drawing on a giant piece of paper that's spread out on the kitchen floor (I have no idea how Mom is managing to navigate). That unfortunately means I can't really delay my homework any longer, even if cracking open my geometry book doesn't mean I'll automatically understand it.

"You okay over there, Kell-belle?" Mom asks, probably because I've been sighing really loudly as I try to figure out what a postulate is and therefore, if one is being applied.

"Geometry is ridiculous." I get up to look through the refrigerator for juice. "And there's no way I'll ever use it in my real life, so don't even try that."

"I wasn't about to. Sara's in her room, why don't you ask her for help?"

"Help with what?" Sara walks in, holding out a Barnes & Noble bag. "Here."

"What is it?"

"You could open it and find out."

I reach inside and find the essay book I'd been considering earlier. "What's this for?"

"Sorry if I seemed rude earlier, okay?" She touches my arm just how Mom does sometimes. "I didn't mean to."

I don't know if I'm ready to forgive her, but it is a pretty decent gesture, plus I do need her help to get through my homework. "It's okay. Did you put this on Dad's card?"

She grins at me in a way that I know she did. Rule-bending Sara, I like it a lot.

"Can you help me with this after supper?" I ask.

Sara glances over my shoulder at my textbook. "Yeah, sure. If you help me pack."

It's like my brain wouldn't let me accept that Sara's actually going away with Camille. But I don't want any more fighting or acting weird between us.

"Ooh, I'm good at packing. I can fold clothes really tiny." A skill of mine that has very little use in the real world, though probably no less so than geometry. People go on trips more often than they need to prove how they'd figured out the area of a cylinder.

"I think that's a fair exchange."

So after dinner I take my geometry to Sara's desk while

she flips through her closet. The clothes are organized by color, which I have to admit looks pretty awesome.

"Are you mad I didn't say something about Oliver sooner?" I ask. "I wasn't trying to be dishonest or anything."

"I'm not mad," she says. "What about this dress? I think San Francisco is pretty casual, but I still want to look nice when I meet him. You're better with clothes than I am."

I nod at the sapphire blue dress she holds out. "It's really good. And, no, I'm not."

"By default you are," she says. "Given that I wear a uniform most of the time. You always look cute."

It isn't that Sara never says nice things to me, but this is an especially good-to-hear one. "Seriously?"

"I'm bad at joking, so *of course* seriously."

"Kaitlyn said—"

"Kaitlyn isn't always very fair to you," she says. "I can say that now, right?"

I hold up my notebook. "Will you check this?"

"Yeah, go find some other things for me to take."

I hop up, handing off the notebook, and pull out two sweaters and a dress she'd already passed up. "The thing with Oliver sort of started back at that picnic. Not really, but... well, it's when we met. He texted me after we saw each other at the diner the other night; I don't even know how he got my number."

"*That's* why Dexter was messing with my phone," she says. "You can blame him."

"No, it's a good thing," I say more emphatically than I'd planned. But it is *such a good thing*, after all. "Do you think it's weird Oliver likes me?"

"No, and I never said that. Why would I? You're cute and

funny, and people always like you. No one would be shocked *you're* dating someone."

I think about how bizarre I'd found it when Sara and Dexter first started going out and feel a little guilty. "No one was shocked when—"

"You're bad at lying, Kell," she says. "You're too honest a person."

I roll her sweaters very tightly, though I realize she'll probably want to wear one of these on the plane. I unroll the pale green one and hang it up on her closet door where she'll see it first thing in the morning. "Sorry, then. I don't think it's weird now, at least."

"It's fine." Sara jumps back up and nods at my additions to her suitcase. "You did that problem perfectly, by the way."

I do a brief victory dance. "Are you nervous about going?"

"Why would I be? We've emailed a lot by now, so I know I'll get along with him."

"Yeah, but…taking a trip with Camille seems kind of like a big deal. Right? Like a total mom thing." I hadn't meant to say that last part, but now it's hard to stop. I can at least steer my tone into *nonchalant*. "Do you feel like Camille's your mom now?"

"Of course I don't." Sara stands up and steers me back to my textbook. "But she's…she's something. We have a lot in common, and it's easy to talk to her."

I want to defend Mom, but Mom is a kooky artsy lady who loves us to death and wants us to be happy. Yeah, those are good things, but I understand. I don't want to have that ping of recognition, but Sara must think that Camille is better than Mom at things that matter.

Because maybe that's true.

"Finish your homework," Sara says. "You understand it better than you think."

Mom really wants to drive Sara to the airport on Friday, but instead Camille is swinging by to pick her up. I'm meeting Oliver to hang out soon, but I wait on the front porch and pretend to be jotting down ideas for next week's story when really I just want to bear witness to all of it. Or stop it completely, like I'm going to single-handedly save my family from the unraveling I see Camille capable of starting.

Camille's car pulls up, and I make very serious business of writing down story ideas so that she won't look over my shoulder and see so far I've just made a list of songs that could play if I ever get around to having sex with Oliver. (I cross out The Beatles' "Why Don't We Do It in the Road?" but I'm still sort of laughing about my genius thought. Is laughing during sex considered bad form?)

"Hello, Kellie," Camille says as she walks up the steps to the porch. She is dressed in jeans like Kaitlyn owns, a pair I remember her using her fancy Amex platinum card on even though I'd insisted her butt had looked just as good in the jeans she was wearing from Old Navy. It's weird I hardly talked to Kait this week. I'd been someone who believed the inherent promise in signing yearbooks and school photos *BFF*. And therefore I had no idea a predator was maybe moving in this whole time: the allure of cool and my terminal resistance to it.

"Is Sara ready?" Camille asks.

I jump up and open the door, where both Sara and Mom are standing. For some reason I have the urge to see Mom throw her arms around Sara and demand she doesn't go, but why would Mom do that? Why *should* Mom do that, except for of course keeping our family from collapsing?

...Is it weird I actually think that?

"Call me as soon as you get in," Mom tells Sara.

"I'll try. It'll be late and—"

"Call me," Mom repeats, touching Sara's face with both her hands. "And have fun, sweetie."

"Thanks." Sara waves at me as she picks up her suitcase. "See you, Kell. Thanks for helping me pack."

"Of course," I say, even though I want to throw her suitcase away from her as a delaying tactic while I beg her not to leave us. "Thanks for imparting your geometry genius."

"Ha." She waves and gets into Camille's car. Maybe I should take comfort that Sara's clearly not making this some big, dramatic good-bye. But I still feel the metaphorical earth metaphorically shifting.

Once Camille's car pulls away, I run up to my room, deposit my notebook safely in my desk drawer, switch my faux-vintage Monkees T-shirt for one from my shopping trip with Mom (brown and fitted with little buttons on the cuffs I think are kind of sophisticated), and dash back downstairs. Probably better to just not think about Sara or Camille for awhile. "I'm going out."

"Wait a minute, young lady."

Young lady? Luckily, when Mom walks into the room, I can tell from her smile she's kidding. "What? I'm running late already."

She hugs me really tightly. "You know about being careful, right, baby?"

Oh my God, did she see my list earlier? "Why are you asking me that?"

"Because you've been out with Oliver a couple times now, and I'm not stupid."

"I'm not stupid, either," I say. "And if stuff started happening—which it hasn't—I know about being careful, yeah. Okay? Can I go now?"

"Be home by one," she says. "And, yes. Have a great time."

"Who doesn't have a great time after talking to their mom about their sex life? Bye." I dash out to my car and back out of the driveway like I'm still running away from that conversation. I wonder if Mom had grilled Sara about her hypothetical sex life. I wonder if Sara *has* a hypothetical sex life. Mostly, though, I wonder if Sara will get to San Francisco and gaze upon the two perfect people who created her and ask herself why she should ever bother with us freaks again.

When I arrive at Oliver's dorm, his roommate is out, but the pizza has just arrived. That means we get right to eating, not making out. Still, after watching my sister leave, it is good to be across town doing something completely unrelated.

"There's some party going on tonight," he says as I'm determining whether or not there is a classy way to lick delicious pizza grease off my fingertips. "You want to go after this?"

"Like a frat party?"

Oliver laughs, but not at all like I'm dumb. He is

seriously The Nicest, and it makes me feel lucky just to know him. "Do I seem like I go to frat parties, Kell?"

"Sorry, I don't actually know anything about college, just some special my mom made me watch last year about fraternities hazing people. And, yeah, sounds good. So, um, I noticed you—"

"Oh." He jumps up from the bed, where we're sitting to eat, and gets a little book off his desk. "I just remembered, sorry. I got you something."

I wipe my greasy hands on a napkin before taking it from him. It's a philosophy book about some guy in a wig named David Hume. Lucky for Oliver I'm not a girly type who figured the first gift from her boyfriend—okay, I said *boyfriend*, does that mean it *is* official?—would be flowers or candy or jewelry. "I hope this is like *Philosophy for Dummies*."

"Well...it—" Oliver laughs and sits back down, but closer to me this time. "It sort of is. I just thought maybe you'd be interested, since you asked me what I liked about philosophy."

"Thanks," I say, and not just because I realize I haven't yet. "Hopefully, I'll understand it, civilian to the philosophy world and all."

"Don't worry," he says. "I like Hume a lot, and I just thought you'd like it, too, what he says about life and all. I mean, it's out of our control, but it'll keep going on, even when things get rough."

I like the sound of that a lot. Also, I like the sound of Oliver's voice, how this old, wigged guy means a lot to him. And I really like that this book is in my hands, and this guy who thinks about things bigger than himself also cares about me. Maybe a lot of the things I'm into aren't very serious, but I still think it's better to really care than not.

"Anyway, sorry I interrupted, what were you saying?" Oliver kisses me right before taking another piece of pizza. "You noticed I what?"

Now that I'm holding this book and thinking how truly much I just *like* this guy, I wish I hadn't brought it up. Just Talk to Him, though, yeah? "Just your, um, your Facebook profile? I saw you put that you were in a relationship."

"Oh." Oliver looks sort of relieved, then confused, and then he takes both my hands in his like we're some cheesy romantic couple who does things like that all the time. "Not cool?"

"I just thought—" I stop and try to figure out the fairest way to say it. Both for him and for me. "I guess I thought we'd talk about it before doing something like making it Facebook official."

"Sorry," he says quickly and takes a deep breath. "I'll take it down if you—"

"No, it's okay," I say. "But I hadn't even told my sister that we were going out yet, and because of you doing that, she found out from Facebook and not from me. If we could just talk about stuff first…"

"Definitely." He's nodding like I do when Mom or Dad lectures me about something where we all know I'm dead, dead wrong. On one hand, awesome that he is with me here on this. On the other, is that really the reaction I want from my boyfriend? "I hear you and what you're saying. I just really like you, Kell."

"I really like you, too," I say. "Also, duh, I was joking about Facebook official being some big thing."

"You are a big thing, though," he says. "To me."

I used to think sincerity was some kind of foreboding of the dorkiest of humanity, but a lot has gone kind of crazy lately, and one thing that hasn't is him. I start to thank him for saying the sweetest things ever, but instead I just kind of pounce on him and kiss him.

It seems to be the right reaction.

The party is in the next dorm building over from Oliver's, and even though it's basically just a ton of people shoved into a few tiny rooms, listening to loud indie rock and drinking crappy beer, I'm glad to be here. College party, keg beer, sneaking gropey moves when people aren't looking, all checked off my list of Tasks to (Hopefully) Accomplish in High School. And Oliver has all these friends who want to talk to him and ask him about classes! He looks so alive when he talks to people, too; he isn't at all someone who could sit back and not care. These days I am over anyone who can do that.

Oliver's friends ask my name and my major—sometimes I cop to being a junior at Ticknor, sometimes I just make stuff up. (Oliver laughs particularly hard when I respond with *oceanography.*) Everyone includes me in their conversations, and it's nice to think that even if I can't get into as good of a school as Sara will that maybe college will still be pretty great for me.

Plus, like all of that isn't fantastic enough, it turns out that Oliver's roommate is gone for the whole weekend. We, of course, decide to leave the party early to take advantage, but even with an empty room and Oliver's cozy bed, I keep getting distracted.

"You okay?" he asks me. "Thinking too much about your

oceanography finals?"

I laugh and shrug. "It's sort of a weird night. All this stuff going on with Sara, it's making me crazy, I think."

"What stuff? You want to talk?"

I start to say *no*, but actually I do. I've been keeping so much of this inside. "Sara's been hanging out a lot with her biological mom. And I just sort of have this gross feeling that the more time she spends with her, the less use she'll have for us. We can't compete with some crazy-smart scientist woman, right?"

"I don't think it'll be like that," he says. "Not to disregard your feelings."

"What if you had some other family member who was super into philosophy?" I ask. "Wouldn't you want to run in their direction? Because if the only family I had was, you know, Dad, and he was still the same, telling me how I'm bad at life, and I had some way out, wouldn't I take it? Maybe Sara's whole life has been like that, being a Normal in a family of—"

"Listen, I get it, trust me. But even if she fits in better with her biological family, I think that just adds to her life, doesn't take away from yours."

I want him to be right, but maybe it's enough that he believes that.

"You need to get home? It's almost twelve thirty."

"I do, yeah." My great curfew protector. "Thanks for listening."

Oliver shrugs. "It's what I'm here for, Kell."

I love how much he really means that.

CHAPTER FOURTEEN

After work the next night, I meet up with a bunch of people from the paper (and some of their significant others) at Mokabe's. There's something about the crowded atmosphere that is kind of what I picture hanging out at a bar is like, so for people in high school, I guess it's the next best thing. For people like us in high school, at least. Kaitlyn probably has a fake ID by now and a regular bartender who makes her some girl drink, pink liquid in a martini glass. I imagine her drinking it alongside Lora and Josie and whoever else and wonder if she would be thinking about me at all, even if it is to speculate about how uncool my night probably is in comparison.

I'm pretty sure I see Oliver walk by, so I make up a lame excuse about phone reception and duck outside. I'd been wrong but not totally off base; it's Dexter who is walking up the sidewalk. "Oh, hey."

"Oh, hey, you." He walks back from his pack of dudes. "What's up?"

"Honestly?" I laugh and hope I don't sound crazy. "I thought you were Oliver."

"I *knew* it, like since when would Kellie Brooks go chasing me down? Sorry to disappoint. Actually, though, while I've got you out here, have you heard from Sara? Since she got to Frisco?"

"I don't think anyone actually says that. And she called my mom to let her know she was there, because Mom said she had to, but that's it. I guess you haven't?"

"I haven't." Dexter crosses his arms, frowns in a way I haven't seen from him. "Not used to her blowing me off."

"I'm sure she's just busy," I say even though I don't like the sound of that at all.

"Yeah, maybe. Anyway. Gonna jet."

I wave to him and walk back inside, where Byron has taken my spot. Adelaide yells at him as soon as she sees I'm back, and Byron hunts down another chair.

"Were you out talking to Dexter?" Adelaide asks me. "I used to think he was really cute, you know."

"Before you met Byron?" I ask.

"That's right, Kellie, once I had a boyfriend, I never looked at another guy again. No, when I first met him. Post going out with Byron, thank you very much."

Adelaide is so mature.

"The thing about Dexter is, though," Adelaide says, "he's a great guy, but he's always trying so hard."

"I've totally thought that, too!" I'm a little thrilled that someone else sees part of life just how I do. Especially someone genius like Adelaide.

"You can't really blame him." Byron appears with a chair he'd commandeered from somewhere. I had no idea he'd been listening. "It's probably rough feeling like you have to make up for your brother's screwups," he continues, which sends jolts through me.

"Byron, did you know Oliver is Kellie's boyfriend?" Adelaide asks way more calmly than I would have. Not that there's any reason for Adelaide to freak out about Oliver being some kind of huge disaster.

I look over to make sure no one else is listening to any of this, because I definitely don't want the whole *Ticknor Voice* staff to think I'm going out with a Huge Disaster.

"Sorry, I didn't know," Byron says. "But—really?"

"Oliver's great," I say. Because he is. Still... "What did he do?" But I don't really want to know. Right now I want to keep Oliver in my life, and if I hear more, maybe I won't.

Or maybe—worse?—what qualifies Oliver as a disaster is just the same set of details that makes up A Description of Kellie Brooks, i.e. worse than her sibling at *everything*. Maybe if Byron and Adelaide knew more about me, they'd laugh at themselves for thinking I was worthy of hanging out with. My new world of achievers and geniuses just got scary again.

"Maybe we shouldn't talk about this." Byron jumps up from his new chair. That doesn't sound like the kind of avoidance you need just for something like *Well, he's a bit of an underachiever in comparison to Dexter*. Avoidance tactics are for bigger, scarier things. "I'm getting some water. Anyone else?"

"Please." Adelaide picks up whatever fancy drink she's working on and takes a giant gulp. I even hear the sound in her throat, *gulp*. "So, what do you think you're writing for next week's paper?"

"What do I think I'm *writing*? Oliver killed someone and we're talking about the stupid *Ticknor Voice*?"

"Oliver didn't kill anyone, Brooks," she says. "Let's just drop it."

"But—"

"Dropping it." Adelaide takes out a giant notebook that was somehow in her purse. She's like the Hermoine Granger of Ticknor, complete with the magic bigger-on-the-inside bag. "Can I run some questions past you that I'm planning on asking your mom for my paper?"

"It's Saturday night," I say.

"What does that mean?"

"It means people don't want to do homework," Byron says, speaking my mind as he walks back with a couple of glasses of water.

I think about bringing Oliver back up, but something overrides the honest and open part of my brain. It'd be different if I wanted to marry him. He's just my boyfriend, and I'm only sixteen, and as long as he isn't a crazy murderer, things are fine.

(Is this what denial is like?)

Before long we kind of disband. Adelaide and Byron are taking off together, which makes me wonder what they're like when no one else is around. I can't imagine Adelaide as someone who does much besides save the planet, but I guess they probably go to Byron's dorm to have sex or at least make out. People can save the planet and still have time to do it, I'm sure.

Mom and Russell are up when I get home, but I just wave a fast hello and head to my room. It's completely normal for me to be home before Sara on a Saturday night, but the house seems extra quiet, and San Francisco feels so far away.

After brunch the next morning, I head back up to my room to work on a few ideas for my next column, but I've barely started when Mom leans into the room.

"Hey, baby. Can I come in?"

"Yeah, sure."

She walks up and kisses my cheek before sitting down on the bed next to me. "So how's everything going?"

"Everything's fine, Mom. Why?"

Mom laughs. Her ponytail swings down and brushes my cheek. "Can't a mother ask how her daughter's life is going? We don't hang out as much as we used to."

"I know. Does that make me a bad daughter?"

"Absolutely not. You're sixteen, you should be going out and having as much fun as possible. How's everything with Oliver?"

I realize something wonderful: if whatever Oliver had done to provoke Dexter's overachievement was that horrific, Mom would likely know and therefore not let me date him. Good deduction, self. "Everything's good."

"So I had a thought. How about tonight, you and I drive to the airport to pick up Sara, and then the three of us will go out for dinner? Girls night out."

"Totally." While I like this whole thing where I have a life and therefore places to be and more people who want to hang out with me (and even one who wants to make out with me on a regular basis), being with my family is tough to beat, too. It's rare that just the three of us spend time together anymore, but it always gives me a good case of nostalgia. Back when Dad had first moved out, I got sad sometimes, but I also loved the slumber party atmosphere that had descended upon our house.

Mom heads back downstairs to hang out with Russell and Finn, so I get back to brainstorming. Luckily my chat blinks, saving me from having to have too many smart thoughts at once.

Oliver McAuley: What's up?

Kellie Brooks: just newspaper stuff. what about you?

Oliver McAuley: Hoping to talk to you actually.

Aloud I say, "Aw!" but I only type back: i am the only point of the internet after all.

Oliver McAuley: Ha ha.

Oliver McAuley: You still didn't accept my Facebook thing. Is there anything we need to discuss?

I read it like five times and blink a bunch, but it never gets less weird to me.

Kellie Brooks: are you serious? it's really not a big deal. it's stupid facebook.

Oliver McAuley: We're not a big deal?

Kellie Brooks: i didn't say that. it's just the internet. and i haven't been on much since we talked.

Oliver McAuley: Fine.

Kellie Brooks: why are you making a big deal about this? i told you i liked you. doesn't that mean more than facebook?

Oliver McAuley is now signed off and did not receive your message.

I slam my laptop shut and walk downstairs and out the front door. It isn't like I have anywhere to *go,* but I can't sit still while my brain overloads with thoughts of Oliver being sort of crazy. So I walk down the block while trying to figure out what to do. Stupid thought or not, I want to call Kaitlyn, because—despite her real-life experience level—she's spent a lot of time and energy thinking about guys. And unlike Adelaide, who'd probably just tell me either that Oliver is crazy or good people and to act on that, Kaitlyn and I could have talked it out. We used to spend entire days just talking things out.

The only thing I hate more than this stupid Oliver situation is how much I miss Kaitlyn.

I head back inside and hang out with my family because they're better distractions than aimlessly walking. Mom ducks out of the living room to take a call from Sara who is on her layover in Phoenix (for some reason no airlines want to fly direct to St. Louis from anywhere useful), while Russell and I continue our game of Go Fish with Finn.

"Hey, Mom," I say as she walks back in. "It's your turn—"

"Kell-belle, let's go into the kitchen for a second."

I don't like her tone or that her blue eyes seem a little dimmed. Close up I can see that the corners of her eyes are damp, and her eyeliner and mascara have smudged all around. If Mom is crying about anything that isn't a touching film or inspiring book, things aren't fine.

"I just got off the phone with your sister. We don't need to pick her up because she's staying a few nights at Camille's."

Okay, I'd totally called it—well, sort of—but I guess I didn't think it was *really* going to happen. If I truly had, this wouldn't feel like a well-aimed punch to my gut.

"Are you okay?" I ask despite all the evidence to the contrary.

"Of course." She cups my chin in her hand. "I just wanted you to know. So how's your evening look? Still want to have our girls' night out?"

Of course I would have agreed anyway, but now there's no answer but yes. I make a joke about a steakhouse in an attempt to make her smile (it works), but it hits us that it is actually a *really good* idea, so that's where we end up. I really want to fix this for Mom, because no one as selfless as her should have to feel like crap, ever, especially for a reason like this. But there is no fix; maybe we're going to lose Sara, and definitely none of us have the useful skills to do anything about it.

At dinner we talk about Mom's latest big projects at work (a half-sleeve of ivy, a line of text up someone's spine) and how much I'm liking newspaper so far. We laugh about Finn's preschool teacher's observation that *he's very much interested in zebras,* and of course, we rave about all the meat we're eating.

And we don't mention Sara at all.

I go up to my room once we're home and I've said good night to Finn, but I feel really restless (also no one of interest is online, and there's no marathon TV worth watching). Mom and Russell are still up downstairs, so I figure a little more quality time with Mom is probably the right way to spend my time (and not just because there's nothing else to do). I stop dead in my tracks on the stairs, though, once I hear Mom's and Russell's hushed voices. Yes, we aren't into secrets or divulging privacies…but that's Mom's rule and not mine.

Obviously, this means I slide to the side of the staircase where I can hear but can't be seen. I only feel a little guilty for not following The Ideology of Melanie Stone.

"…doubt it's like that, Mel," I hear Russell say. I've always liked that Russell is the voice of reason. Sometimes— by which I meant *often*—I'm jealous of Finn for having one very reasonable and one ridiculously reasonable parent.

Mom says something really muffled and tearful, which just about breaks my heart even though I don't understand a word of it.

"No one thinks you're an idiot," says the slow, assuring voice of Russell. "Least of all Sara."

Unlike my hair and my height, feeling like an idiot is not something I like sharing with Mom.

"I can't compete with her," Mom says. "If that's what Sara needs—"

"Mel," Russell says. Right then I don't find his steady brand of calm comforting at all. Why aren't they *doing* anything? As far as I understand ages and milestones, turning eighteen might mean you can legally smoke and vote and sign up for the Army and get a tattoo and meet your biological mother. It doesn't mean your parents have no say at all in your life anymore.

Does it?

Russell clears his throat, and I realize the sound is coming from somewhere much closer to me. I guess he'd

gotten up for whatever and spotted my hiding place. I shrug
and try really hard to look apologetic, and I guess it works
because he laughs and keeps walking to the kitchen. I get to
my feet and stomp around a bit to make it sound like I've
just walked downstairs. Mom glances up at me with a smile,
which makes me sad, since I know she's faking it. I don't
want anyone faking it for me.

"Still up, Kell-belle?"

"It's only ten, Mom." I sit down across from her and
think about saying some of it, like that her and Dad and even
Russell have the right to tell Sara not to leave us. Maybe kids
don't have the right to tell their parents that stuff, though.
Normally, I can at least fake it, but right now I have no idea
what I should and shouldn't say.

"Russell and I were going to make popcorn and watch a
movie. You should join us."

I'm not entirely sure if maybe I'm intruding on some
sort of date night for them, but if Russell picks the movie, I'll
probably like it. And now that I've heard the word *popcorn*
I catch a whiff of it from the kitchen, and who am I to turn
down the best-smelling snack food ever? It's definitely a
better option than holing up in my room and thinking about
everything else.

CHAPTER FIFTEEN

The first issue of the paper that'll feature my column is out on Monday, so at lunch I head straight to Jennifer's classroom and grab one off the stack before they go to the general public. I'm there in real black and white.

THE TICKNOR TICKER
THE SCENT OF GROWTH?
By Kellie Brooks

The grounds of Ticknor Day School boast native Missouri plant life immaculately maintained by a hardworking grounds crew. Surrounding our students in such an environment is just one way we at Ticknor strive to not only provide a quality education, but the best setting possible for academic growth.

So begins the "Campus Grounds" section in the Ticknor Day School promotional brochure, a paragraph those who spend each weekday at T.D.S.

might find difficult to take seriously. After all, is the word "immaculate" synonymous with "poop-smelling"? Is "the best setting possible" an area that smells like the elephant pen at the zoo?

Due to the unseasonably mild weather, juniors and seniors have been fortunate enough to take advantage of the Upperclassman Courtyard Dining Area throughout this often-chilly month of October. But unfortunately, this has not been the serene lunchtime experience it once was. Thanks to the new trees provided to the school by the T.D.S. Alumni Association, anyone spending lunchtime in the Courtyard is greeted not by the fresh smells of nature but the not-so-fresh stink of manure.

As a junior, I spent two years looking forward to the opportunity to get in touch with nature during the very limited window of time that is even possible thanks to the roller-coaster ride that is Midwestern weather. This literal change of scenery has brought my vision to a screeching halt and my nose wanting to go on vacation from my face.

If T.D.S. is as devoted to the mental well-being of their students as their brochures and website claim, they would seek out manure alternatives that nurture not just a growing tree but the well-being of their students and their olfactory senses. If you can't depend on your school not to smell like poop, what can you count on in life?

"It's me," I say to no one in particular. "My column!"

"Yes, Brooks, all our columns are magically in the paper," Adelaide says as she's dispatching freshmen to distribute the paper around school. But she grins at me and I think she gets that for me this is a big deal.

"Congrats." Paul gives me a high five. "It's really funny."

"Thanks. I'm working on being funnier," I say, which is a weird goal but a real one. "But thanks."

"It's the right tone," Adelaide says. "Yes, it's a humor column, but this is still a professional publication."

"I feel like professional's pushing it a little," Paul says. "Is high school professional?"

"It's as professional as we make it," she says. "So, yes."

I can tell Paul wants me to roll my eyes with him over Adelaide, but considering that she thinks I found the right tone, I just can't. I take my copy of the *Voice* with me and head into the hallway. My phone buzzes as I'm en route to the cafeteria, and I'm super relieved to see it's from Oliver, since we haven't talked since our argument-via-chat. *Sorry. Bad weekend. You okay?*

In some ways, like that Sara's at Camille's and Mom's heart is broken and that I can't believe Oliver and I had a stupid fight online about frigging *Facebook*, I am maybe not entirely okay. But I really only do feel relief at this moment. *i'm ok. u too?*

I'm so glad when he sends back a *Yes*.

I go to Dad's after school, though it's weird to be there without coordinating with Sara. Mostly it's because I don't want to let him down even if she is, but also I have some tangible proof I'm more than a B student who does little else in school. Dad should see it.

I mean, it's fine for Mom and me to goof around about being useless, but she *can* joke. She's an artist with a passion. (And expensive hourly rates.) Being useless is a lot less charming when it's less of a joke and more of a truth. But today I don't feel useless at all. My paper is real, and multiple people complimented me on it. People I don't even know well said nice things.

So I open up the *Ticknor Voice* to my column and leave it on the front table before settling in the living room with my homework, laptop, and Dad's glorious big-screen TV. And, of course, my phone, which I'm using primarily to text Oliver.

When I hear Dad walk in, I listen closely to make sure he's taking enough time to look at my column. When it seems like he is, I listen even more closely, which is goofy because it's not like you can hear someone reading.

"Hey, there she is." Dad walks into the room and sits down in his usual chair, without the paper. "How was school?"

"It was fine. Did you see my article?"

"I did. Glad to see you're getting more involved in school, kiddo."

I shrug, even though maybe it's dumb to pretend that I don't care. "Newspaper's actually sort of fun."

"Yeah, I can see that. Maybe next time you'll focus on something a little more serious."

"It's a humor column, Dad."

"Ah. So, what sounds good for dinner tonight?"

That's *it*? I applied and got accepted and then had my article *published* and I'm still just basically a joke to him? (Okay, yes, *yes*, it's a humor column, and *yes*, it mentions poop more than once, but *still*.)

"I don't know if I'm that hungry," I say while texting Oliver to see if he wants to hang out. The *Yeah, of course* comes back really quickly, so I make excuses (or, well, *lie*) to Dad about newspaper staff stuff and drive up to Oliver's dorm.

"Sometimes I hate my dad," I tell him, and then wish I could rewind and make that sentence not come out of my mouth because it doesn't make me look mature or ready to make out, one of which I want to be and one of which I definitely *am*. "Sorry. Never mind."

I reach up to slide my arms around his neck (my standard Making Out Position Number One), but he stands still instead of placing his hands on the small of my back (Oliver's standard Making Out Position Number One).

"What's up?" he asks, touching my face. "We can talk, you know."

"I know, I just…" I roll my eyes and try to make it clear that I am the subject of said eye-rolling. "I don't know why I've known my dad my whole life and still get my feelings hurt when he acts like he always acts."

"Because it still sucks?" he offers, which, true. "What happened?"

"He didn't care about my column," I say. "And, ugh, seriously, my column is about our courtyard smelling like poop, which—"

"I know, I read it when you sent it to me." Oliver grins and sits down on his bed. "For the record, I liked your poop column."

"Gross, don't say 'poop column'!" I laugh and pretend to tackle him back, which of course turns into fake wrestling, which *of course* turns into making out.

Now that we're together, and Oliver is my boyfriend (and I even made that Facebook official earlier this afternoon), I'm so glad that more didn't happen back in May. Kissing him then had been exciting. Having his hands all over me had been exhilarating. Feeling his bare skin pressed up against mine was almost otherwordly.

But, also, it had all been kind of scary. My breath had caught in my throat countless times, and not just because things were sexy and mind-blowing. I'd barely known him, and I hadn't really wanted to be doing much sexy and mind-blowing with someone I didn't know.

But now I know Oliver. Now when his hands skim over me and our bodies are smooshed all sexily up against each other, my breath catches only because this feels amazing. Because he's safe and because I trust him.

"I'm still not ready to have sex with you," I tell him, though I do try to sound worldly and experienced. Lots of my clothes are off or moved aside, so it's easy feeling these things. "Is that okay?"

"Of course it's okay," he says, though I'm pretty sure he was hoping I'd feel the opposite. "If you're—"

I'm really nervous he's going to actually say *a virgin* and I'll feel like a baby, so I jump up and get dressed and make a big deal about checking my phone for messages. "I'm fine. Just, it's a weeknight, my dad might call, all this stuff with Sara..."

"Kellie, it's fine," he says. "I'm not going to push you into something. I respect your feelings and your boundaries. Do you think I don't?"

"Of course not. You're like the nicest guy ever." I walk back to him and kiss him. Will something click when it's time? Will I just know? How does a person just know? Is it like when your phone beeps and you know you've gotten a text? Ugh, I have no idea who I could even ask about a thing like that. "I'll text you when I get home."

"I'll walk you to your car. Hang on."

Our hands are clasped as we walk across campus, and it's like his touch is holding off the rest of the world. At my car we kiss a few more times, and I feel like if I let myself I could just melt into him. And there'd be nothing left, and I wouldn't know to care. But instead we say good night for real and I get into my car, and as I drive home, I think about Dad and Sara and Kaitlyn and how much of my life isn't at all how it's supposed to be.

And I guess the truth is that right now I wish I'd melted instead.

CHAPTER SIXTEEN

I wait at Kaitlyn's locker the next morning, even though I can feel how that's dangerous. But we've said nothing official, and maybe I'm not being fair. Maybe it seems to her that I'm blowing her off, too. Okay, I don't really think that, but I need to talk to someone about Sara and Dad and Oliver and of course, my impending sex life. Kaitlyn's good at all that stuff. Who else is going to weigh in on if I actually do need to buy fancy underwear or not?

"What?" Kaitlyn asks as she walks up.

"*What?* Is that how we're saying hi now? Okay. How are you?"

"Don't be so weird," she says, pushing past me to reach into her locker. She looks exactly the same; her hair is beautiful, and her outfit is one we picked out together at West County mall, and she's been carrying that overpriced Coach purse for six months now. But also she's not the same at all, and I can feel that.

"Never mind," I say, because this Kaitlyn isn't going to have anything useful to say to me, even about sex underwear. "I just—"

"Don't you get it?" she asks. "We're not friends anymore, Kellie."

"We were friends last week," I say.

"I guess. Stuff changes." She stares at me, hard. "Don't be such a baby about it."

Lora walks up and gives me a side-eye. "Everything okay here, Kait? Is she bothering you?"

"Oh my God," Kaitlyn says, *and giggles*, and then they're off down the hallway together. What the hell?

I find Adelaide, hoping she'll pick up on my mood and say the right genius thing, but she just gives me a flier for an art show/political rally happening on Saturday night.

"Kaitlyn's being..." I try to communicate with my eyes how I feel.

"Are you feeling okay, Brooks?"

I think Adelaide has at long last picked up on an emotion of mine, but she just gives me a travel pack of Kleenex because I apparently look like I'm suffering from allergies. I want to be annoyed, but having a friend who keeps an eye on my health and well-being is a good thing. And I can't be mad at Adelaide for not being more like Kaitlyn, when isn't that the point anyway?

Dexter, weirdly, texts me at lunchtime. *Yo Kells it's Dex. What's up with Sara?* I respond right away. *no clue, haven't seen her since friday. why?*

"Is it true you have some college boyfriend?" Chelsea asks me while I'm willing my phone to beep with Dexter's response.

What a weird thing to be true, and also to be asked about, like Oliver and I were photographed in the latest celebrity tabloid or something. Canoodling! "It's true."

Chelsea has all the standard questions, from his name to his major, which I'm fine with giving. Still, I get the feeling she thinks I should be gushier or full of bigger details, and I just don't feel like going there. Having a boyfriend shouldn't be about bragging rights or gossip possibilities, just tons of making out and talking and listening to music.

Though I guess to be honest, I do hope it trickles up to Kaitlyn and her table, and she'll have to admit her supposedly uncool and immature former friend is practically doing it with a college guy. I try to look a little more mysterious to Chelsea and Mitchell in case "mystery" = "practically doing it."

Newspaper feels like something I've been doing for a million years by the time it rolls around after school. I'd already discussed my potential ideas with Adelaide, so I just let her select my lunch options idea and watch as it's written next to my name on the board. (Of course I do get that the people writing timely and hard-hitting stories like about the upcoming Halloween Ball or changes to next semester's curriculum have a little more pressure to deal with.)

Chelsea announces she's having a party next Friday because her parents will be out of town, and we all get really excited even though I think most people in this room are real rule-followers who aren't going to start experimenting with sex or drugs. Parties are still good news, and it'll be close enough to Halloween that we decide costumes are mandatory.

It's my night to pick up Finn from daycare, which is

good timing because newspaper kept me distracted enough from my life's drama. It's basically impossible dwelling on anything annoying when you're running around a park and seeing if you still fit down the kiddie slide (just barely). Dexter calls while I'm showing Finn some ninja moves like sneaking around a telephone pole, so I tell Finn it's his turn, and I park myself on the ground so I can keep an eye on him while I answer my phone.

"I hate texting," he says. "So I didn't wanna type any more to you. But you wanna grab a cup, talk about crap?"

I know it's pretty weird to get coffee with your sister's boyfriend-slash-your boyfriend's brother, but if anyone will understand how crappy stuff is getting with Sara, it's him. "Um, yeah. Later? Right now Finn and I are hanging out at the park." I grin at Finn, who mimes throwing a ninja star at me. I mime catching it in my teeth, which makes him burst into giggles. If only I could keep Finn around at school; he is totally my antidepressant of choice.

"Yeah, yeah," Dexter says. "Call me when you're free."

I agree to that and go back to ninja moves until it starts getting dark. Mom is home by the time we arrive, which is great, because there's sesame tofu nearly ready to eat, and also because as soon as I'm done with that, I'm free to meet up with Dexter. Hanging out with Finn is almost always awesome, but it's a relief that at the end of the day, literally, he isn't really my responsibility.

Dexter and I make plans to meet up at The Beanery, and we end up walking in at practically the same time. Dexter is still in his uniform but has his blazer on inside-out so the pattern shows instead of it being navy. I guess that's how hipsters make dressing like everyone else work. We step up to the counter together without a word, and I order.

"Hey, Kellie."

I turn around and see that Paul from the paper is sitting at one of the front tables with a couple of his non-newspaper friends. "Oh, hey."

"You going to Chelsea's party on Friday?"

"Yep."

"Wearing a costume?"

"Well, it's mandatory, so, yes. Mandatorily." I wait for Dexter to order before walking to the end of the counter for my drink. He shoots me a smirk. "What?"

"Like you don't know."

I really don't. But once we're settled at a table with his black coffee and my vanilla hot cocoa, he leans in conspiratorially and gestures in Paul's direction. "That guy's really into you."

"What? He's not, he's just some guy from newspaper."

"A guy from newspaper who wants to jump you," he says. "What? I'm not gonna tell Ol or anything. Who cares if I even did? I didn't say you wanted to jump him."

"Stop talking about jumping people," I say. "What's going on with you and Sara?"

"Nothing, *nada*," he says. "All of a sudden she's too good to return my calls or texts, too busy, I dunno. She said anything to you?"

"That would be hard considering I haven't even seen her. She's staying at Camille's," I say. "Just one more crappy thing about this crappy week."

Dexter lets out a whistle. "Tough talk, Kells. Things that shitty?"

I shrug, weighing how I don't really know Dexter that

well against the fact that it's absolutely useful to be around a guy who isn't my boyfriend and therefore, will not distract me with magical sexy powers. (Also I really don't care how whiny or immature I seem to Dexter.) "My best friend's totally cut me out of her life for no real reason. Well, the reason is she wants to be cool, and I'm uncool—"

"What? Kells Brooks *uncool*?" He raises his eyebrows like he's an ultra-suave Muppet. "Who said that? I will defeat them."

"Shut up, and you know what I mean. I don't have any shirts made out of gold glitter, and I don't feel like sneaking into any clubs."

"Where the hell is that written down in a list labeled as *cool*?" Dexter shakes his head. "I thought Ticknor was one of those goddamn hippie schools. I figured the cool kids started drum circles and smoked a lot of weed."

"If only," I say. "Well, that sounds awful, too, but less so. Also, my dad."

"What about your dad?"

"Just how I'm this huge disappointment to him and Sara's his shining star." I shake my head like the conversation is an Etch-a-Sketch and this'll clear it. This is one topic I don't want to bring up to the guy who's the shining star in his family. "So, um, are you still trying to get in touch with Sara? Or just ignoring her, too?"

Dexter makes a grand gesture, takes out his cell, and dials Sara. I hear her voice mail pick up, and he clicks off the phone. "Listen, I'm trying. You hear from her, let her know, okay?"

A tiny and dramatic part of me worries I won't hear from Sara any time soon and won't get a chance to pass on the message, but I don't like how defeated Dexter seems. "I'm sure I'll hear from her soon, and of course I'll let her know."

Since Mom and Russell are still acting like nothing unusual or apocalyptic is going on in our family, I decide to take things into my own hands. I won't just act brave; I will be brave.

I go back to Dad's on Wednesday.

"You here for the night again?" Dad asks, looking surprised but honestly not unhappy. "We could order something for dinner or go out, your choice."

"Whatever you want is fine," I say, not feeling deprived at the moment thanks to dinner on Sunday. Living with a vegan is fine as long as you can occasionally make a great steak escape. "Um, so have you talked to Mom this week?"

"Uh, no, I don't think so." He riffles through his mail and looks back to me. "Why did you think I would have talked to your mother?"

"Sara got back into town Sunday, but she told Mom not to pick her up at the airport because she'd be staying with Camille for a few days."

Dad's eyebrows draw together. "And Mel said okay to that?"

"You know Mom, she wants everyone to be happy and making independent choices or whatever." I make it sound really casual, because Clayton Brooks hates casual. I will scare him to his core and make him the one who reacts.

"Right," he says, when I know he means something more

like, *Yeah, that crazy woman.* "I know Sara's really enjoyed spending time with Camille, and when has Sara ever made a bad choice?"

He does have a point, even if it isn't one I necessarily want to hear from him. Where is my control freak dad?

"We haven't heard from her since," I say.

"Well, that was just Sunday," he says. "Today would still be included in 'a few days,' wouldn't it?"

I have to admit he's right.

"Dinner thoughts?" he asks, and I hope he'll ask me *anything* about *me.* What am I working on for the issue of the *Ticknor Voice*? How are my friends? (Ugh.) Even how are my grades? I try to send little mind beams to him: *ASK ME SOMETHING.*

But obviously, I don't have magical mental powers (or a dad who cares that much about my extracurriculars). At least he lets me pick the restaurant, burgers in U City at Fitz's, where they brew their root beer right there on the spot. (That makes it just as much better than regular root beer as you'd think.) Dad isn't usually one for driving more than a couple miles or going anywhere that actually qualifies as cool, so it feels like almost as much of a victory as if he'd asked about the paper.

Almost.

"This is actually really good," Dad announces as we're eating our burgers. Probably I should have been offended at his incredulous tone, but I'm so used to him that I'll just take his shock that I could have good taste in dining establishments as a compliment. "Great idea, kiddo, glad you came over tonight. I know it's tough between my schedule and yours."

"Yeah." I feel sort of awful that it took the Sara drama to get me to his place tonight. Honestly, once Sara and I started driving, we haven't exactly stuck to the stricter schedule of seeing him at least one-point-five times a week we'd upheld before. It truly isn't about how sometimes hanging out with Dad is the emotional equivalent of getting needles poked under your skin, and not in the good acupuncturey way. (Usually.) At this point I'm just ready to have one place to live. Mom and Russell are much closer to school, and also they rarely say anything about my college chances or my attitude toward school and hard work, so I guess there is also that.

"So, uh, your mom said something to me about you..." Dad gulps his root beer like that will fortify him. "Dating someone."

Dad knows this, but not that Sara is totally leaving our family for possibly forever? Mom and her open communication! "I guess I am."

"Mel seems to approve, so..." Dad shrugs, like it's perfectly normal for him to basically say, *If it's fine with your mom, it's great with me.* "And you know a guy has to treat you well and respect you and all of that, right, kiddo?"

"Of course, Dad."

"Well, I hope he's good enough for you," Dad says, which is such a cheesy and clichéd thing a dad would say on a TV show that I feel way less like his biggest disappointment.

Back at the house, though, he immediately (before I'm completely inside the front door counts as *immediately* for sure) tells me to work on my homework, so we're back to business as usual, and then he walks into the kitchen yammering on about something to do with college. Good thing you didn't get too cool all in one night, Dad.

"I'm only a junior," I say, my default response to anything containing the words *college*, *university*, *GPA*, or *extracurricular*.

"It's never too soon to start looking, though." He plunks down this giant book on the table in front of me. *Your Guide to the Best Colleges and Universities FOR YOU*.

"Whoa, the all-caps are a little freaky," I say.

"I got it for you this week, thought it might be helpful."

"What is it, some book for weirdos?" I check the back of the book, and after mentions of *creative* and *against-the-grain* and *non-traditional environments,* I realize I'm right. Honestly, if you're really at home at Ticknor, you're probably not going to exactly fit in at your average college with a Greek system and organized sports and whatever else. I'm not really ready to start actually narrowing down college choices, but I guess it's nice Dad knew not to get whatever genius edition he'd gotten for Sara. For once the differentiation doesn't feel like an insult. "Thanks, Dad."

"Sure, kiddo. You want to start looking through this? Maybe over the summer you and I can take a trip and tour some of your favorites. What do you think?"

A million thoughts fly through my head at once like in movies where your whole life flashes before your eyes (though luckily without the accompanying near-death experience). Dad and I on a trip together is a recipe for disaster! A vacation that doesn't involve making sure Finn doesn't run into traffic or the ocean sounds relaxing! Wait, college is actually this completely real thing that I'll go away to in a couple years and I have a say in it?

"You know." Dad sits down across from me, backward

in the chair like rebel kids on bad TV shows. "You've got to give Sara a break."

"What?" *What?* "I didn't say anything about Sara."

"I'm sure getting to know Camille is really validating for her," he says. *Validating?* "You wouldn't know how hard it is to not fit in."

I think there should be a law that if any adult says that to someone in high school, they can be declared mentally incompetent.

"You and your mom have so much in common," he continues. "Sara's never had that. Think about what that would be like."

I'm not a violent person, but I have to get up because right then I really want to punch him in the face. Think about what *that* would be like, Dad. "I'm going to bed."

"Kellie—"

"I'm tired." I leave the college book on the table and carry everything else to my room. It isn't even ten yet—of course I'm not tired—and I have all this additional energy thanks to getting riled up by Dad and his crazy talk.

I get online, figuring at least maybe I can distract myself somehow. Oliver is logged in, which is just about the best distraction I could get.

Oliver McAuley: Hey.

Oliver McAuley: What are you up to?

Kellie Brooks: ignoring my dad. you?

Oliver McAuley: Procrastinating from reading. Hoping to catch you.

Oliver McAuley: What's up with your dad? The usual?

Kellie Brooks: sort of.

I think about mentioning Sara then or Mom's reaction—well, lack of—or Dad's wrongheaded thoughts of almost everything. Oliver will be there for me, of course, but I'll still have to dwell on all this stuff. And, ugh, could I just not dwell on stuff?

Oliver McAuley: Sorry to hear it.

Oliver McAuley: Mine just emailed me an article about some Philosophy major who graduated from SLU last year and still can't find a job.

Kellie Brooks: our dads should team up.

Kellie Brooks: they could be REALLY disappointed with their powers combined.

Oliver McAuley: Not sure the earth could withstand that.

Kellie Brooks: apocalypse dads!

Adelaide starts messaging me, and even though I also briefly think about dumping all my brain's issues on her, I decide to keep taking distraction where I can find it. And, anyway, Adelaide is detailing the blog posts she'd made that have gotten the most hits (which means I'm mostly typing lots of oh and awesome and the occasional they really test THAT on animals??). Oliver can at least be counted on for actual conversation.

Oliver McAuley: No, as far as that's concerned, I think you're insane.

Kellie Brooks: there is NO WAY the stones are better than the who. you're the one who's crazy.

Oliver McAuley: Now I'm not sure if I can trust you regarding anything.

Kellie Brooks: i was just about to say the same!

Kellie Brooks: so do you want to go with me to a friend's party next week? or are you totally above high school parties?

Oliver McAuley: I don't make a habit of frequenting them.

Oliver McAuley: But sure I'll go. It'll be good to meet your friends outside of Adelaide.

Kellie Brooks: i don't really seem to have THAT many friends outside of adelaide anymore.

Kellie Brooks: terrifying thought I know.

Oliver McAuley: I can think of worse scenarios than that.

Kellie Brooks: i guess.

Kellie Brooks: it's a halloween party so you have to wear a costume.

Oliver McAuley: I can handle that.

Kellie Brooks: oh, and please don't tell anyone about your stones opinion or i'll completely deny i know you.

CHAPTER SEVENTEEN

Sara is, miraculously, home when I get there after school the next day, and since Finn is zooming around playing pirates and zebras, she clearly lived up to her assigned duties and picked him up from daycare.

"Hey," I greet her, trying to seem like she didn't just go AWOL on us. My voice sounds a little screechy, so I'm not sure I pulled it off.

"Oh, good, you're home," she says. "I need to work on homework, so Finn's all yours."

"But I haven't seen you in days." My voice is still screechy. Get it together, self. "Can we hang out?"

Can we hang out? Ugh, I sound like such a dork.

"I really don't have time, Kell," she says and disappears up the stairs. I put my energy into joining in the game of pirates v. ninjas instead of dwelling on Sara v. the rest of us. Luckily Mom's home before long, because honestly the not-dwelling isn't going that well.

"Hey, you two." Mom drops to her knees to hug Finn, then stands and hugs me. "Could you do me a huge favor and cut up all those veggies on the counter for the salad?"

The thing is, I have homework, too, but I've never figured out how to refuse Mom without being a huge brat. So I just pick up a cucumber and a knife and start chopping.

"How's school, Kell-belle?"

"It's fine," I say, because the actual school part is, and I know it would make Mom really sad to know lately the Kaitlyn stuff isn't. Mom has enough to be sad about these days without me adding to that crap pile. "How was work?"

"Exhausting. I started on a girl's backpiece that's going to take several sessions, but believe it or not, I got the whole thing outlined."

"That reminds me, the other day I was thinking how you and Russell are almost to the point where you only have appointments people make in advance, so maybe you should hire someone else for all the walk-ins, at least on your busy days like the weekend. You do have an open station, two when the freelance lady isn't there."

"That's a great idea." She slides a casserole dish into the oven. "I'll talk to Russell and see how he feels. We've definitely turned away more people lately than we've liked."

"Mom! Mom!" Finn runs into the room with a bunch of Sara's highlighters. "Can I have paper so I can color?"

"You'd better give those back to Sara," I say. "Or risk being torn limb-from-limb."

"Let's not talk about dismemberment so close to dinner," Mom says. "Finn, did you ask Sara if you could borrow those?"

He shakes his head, so we make him return them. Mom

gets another knife from the fancy set she'd given Russell for Christmas the year before and grabs the carrots. "Want some help?"

"Thanks, Mom."

"I'm impressed with you. It really is a good suggestion for the shop."

"Guess I'm not as useless as everyone thought." I smile so she'll know I mean her brand of useless and not Dad's. (Truthfully, I mean both.) "Can I get some more hours next week? I'm not having any issues balancing school or anything."

"Sure, baby," she says, but her focus seems to be on the carrots and the sharp, sharp knife, not me. "How's everything with Oliver?"

"Good," I say, instead of *I can't believe how cute and smart he is and how good kissing him is.* "Can I go out on Friday night? And then Saturday after work—if I can work Saturday—some people from newspaper are going to hang out in The Loop. Okay?"

It takes a long time for Mom to seemingly even realize I'm talking to her. "Mmm hmmm. Sure, Kell."

At this point I feel like I could get her to agree to giving me a million dollars or letting me skip town for a year or tattooing a full backpiece on me. But I just excuse myself from vegetable chopping instead of taking advantage.

Okay, I guess getting out of vegetable chopping *is* taking advantage. Just to a very mild degree.

Sara's door isn't shut, but I still knock before sticking my head into the doorway. "What's your deal?"

Okay, not exactly good negotiation tactic there, self.

She's sitting at her desk, surrounded by textbooks, novels,

and notebooks. "Kell, seriously, not now."

"It seems sort of...I don't know, just, like." Terrible timing to become extra-inarticulate. "You're choosing her over us."

"That's a stupid thing to say."

I really hate when Sara uses *stupid* or any of its synonyms regarding me. She might as well have slapped me.

"I'm—" She looks up at me. "I'm sorry."

"I'm sorry, too," I say, not because I really am, but because I don't want to fight with her. I just want things to be okay again. I don't have to be right.

"We had a lot to talk about," Sara says. "Eighteen years, and more, after the trip. I didn't feel right just leaving."

"But you felt fine *just leaving* us?" I try to make my voice mellow and open, the way Mom always sounds.

"I didn't leave," she says. "And I'm back now, aren't I?"

"I still feel like you're still shutting me—shutting *people* out." I might have said more then, but I feel weird admitting I've been talking to Dexter about her.

"Right now I just need to do my homework," she says, which is such a normal Sara thing I know I've pushed enough. "All right?"

"Fine." Of course I wanted more from her than dismissal, but it's like I'm not programmed for real conflict. Sara's always been the easiest person in my life. I can't just switch over to dealing with her as the unknown...or the enemy.

I walk back downstairs, where Mom's making homemade salad dressing and not looking overly concerned at the state of our family.

But the next night, Sara doesn't come home, and I guess the truth is that no one is surprised. Least of all me.

I pick up Oliver from his dorm on Friday night, even though by now I still haven't seen a trace of Sara, and I feel weird leaving the house dark and empty. I'm torn between assuming we'll just never see her again and staring out the windows for her imminent return. But I'm determined to be fun tonight, and not to get distracted by my drama, family or otherwise. I feel like so recently I was 95 to 100 percent fun!

I drive us over to Cherokee Street (after a reasonable amount of time spent making out, of course), where vintage and antique shops line up against hipster coffee shops and old-school traditional taco places. We grab coffee and cocoa right away before dropping into Apop Records (Oliver insists on buying me Buddy Holly & the Crickets on vinyl, and I let him because he seems so excited to do it), and then to a handful of vintage shops and the store that sells only stuff made in or about St. Louis.

I wonder if I should still be so surprised that, in general, having a boyfriend is really easy. This is completely the kind of night I'd want to have anyway, but I'm with someone who's interested in all the same places I am (well, I was way more excited about the music, and he was more interested in looking at dusty old books, but it evens out), plus there's the bonus of holding hands with him and knowing that, post-tacos, we will be making out again.

"What's your next column about?" Oliver asks me over the giant plate of tacos we're sharing.

"Vegetarian options in the cafeteria," I say. "It's kind of goofy, too."

"Yeah, but isn't that the point?" He grins at me. "What are you doing tomorrow night? They're playing some old movie on campus, thought you might like to go."

"I'm hanging out with Adelaide and some newspaper people," I say.

"Oh," he says. "Want me to come?"

"No, I'm good," I say, like he's being nice to offer, but his eyes dim a little, and I realize he's disappointed. "Are you okay?"

"I'm fine. Just to be honest, it'd be nice to see you more."

"You're seeing me now," I say. "In combination with tacos. Pretty great, right?"

"Ha," he says.

I don't want to flat-out say that he isn't invited, and I don't want to comfort him even though maybe I should. I'm still learning the good relationship rules, so how would I know the other ones yet? If a guy wants you to spend all of your free time with him, is that nice, or is it too much?

I hear a tiny Adelaide in my brain yelling, *Just talk to him, Brooks*, but she's pretty easy to ignore when she's not around.

"Where do you want to go after this?" I ask. "Is your roommate out?"

"He's there," Oliver says.

"Okay," I say, trying to seem like things didn't just get kind of weird. "I guess I could just drive you back."

"Sorry." He takes my hand despite taco grease. "I just like hanging out with you. You're one of my favorite people."

It's intense. Oliver is *intense*. But lately I haven't felt like anyone's favorite. Why would I refuse this? I'm one of his favorites, *and* he doesn't let a little taco grease get in the way of anything. That's basically perfection.

Sara's door is shut but her light is on when I get home, and I take a chance and knock softly.

"What?"

It's the same way Kaitlyn answered when I tried to talk to her, and I wonder why lately conversation with me is such a horrifying option to the two people I used to talk to the most. Still, I open Sara's door and lean in. Of course I'm hoping to catch her in some secret moment, something telling or meaningful or new. But she's just hunched over a textbook. She's just Sara.

"I said *what*, I didn't say *come in*."

My mouth actually falls open because she sounds so mean. I catch sight of myself in the mirror, and I look ridiculous. But it's Sara! Sara's made me look ridiculous!

"I wanted to talk to you," I say, even though I didn't knock with thoughts of Oliver in my head. I knocked because this is *Sara* and that sentence should get to end there. Now that I'm here, though, I might as well ask something like, *What if a guy is clingy and intense, but also intense in a good way?* Seriously, since when do Sara and I need reasons and excuses for each other? Especially when we haven't seen each other in days?

"I'm busy," she says with barely a look to me. The only positive thing about that is hopefully she missed me looking ridiculous. "It's one in the morning, Kell."

"Right...and I want to talk and you want to do homework. Which is weirder?"

She doesn't look up and so I can feel that the

conversation is over, whether or not I'm still standing there. Still, I give it a chance, wait a minute to see if maybe something will snap into place in her brain and she'll be normal Sara again.

But nothing snaps, and nothing happens. It gets awkward that I'm still standing there, so it takes me a few more moments to leave the room and head to my own. I turn on music (a Herman's Hermits album, even though even for *me* they're pretty dorky) and scan through a list of people in my head I could text at this hour about how things with my boyfriend are sometimes weirder than I want them to be and of course that my sister's pulling further and further away. But Kaitlyn and Sara were my one in the morning people. Oliver's the closest thing I have now, and not really.

I can remember how I felt when I applied for the paper. It was straight out of a self-help book. (Mom bought us plenty of those after the divorce.) I'd thought, *I want to be more*, like my hard-hitting editorial on the smell of poop was some big step forward for mankind. But right now, I don't feel like more. Right now even with my column and new friends and Oliver, my world seems a lot smaller.

The next day after work, I meet a bunch of people from the *Ticknor Voice* at Pin-Up Bowl, where none of us actually want to bowl. After hours it's a bar, but before nine they don't care if you're twenty-one or not. You can't drink, but you can hang out. There's red velvet everywhere and shiny red couches, where we pile in to drink soda and eat homemade gourmet Pop-Tarts.

"Have fun, Brooks." Adelaide shoves Mitchell, who's sitting on my left side, and squeezes in. I guess it's funny we just let her, but with Adelaide, you *just let her*. "What's with your face?"

"This is just my face," I say, even though of course I know despite the soda and the pastry and that I'm literally surrounded by new and old friends, I am not in my best mood ever. I am not even close.

"Aw, leave Kellie alone," Chelsea says, a brave move countering Adelaide in any matter. "She's fine."

Chelsea's sat at our lunch table since she started dating Mitch last year but clearly can't tell my moods apart. She could never be a one in the morning friend, Adelaide-bravery or not.

I get out my phone to text Oliver. Even if maybe he's being kind of clingy, I know he'll respond with lightning speed and I'll have tangible proof I'm important to someone right in this moment.

Ugh, I sound so pathetic. Only in my own head, but still.

"How's the boyfriend?" Adelaide asks.

"He's fine," I say, then reconsider because *fine* sounds like how your grandma's doing, not the guy you're making out with. "He's great. How's Byron?"

"Also fine and great," Adelaide says.

"It's so cool you guys have college boyfriends," Chelsea says.

"What about me?" Mitchell asks. "Aren't I cool?"

We all laugh because even though Chelsea's in love with him, none of us would exactly use the *cool* word as a descriptor. And Oliver texts back that I'm right about the awesomeness of Pop-Tarts, gourmet or not, so I guess I'm back to thinking he's, for real, great and not just fine.

After we get kicked out of Pin-Up Bowl, Adelaide wants to see a foreign film at the Tivoli, but the rest of us talk her out of that and we get food at Blueberry Hill instead. The truth is that their food isn't that great, but it's practically a music museum, so we pretend it doesn't matter that as far as the eating's concerned we might as well be at the school cafeteria.

My phone buzzes again, and I assume it'll be Oliver being cute again, but instead it's his brother. *Yo Kells. Any word from Sara?*

I don't want to, but I understand Sara pulling away from us. She's like a little perfect piece of metal being drawn back to a perfect magnet. But what did Dexter do? He's in her perfect orbit.

she's home but barely talking to us. sorry!!

It feels weird that a guy like Dexter needs me, but I send a second message, just to be nice. *i don't get it. she has no reason to ditch u.*

My phone buzzes just a moment later: *She has no reason to ditch you either, Kells.*

CHAPTER EIGHTEEN

THE TICKNOR TICKER
THE DEFEATED MEATLESS
By Kellie Brooks

Ticknor Day School has a certain "reputation" in our community. Other schools might brag about test scores and sports teams, but here at Ticknor we're independent and free thinking.

One thing that seems to go together with a lot of free-thinking people is being a vegetarian. And Ticknor recognizes this, even including mention of it on their website: "Vegetarian students will be excited by the array of meatless options!!"

In addition to the fact that I don't know anyone literally excited by cafeteria food or the startling use of the double exclamation point, this statement doesn't exactly ring true. Here's what I had to choose from for lunch yesterday: pizza, salad, chicken tenders, tiny cheeseburger. (Side note: has anyone noticed how tiny the cheeseburgers are at Ticknor?)

Here's what my hypothetical vegetarian friend Leafy McGreens had to choose from (no, Leafy doesn't exist, but there are vegetarians here, just none I am personally friends with): salad with fewer toppings, tofu tenders, pizza if you're comfortable ripping off the sausages and pepperonis. Not even a tiny tofu burger! My stepdad is a vegan, and I'm not sure he'd have anything to eat at our school besides plain lettuce. What kind of existence is that?

Ticknor, everyone thinks of you as the weird hippie of schools. Shouldn't the weird hippie be the first one to let our non-animal-eating friends have more to eat?

Chelsea's party is in—is *full swing* what parties get up to? well, okay—full swing by the time Oliver and I arrive on Friday. We would have made it there sooner, but we got pretty distracted when he picked me up, considering Finn was at Russell's mom's, Mom and Russell were both still at the shop, and Sara was—shocking to no one—nowhere to be found. (Also then we had to repair our costumes from making out damage. Oliver's zombie makeup got rubbed off, and therefore, I had his zombie makeup on my face and a few areas of my Batgirl costume to wipe off.) Yeah, this is a party, so obviously if Oliver and I really want, we'll have ample opportunity to—well, not *be alone* but at least make out all we want. Maybe it's because he's in college or maybe because I don't like the thought of people from school being able to walk in on me making out, but I feel like we're beyond that.

We squeeze past the group on the porch, smoking every variation of whatever could be smoked besides, you know, crack, and make our way inside, where Paul is playing a weird, beaten-up guitar, the kind that has crazy strings popping loose like a hairstyle gone bad, and along with Scott and a few other guys from newspaper, singing with the stereo.

"Hey," everyone kind of greets me in grunty dude unison. One of them hums the Batman song, but it's done so half-assedly I can't even locate its source.

"Hey. This is Oliver."

I introduce Oliver to all of them, and he shakes their hands, which makes Oliver look like a huge nerd, so I sort of make a joke out of it before pulling Oliver with me in search of the rumored keg. It's in the kitchen, along with a dozen liquor bottles each holding a few inches of something.

"Here." Oliver hands me a cup of beer and gets one for himself. "You want to go out to the backyard? Looks like that's where everyone is."

I agree and follow him out. Mitchell and Chelsea are there. Oliver says hi to them with more handshaking, like he's interviewing for a job and not just some guy dating their friend. But neither of them acts like he's weird, so that's a relief.

"Kellie Brooks." Adelaide appears out of nowhere, trailed by Byron. I'm pretty sure she's dressed as Eleanor Roosevelt. "I'm glad to see you, this party needs more than culturally unaware pop-punk-listening drones competing at who can be the drunkest."

"Hey, Adelaide," Oliver says.

"Hello, Oliver. It's good to see you, too. See, Byron, I told you someone else who'd already graduated would be here."

"Solidarity," Byron says, tapping his fist against Oliver's.

"Why are you Batgirl?" Adelaide asks. "What's the significance?"

"My little brother had most of this stuff already," I say. "The significance is laziness."

Adelaide loops one of her arms through mine and tugs me away from Oliver. "Just so you know, Kaitlyn's here."

"What?" I follow her line of sight. Kaitlyn is standing there like she belongs, which feels pretty dishonest when she's put all this effort into leaving us behind. She's dressed as a "sexy" pirate. "Why? Isn't this stooping way too low socially for her?"

Adelaide shrugs. "There are a lot of people here, Kellie. News of free booze spreads fast."

"'Booze'?" I laugh, even though I also want to puke. Josie is talking right into Kaitlyn's ear, and they both laugh in a stupid, uproarious way. No one's ever as funny as you want other people to think you are. "Maybe I should go."

"I'll kill you if you do," she says.

I stick my tongue out at her but return to the crowd, leaning back into Oliver like we're the kind of couple we actually aren't. But if Kaitlyn catches one glimpse of us, I want to firmly control that glimpse. Probably that isn't any better than uproarious laughter, but I'm only so strong.

When our beers are finished, I volunteer to head inside to refill our cups, which makes Oliver laugh and run after me. Inside the kitchen we sneak in a few kisses in the rare moments we're actually alone.

"Ahem," someone says, like someone actually says the

word *ahem*. I pull away from Oliver to mock whoever it is, but who it is turns out to be Kaitlyn.

"Oh," I say. "Sorry. We were just—"

"I'm getting a drink," she says.

"So were we." It is a dumb thing to say because clearly we were doing more than that. I can't even stand the thought of being in the same room as her, so I grab Oliver's hand and pull him into the next room, which has also emptied out. People seem to be either out on the front porch or in the backyard, with only a few in here intent on whatever is being played on the Xbox involving vampires and several buckets' worth of blood.

"Everything okay?" Oliver asks me.

"Sure, except I hate her." I grab the collar of his jacket and pull him to me, kiss him like life depends on it.

"Hey." Oliver jerks back from me. "We can head out if you want to mess around or whatever, but—"

"'Mess around'? This is what we always do."

"Yeah, in my room or your room or our cars. Just—" He shrugs. "Who are you doing this for? Doesn't seem like me."

"I don't know what you mean," I say, even though I know *exactly* what he means. Of course Oliver deserves to be made out with only when I actually want to, not when it's to prove to Kaitlyn I'm doing just fine.

I am a jerk.

"I'm getting a beer," he says and walks back into the kitchen.

I just stand there waiting at the edge of the room, vaguely keeping an eye on the Xbox. When someone steps close to me, I assume Oliver is back to apologize or see if I want a beer or who knows what else. But it's just Paul.

"Hey," he says softly, and now I wonder if Dexter was right about him. After all, I'm absolutely positive he heard Oliver and me. Sure, I knew he checked me out when he could, but I guess his interest is a little stronger than just that. "Everything cool?"

"Everything's fine. How's saving the princess going? Or whatever you guys are doing over there?"

He laughs and shakes his head, honestly looking pretty hot in the tall, dark, and handsome way (well, for a dude happy to sit and play video games at a party where there are both girls and alcohol). I have no idea what he's dressed as, just some medieval-looking stuff, so I'm assuming it's a *Game of Thrones* reference I am not catching.

"It's okay," Paul says. "So that guy your boyfriend? Or just some guy you know picking a fight with you for kissing him? Not that I was spying or anything," he adds when I probably looked slightly horrified.

"Yeah, not at all. And, yeah." Paul should know that I am not someone up for consideration. But I can't lie and say I don't like being up for consideration. I know the kinds of things about me that Kaitlyn thought she had to leave behind, even if she didn't say them aloud. And I may always be a dork who'd rather drink cocoa and listen to The Who than wear something tight and sparkly and party it up at a club. But it doesn't mean I'm not growing up, too.

Ugh, I sound too lame and cheesy, even for the insides of my own brain.

"I guess I should go talk to him," I say to Paul, though I don't wait for his reaction.

Oliver is in the kitchen, *talking to Kaitlyn*, but at least he smiles when I walk in so hopefully that doesn't mean she was telling him terrible things about me—or if she was, that he was believing them. "Hey."

"Hey. Keg assistance please?"

"Sure," he says, then to Kaitlyn, "Good meeting you. I'll see you around."

She is staring sort of bug-eyed at me, her immature former friend who just happens to be there with a cute college guy, the cute college guy she was clearly flirting with. It's thrilling, except I remind myself not to be a jerk.

"Come on," I say, and pull him to the backyard. "Sorry if I was being—"

He hugs me tightly. Sometimes Oliver is just *so nice*. "You want to go somewhere and talk?"

I shrug because I still haven't fully accepted Oliver as some sort of option when my brain gets way too full of crap to deal with. "I'll be fine."

"You sure?"

I shrug again, watching as Kaitlyn walks across the yard to the oasis of cool in the sea of the rest of us. If aliens landed right now, they'd know right away who's powerful here. "She used to be my best friend. It's really hard. And Sara's still...I don't even know *what* Sara's doing."

"People mess up, Kell," he says, with one of those Looks I know is Significant. "That's a normal part of life. Right?"

"Right." I hug him back. Even though he's kind of on the skinny side, he's like a solid wall when I throw my arms around him. "I'm not normally like this. Things are just kind of crazy, and I think it might be making me crazy, too."

"Listen, I've been there. You can talk to me." He holds my face in his hands, right next to his, which kind of overwhelms me at how close we are to be talking and not making out. "Don't hurt me, but Kaitlyn seemed okay. Maybe you guys can talk?"

I elbow Oliver in the stomach. (I was aiming for his ribs but he's like eight inches taller than me.) "Seriously, I don't think she'll ever want to. It's like she's this new Kaitlyn, and I can't even see the one I was friends with anymore. You know?"

"I guess." He shrugs, just a little. "Sometimes it's tough when people are changing. Doesn't mean you can't be friends, but sometimes there's adjusting before you can line up again."

I remember that Sara said something not unlike that, though she hadn't believed the lining up again was as inevitable. I guess I don't, either, but it's nice that Oliver feels otherwise. "Did you learn that from Hume?"

Oliver laughs and hugs his arms around me. "I learned that from life."

I love it when people say things that make you feel possible again.

"You want to go?"

I don't, not really. More people have shown up, and it's easier to forget that the ones I don't want to see are there. So we stay, and I drink a little more, and okay, Oliver and I do sneak off to make out, but it's due to beer and standing so close for so long, and definitely not showing off for anyone. The only bad thing about it is it's definitely the catalyst for our conversation in the car later, a conversation I'd hoped wouldn't actually come up. Couldn't things just happen organically without needing to talk about them?

"So I was..." Oliver cups his hand over one of my knees. I'm wearing thick tights but I can still feel the little paths his fingertips make. I'm dizzy from it. "Wondering. Maybe sometime we could…?"

"Have sex?" I ask, because I hate all of those stupid euphemisms like *take this to the next level* or *get intimate*, and if one thing could make me not want to sleep with Oliver, ever, it'd be him saying something like that.

"Well, yeah. I'm not trying to push you or anything, just…"

"No, I know." I think about how close we'd come back in May and how freaked out I'd been then. Of course I haven't been scared again, not even once, but I've put up stopping points and kept him aware of those. And maybe that's why it feels like I'll never freak out again. What if our clothes all come off with sex firmly on the agenda and I'm still the same way? It's bad enough I reacted like that then; if I start crying about *having sex with my boyfriend in front of him,* I will likely never recover. Lately, I can't exactly trust myself to contain my emotions. "Maybe I should go on birth control first or something." Ooh, great idea, self. Buying time *and* preventing teen pregnancy in one fell swoop.

"Good plan," he says, as he pulls up to my house. "Sorry I got you back late."

"It's one oh one." I laugh and lean in to kiss him. "My mom's not that strict."

So we kiss for a while before I get out of the car and quietly let myself into the house. Mom is up in the living room watching TV, but she switches it off as I walk in the room. It's weird that she's up, but back before she had her own shop and a little kid to look after, Mom was always up late. So maybe she's just reclaiming her old ways.

"Hey, Mom."

"Your curfew's one sharp, Kell-belle. That doesn't mean a little after one."

Since when? "I'm sorry, we just—"

"I don't know when you girls decided curfew was flexible, but we need to get back to following it. Okay?"

Oh, there we go. Mom's complaint list for my sister is growing by the minute, but I'm the one who's here. "Okay. Sorry again, Mom."

"Do you want to open the shop tomorrow?" Mom asks, her tone like an apology for yelling at me. "I have a couple errands I should run in the morning."

"Sure," I say as Mom gets up and hands me her Family Ink key. "Can I keep this?"

"Of course. I've got spares." She kisses my forehead. "Get some sleep."

I stop by Sara's room on the way to mine. Totally empty. She'd better shape up soon, or Mom will go so crazy with rules I'll never manage to have sex with Oliver. *If* I am going to have sex with Oliver. I'm not going to make that decision tonight.

CHAPTER NINETEEN

Even though I don't get to sleep in as late as usual, I'm excited to open the shop on Saturday. Keeping to Mom's traditions, I stop off first for coffee and donuts, making sure to get some vegan ones for Russell. When I get to The Family Ink, I think about unloading Russell's CDs from the stereo for mine, but the truth is when people are getting tattooed, they're probably expecting to hear The Ramones or The Misfits or The Damned or that creaky old-timey piano music while that guy with the old-man voice drones on about the dregs of society, and not the happiest pop music in the history of the world.

Russell shows up before long, grinning when he sees the coffee and donuts. "You already accomplished the most important job of the day. Any calls?"

"Just people checking the hours, no appointments. You're pretty booked today, though."

He sits down at his station and opens up the newspaper. "Don't know if your mom talked to you or not yet—"

"She did. I'll be better about my curfew."

"Not that. Sara's at Camille's for a few more nights. Just so you know."

"She might as well move in with Camille." I feel mean but not wrong. "I mean, obviously she's going to."

Russell sighs, not looking up from the paper. "Let's hope not. It's her decision, though, Kell, she is eighteen."

"It's so dumb. Like you turn eighteen and you magically make good decisions."

"I didn't say that. I'm saying she's allowed to make those calls for herself." He's still looking at the paper and not me. "And you might want to keep in mind this isn't exactly easy on your mom and give her a break."

Of my parental units, Russell is definitely the least annoying. So clearly there's a first time for everything.

I check my email instead of trying to talk any more with him, and luckily within a couple of minutes, both his first appointment and the freelance artist walk in, so I don't have to anyway.

I spend my lunch eating pho and reading about Hume, and when I get back (completely on-time), Mom is at the front desk working on an elaborate floral design. She smiles at me like all is fine and I hadn't gotten a ridiculous curfew lecture and Sara isn't slowly leaving us. "Hey, baby. Good lunch?"

"I guess. So is it okay if I go to a movie with Oliver tonight?" He'd texted me during lunch, and despite our sex conversation and my lack of love for most new movies, it sounds like a good way to spend my night.

Mom frowns. "Normally of course I'd say yes, but Russell and I both need to stay until closing, and Russell's mom had

Finn since this morning."

"Mom, I babysat like almost every night this week," I say, not bringing up the fact that I'd basically taken over Sara's one measly night, too. "What about his sitter?"

"She's busy, and this isn't up for debate."

Russell looks up from the drama masks he's inking and shoots us both a look. I can practically read his mind: *No domestic drama in the shop.* So I step out front, and Mom follows.

"It's not fair if—"

"No, it isn't fair, but that's what being part of a family is, it's pitching in and helping when you're needed. And you're needed."

"You're ruining my social life," I say and cringe, like who am I to say something straight out of a teen movie?

"I highly doubt that." She ruffles my hair. "I'll make this up to you, okay?"

"With time travel to give me the night off later? It's fine, I'll do it. I mean, I don't have any choice. It's not like it's Finn's fault."

"You're the best, Kell-belle," she says, but I don't want to hear it, just want to get inside and break the news to Oliver. I feel like a bad girlfriend *and* a bad sister for being disappointed at spending the evening with Finn.

It hits me that Mom probably feels guilty enough about my canceled plans to let me have company. I text Oliver to see if he wants to come over instead (and he does) before ambushing Mom in the back room between appointments.

"So would it be okay if Oliver came over tonight?" I ask. Probably this is a little riskier, one night after The Conversation, but it's not like I would have had time to go on birth control in the past twenty-four hours or anything. "I won't neglect Finn or anything, I just thought maybe because I can't go out…" Guilt trips aren't really respectable, but the thing is, when used in moderation, they work.

"Sure, baby." She cups my chin with one of her hands. "Are you two having sex yet?"

Yet? Add my mother to the list of those who think it's a foregone conclusion. "Mom—"

"I was sixteen once, you know. If you need to go talk to a doctor about birth control, I'd be more than happy to take you."

Obviously, I do need to go talk to *someone* about birth control, but I have this unsettled feeling somewhere between my heart and my brain about Mom, like that she would be so, so proud of this beautiful, shining moment where I go to see her gynecologist and she gets to be the cool, open-minded mom.

And right now I just don't want to give her that.

"We're not, Mom, and I'm fine."

What a lame way to make a point. Now I have to figure out how to do this without Mom's help or else totally backpedal later.

"Well, either way, of course Oliver's welcome to come over tonight," she says and kisses my cheek while I stand there, completely unprotected. And it's all my own fault.

Oliver apparently has a ton of homework, so once he arrives and says hi to Finn and me, he plunks down at the kitchen table with his laptop and a bunch of books about Nietzsche. Rocking Saturday night. Finn and I play catch in the backyard, with a ball I'd painted in zebra stripes for him, while I try not to think about how much fun I'd be having out with Oliver, where he'd get to ignore his homework in favor of me for awhile.

After I give Finn a bath and read him three stories of his choosing and one that I make up about Marvin vs. a pack of wild pirates (obviously, the pirates are no match for Marvin), he's finally ready to sleep. I don't want to say I'm anxious to spend time with my boyfriend because that probably makes me both a bad sibling and babysitter, but honestly, I'm anxious to spend time with Oliver. And I'd just seen him the day before. And from the next room all evening. I am in some Serious Like with him.

"He's asleep," I say, walking into the living room, where Oliver is flipping through the channels.

"It's a lot of work," Oliver says. "I would have killed my parents if they had a kid four years ago."

"Yeah, that's probably the normal reaction, but I was just really excited. I figured my mom couldn't have more kids because I was a miracle or whatever."

Oliver brushes my hair back from my face and grins, the special Oliver grin reserved just for me. "You were a miracle?"

"Yeah, Mom and Dad thought they couldn't have kids, that's why Sara's adopted, but then I happened, to everyone's shock. So I guess Dad was the problem, because no one seemed that surprised when Mom got pregnant with Finn. Sara was totally horrified at first, but I figured it'd be cool, and it is."

"Except for when you get stuck home on a Saturday."

I shrug. "Sort of, sure. Maybe this makes me a huge loser, but I still had fun."

He turns that into a joke about how much fun we *could* be having, so of course we start making out. Everything in my head has sort of turned into a pro/con list regarding sex with Oliver, except I can't actually think of anything to put on the con side. I mean, am *I will be someone who's had sex* really a con? My brain just can't really wrap around it, like here is this major life step I can totally take, but it would change this fundamental thing about me.

Though, really, is lack of sex a fundamental thing?

"Have you had sex with a lot of girls?" I ask him when we pause for air. Also I want to get my lip balm from my purse. "I don't care, I just wondered."

"Not a lot," he says. "Unless you think two is a lot."

"Two is definitely not a lot. Was one of them Sophie?"

"Well, yeah," he says, like, duh, who wouldn't sleep with Sophie? I'd probably at least seriously consider it if it was an option. "Is that a problem?"

"No, I'm just nosy."

"What about you?"

"What about me?" I remember the time we made out in his room, and I told him I didn't normally freak out about sex. Of course that would catch up with me. "No girls at all."

"You're hilarious." He smiles, though. "And you don't have to tell me if you don't want to. People are allowed to have privacy."

There are definitely two choices right in front of me: tell the truth and look like an idiot or lie and therefore, look like one later when I have sex with Oliver. I hate both of these choices.

"Hey, kids," Mom calls to us as she walks inside. "I didn't get a chance to eat dinner, so I brought home Vietnamese."

I'd eaten when Finn had, but just soup and a sandwich, so I'm thrilled to take a summer roll and a big serving of lemongrass chicken. Also, obviously, thrilled that I've managed to escape further discussion or distortion of truths regarding my virginity. Oliver watches me loading up my plate but doesn't say anything until Mom dashes upstairs to peek in on Finn.

"Your mom's cool with me being here?"

"I told you."

"I thought she'd be out later. My parents really wouldn't have been cool with me hanging out alone with a girl back when I was sixteen."

"Right, back in the olden days. Mom doesn't think it's the end of the world if people have sex, so what else is she worried we'll do? The liquor cabinet's had a lock on it ever since Finn helped himself to whatever that purple stuff is."

"Oh gosh." Mom laughs as she walks back into the room. "I'd forgotten about that. How long did it take us to clean that purple puke out of the carpet, baby?"

"Let's not talk about that while we're eating, Mom."

"I think I'm going to head out," Oliver says.

"I hope I didn't scare you off with the puke talk," Mom says, but Oliver assures her she didn't, gathers his books into his backpack, and walks to the door. I jump up and walk him outside to his car.

"You really don't have to go because my mom's home."

"No, I know, but it's like your family time, and...I don't know." He shoves his hands into his pockets. "I don't do that well with moms. If she only gets little doses of me, she'll still think I'm good enough for you."

"Oh, right, like Mom would ever think you're good enough for me." I laugh and wrap my arms around him, rising up into Tall Enough to Kiss mode.

Okay, we accidentally kiss for like ten minutes, but Mom doesn't even tease me when I walk back inside. Maybe that's why my resolve goes down and we have a conversation like: Me: *Maybe I should go on—* Mom: *Oh! Did—* Me: *No, but—* Mom: *We can go to the doctor next week.*

But then the previous week's events kick in. "Can I just go on my own?"

"Oh," she says, like she'd never even heard of people going anywhere on their own, much less a totally personal sort of doctor's visit. "Sure, Kell-belle. If that's what you want."

What I want is to be out of the house tonight and to have had more hours at the shop that week and for Sara to be home or at least on her way. I just have to settle for Tuesday afternoon at the gynecologist.

Of course on Monday morning, Kaitlyn tracks me down regarding what she must have seen as an important matter. She is seriously bad at this whole not-being-friends thing that she'd been the one to initiate.

"So is Dexter's brother actually your boyfriend?"

"No, he's my guy prostitute, that's why I had to start working at Mom and Russell's shop. His rates are—"

"Stop it," she says. "Why can't you ever be serious?"

"Why do you care?" I spot Mitchell across the hall and make a beeline—well, a straight line and not some kind of crazy curlicue path an actual bee would take. "What's her problem?"

"She's not that bad," Mitchell says, which makes me elbow him. "What? She's not. Everyone had fun on Friday."

"What does that mean?" I ask.

"Nothing. What's with you?"

"You always make fun of Kaitlyn, too."

Mitch shrugs one of his slow, slow shrugs.

I don't even know why I want to pick a fight except that every sane person should hate her with the same burning passion I do. "Don't you care that she's mean to me?"

"She's mean to you?" he asks, like, hello, Mitch, welcome to life! "I just thought you guys fought all the time. Girls, uh, seem to do that."

I don't want to call him sexist because basically it's true.

"Well, uh, sorry about Kait." He sort of pats my elbow, like it's a safe area to touch as a friend. "That guy seemed cool and all. Except for shaking my hand. What was *that*?"

"Oh my God, *I know*." We exchange grins, and I'm suddenly glad more of my friends have met Oliver now. I've needed people to occasionally make fun of my boyfriend with.

I wave good-bye to Mitchell and round the corner, where Paul practically runs right into me.

"Hey," he says, like it's some big surprise to see me and that I didn't see him practically choreograph this collision. "Everything cool after Friday?"

"Everything's great," I say.

"I just got around to reading your latest article," he says. "That's the most I've ever thought about laptops."

"Mission accomplished, then." I sort of wave and duck into my class, where Adelaide immediately starts asking me opinions about different cover stories for next month's Thanksgiving issue. I don't care that much, but it's way better than dwelling on Kaitlyn or Paul or you know, anything else stupid in my life right now.

THE TICKNOR TICKER
LACKING LAPTOPS
By Kellie Brooks

We're supposedly living in the 21st century at Ticknor Day School, where our library features a digital room and all classrooms feature computers that can directly display on a projection screen. *The Ticknor Voice* even has one iPad Mini for its use, though I'm still low enough on the totem pole to have never used it for anything.

So what I don't get is that if we're living in such a technological wonderland, why aren't we allowed to bring laptops to school? Instead of typing up my notes confidently, I spend classes desperately scrawling down everything I think my teachers say and then spend my evenings decoding my own handwriting. And hand cramps and carpal tunnel syndrome are real things. I don't have a serious hand condition yet, but with all of this frantic writing, could it be far away?

The administration claims we cannot use laptops

in class because they could not "prevent the use of unauthorized websites and programs by students," which we all know means they're afraid we'll look at pornography. I don't understand why anyone would want to look at pornography at school when really that's something people probably enjoy more in the privacy of their own homes.

So it seems an unduly harsh restriction not to allow any laptop use when likely only a very small percentage of Ticknor students would fall into the group of people who don't mind looking at porn in public. Most of us just want to take better notes without any hand cramps.

CHAPTER TWENTY

I actually get to work at the shop that night after school, because even though Sara is still at Camille's, Mom and Russell have found someone else to watch Finn (probably Russell's mom). Weeknights are pretty slow, but they still need someone at the front desk all the time. Luckily, no one cares if I'm on the shop computer.

Oliver McAuley: What are you doing this weekend?

Kellie Brooks: probably babysitting and working. what's up?

Oliver McAuley: Roommate's going on some road trip. You could come over.

"Kell-belle?"

I minimize my chat window and look up at Mom. "What?"

"Can you run down the street and pick up dinner?"

Normally, I'm thrilled for any errand that takes me away from the desk for a few minutes, especially when everyone's too busy to babysit my half-block stroll and I can spend my walk imagining how Dad's head would explode if he knew.

But I'm getting asked to have sex. Can I just *brb* that?

"Kellie?" Mom waves a couple bills in front of my face. "Go, we're hungry."

So I have no choice. I bring the window back up.

Kellie Brooks: brb. getting dinner.

I don't even have time to grab my phone, just rush down to King & I, pay for the giant order I assume is going to function as lunch tomorrow as well, and get back to the shop as fast as I can. I help dish out the food so Mom and Russell can scarf it down during a break, and finally sit back down with a carton of pad see ew. Oliver has signed off, but at least I have an email from him.

> TO: kellbelle@familyink.com
> FROM: mcauleyol@slu.edu
> SUBJECT: (no subject)
>
> If you're not ready to have sex you could just say so, not invent an excuse to avoid me.

Okay, here it is, the second time I think Oliver is sort of crazy. The third? Does it count that maybe he's done something like murder someone and I don't even know? Should I know? I should, shouldn't I?

I probably do look like I'm lying to get out of it, but normal guys don't just fly to Crazy Land so quickly, do they?

"Kellie?" Mom walks over, Thai iced tea in hand. "Baby, you haven't restocked anything up front tonight. I know it's slow, but that's exactly what we need to use the slow time for."

I know I'm slacking off because I'm so distracted by

Oliver, not that Mom is expecting too much out of me. So I keep myself busy for the rest of the night making sure there are enough gloves, plastic wrap, and cups for water, and don't get back online until I'm home.

Adelaide Johansson: What do you think about a green issue?

Kellie Brooks: like green paper?

Adelaide Johansson: NO. An entire issue devoted to environmental matters. You could write the green policy humor piece we talked about.

Kellie Brooks: sounds fine to me.

Kellie Brooks: do you think oliver's sort of weird?

Kellie Brooks: crazy i mean.

Kellie Brooks: no, i just mean weird. do you?

Adelaide Johansson: Well YES.

Adelaide Johansson: But so are you.

Adelaide Johansson: Green paper is actually not a bad idea, as far as gimmicks go.

My Friday is somehow free of both work and babysitting, but I still feel weird enough about Oliver that I don't think it's necessary to ask him to do something. I'm sort of hoping he'll reach out to me first and be all charming and adorable and hilarious, the way I like him, but that doesn't happen. Since I don't want to give up my freedom, I stay out after school, and after working on a potential column at The Beanery, I decide just to walk around for awhile. Yeah, there are other things to do if I just drove a little, but with all the cute shops and quaint restaurants lined up in nostalgic fashion, I guess I'm not totally immune to my town's charms.

My cell phone rings while I'm rummaging at Euclid Records to check out some old vinyl. By now I guess I'm not really that surprised to see it's Dexter calling. "Hey."

"Yo. Talk to Sara lately?"

"Nope," I say. "You?"

"Negative," he says, the Dexter quality of his voice very much dimmed. Impossibly, I think he's falling apart more over this than I am.

"Do you want to hang out tonight?" I ask. "I'm at Euclid Records."

"Cool, I'll be there in a jiff," he says and hangs up. I finish checking for sixties stuff I've been looking for, and by then Dexter's walking in.

"Hey, lady." Dexter is wearing his uniform shirt (tie askew as always) but with jeans and Converse today. "What's the haps?"

Only Dexter can get away with saying something like that.

"Just looking for a few things," I say.

"Yeah, Ol's said your music taste is pretty eclectic," Dexter says. "But like that's a really hot thing."

"It *is* a really hot thing," I say instead of getting all embarrassed or melty hearing that. Okay, in addition to getting a little embarrassed and *completely* melty. Does this mean I can stop feeling weirded out by Oliver?

"Clearly," he says. "Are you buying anything? I say we take off for some fine chow."

"Sure," I say. "We can get whatever fine chow you want."

Dexter isn't satisfied by the billions of places we could have walked to, so instead we get into his car and he drives to the City Diner, which is crazy packed on a Friday night.

"Things sound cool with you and Ol," he says.

"Yeah, I guess they are." It comes out a little shorter than I'd meant, but I worry if I don't go for the brief version, I'll blurt out that sex is coming down the pipeline and the previous almost-sex has me more than a little nervous about it.

"Dexter, if you had your place to yourself and you asked a girl to come over, and she said *brb* because she had to get Thai food, what would you think?"

It's a regretful question the second it's out of my mouth. First of all, Dexter isn't stupid and will understand this is not a hypothetical and is in fact about his own brother. Secondly, he's dating *my sister*, so this is double-TMI territory.

"I'd probably think she was trying to get out of it," Dexter says.

"Sometimes people really do need to go get Thai food," I say.

"Sex is usually more important than Thai food."

"Usually."

Dexter laughs. I laugh. And we somehow both know we're going to stop talking about my hypothetical sex with his actual brother.

"So Sara even around much these days?" Dexter asks.

I fiddle with the corner of my menu. "Definitely not."

He takes off his glasses and rubs his temples. I can just tell from that and him bringing it up at all that he's worried about this, but at the same time it's still tough thinking of someone like Dexter worrying about anything. "Think she's gonna cut me loose?"

"I have no idea what she's going to do about anything," I say, which is probably no comfort at all. Still, I care way more about my family than his relationship. Priorities. "Sorry, I just—"

"Honesty's cool." He shoves his glasses back on. "What's she said to you?"

"Probably less than to you." I can't sort out if I feel better or worse about Dexter being as left out in the cold as the rest of us are. If Sara leaves her boyfriend behind, it doesn't exactly seem likely that everything else won't change, too.

I mean, I don't look down on all change; some of it brings me things like Oliver and the discovery that I don't totally suck at everything, and some of it is just necessary to get through life and somehow emerge a grown-up. Losing Sara isn't on either of those lists, though. Normally, I can separate stuff into different rooms in my brain, the crap to worry about locked away while I'm out having fun. Lately, the hinges have all come loose.

After we eat, Dexter wants to go to the bar upstairs from the Vietnamese place with the best spring rolls, but I'm not in possession of a fake ID, and I am a little nervous that if we somehow successfully get in anyway, I'll never get home before one a.m. Worrying about curfew is really sucking the life out of me.

We drive back to Webster. The music's off, but Dexter's tapping out a rhythm on the steering wheel with his hands.

"Whoa, is that 'Baba O'Reilly'?" I ask, because it sounds a lot like the drum part to one of The Who's songs.

"Kells, I'm gonna blow your mind and tell you how people're still making music in the present day, and that's from a song that came out this year."

"Maybe it was a time-traveling song."

Dexter laughs and makes a time-travel-y sound effect. *Whoosh!* "You wanna go see who's hanging out at the gazebo?"

There's a creepy gazebo in front of the Starbucks where people, sometimes cool, sometimes terrifying, hang out at basically all times of the day and night. I myself think most towns could do without a creepy gazebo.

"I know it's lame, but I should probably go home," I say. "My mom's been weird with my curfew."

"You're just scared of the gazebo."

"I wish this was purely gazebophobia."

Dexter drives to the lot where I'm parked, but before I can even touch the door handle, he sort of grabs my wrist. "If you and Sara talk, and I come up or something, you'll let me know. Yeah?"

"Yeah, sure," I say, even though I can't picture myself running to the phone to keep Dexter in the loop. I've always liked him just fine, but he is probably the most popular guy in his school, who is perfectly matched up with my perfectly perfect sister. It is an odd thing that rules about who gets to socialize with whom seem to be disappearing.

I decide not to leave just yet. "What do you think about Sara? Is she leaving us? Do you think she at least wants to?"

Dexter shrugs. "Doesn't everyone at least *want to* sometimes?"

I shake my head. "Not me."

"Take it easy." He gives me a little salute. "Give my

regards to Ol, sure you see him more than I do."

"Will do." I open the car door and plant one Chuck Taylor on the sidewalk. "I hope things are okay for you and Sara."

He clinks an invisible glass in the air near where I'd hypothetically be holding an invisible drink of my own. "Kells, you, too."

CHAPTER TWENTY-ONE

I nearly dial Sara approximately eleven times the next day, but I can never bring myself to actually click the call button. But I get off work, drive straight home, since I'm a dork without plans on a Saturday night, and almost walk right into her.

"Oh, hey," is all I think to say.

"Hi." She isn't really making eye contact. "I'm just getting some stuff."

"What, are you moving in with Camille or something?"

"No, I—I don't know. Don't make such a big deal out of everything." Sara isn't really paying attention, just walking to her room, opening up her closet doors. It's like she was replaced with some kind of pod person, because even though Sara can get distracted with homework and other responsibilities, Sara always found time for me. Seriously, she at least found time to explain why she didn't have time. The new Sara barely seems like my sister, which of course is the biggest, scariest part of all.

"I need to talk to you," I say at the same time I'm realizing it. *Of course.* Considering my relationship is out in the open, no matter what Sara and I didn't discuss before, she'd know what I should do. Or shouldn't do, I guess. "Oliver wants us to have sex—well, I guess I kind of want that, too—but—"

"That seems like a personal thing." She takes out some sweaters and jeans from her closet, folds them while standing like she's employed by the Gap. "Why would you think I'd know what you should do?"

Here are some things I wouldn't know without Sara: how to tie my shoes, how to alphabetize my bookshelf, how to drive a stick (Mom herself doesn't know how, and Dad and I didn't exactly have productive driving lessons), how to read Shakespeare without using Cliff's Notes or Wikipedia, how to put on blush without looking like Craze-o the Clown. Okay, most of those things I would have eventually learned from someone else, but I *liked* learning them from Sara. I like how knowledge can be a gift, and when I'm not running around being a pirate, I really do try to remember that around Finn.

"Seriously, it isn't okay," I say. "What you're doing. Mom and Dad are your *parents.* Just because Camille—"

"Don't finish that sentence." She retrieves a handful of underwear from her dresser, tucks them into her bag beside the sweaters and jeans, and zips it up. "I can't talk about this with you—"

"Right, my useless brain can hardly grasp such—"

She brushes past me to get to the bathroom to pack up some of her face and hair stuff and brushes right back in. "When will you stop it with that? You have it so much easier than you think you do."

Weird for me to be speechless, but that totally does it. Even if she's completely wrong.

"Please don't tell Mom I was here." She runs downstairs, and I stay on her heels. She switches her bag from one arm to the other as she riffles through the mail on the front table on her way to the door, which suddenly makes this seem a lot less like a great escape.

"Sara—"

"I'll see you, Kellie."

I sort of wedge myself between her and the door. "We could talk, you know. How you're crazy about everyone liking me or how I hate how things seem when you're not here or that Mom's totally going—"

"*Kellie,*" she says, but softly and gently. "Later. Now I have to go."

She doesn't just dash off to her car like I expect, though. Her gaze shoots past me, at the big painting on the wall of the big heart (Valentine's style not anatomical) Mom painted in her first art class. People always ask if it's by a famous artist. Next to the heart is a handmade frame, put together by Russell out of extra materials from building The Family Ink, holding the same picture that hangs in the shop's front room.

Funny thing is that when I really see the picture, as a third-party observer or whatever, this little voice in my head reports that it totally gets it. Russell and Mom, looking like a match made in heaven or I don't know, *Who Wants to Marry a Tattoo Artist?* Finn is the exact blend of them, and I look plenty like Mom, plus I'm wearing a T-shirt of Russell's. Then there is Sara in her J.Crew and glow of rosy perfection.

The front door slams shut. And Sara's gone.

So here are my options: A) stay here doing nothing, feeling kind of abandoned, and being a loser; B) see if Adelaide is free so we can, I don't know, talk about the *Ticknor Voice* instead of how my family is falling apart; C) report in to Dexter about Sara; or D) call my crazy boyfriend and either explain my run for Thai or ignore that entirely and make plans to *maybe have sex*. I did have a successful visit to the gynecologist and am now armed with birth control pills and condoms.

Obviously, a half hour later I am on my way over to Oliver's dorm.

I say, "Hey, I'm having a really bad night."

He asks, "Why, what happened, do you want to talk?"

And I don't. There isn't anything more I can say about Sara—and if there is, I don't want to hear it aloud. Instead: "The other night I really did have to pick up dinner. Mom and Russell get really demanding."

"Oh," he says, and, "right."

"Also," I continue, "I haven't had sex before, which I just should have said a million years ago, but now you know."

"Oh," he says again.

"Right," I say this time.

"I'm glad you're here," he says.

I grin at him. "I'm glad I'm here, too."

And we look at each other for maybe three more seconds before flying into Making Out Mode, and this time when I end up in Oliver's bed without my clothes, I don't want to cry and I don't want to leave.

It all goes sort of like I thought it would. We've been messing around enough by now to know at least the basics about each other, and I've only read a thousand articles online, thanks to Adelaide and my own Googling skills.

"You know," Oliver says, right afterward, "I love you."

Okay, bad form, but I totally snicker. "You do not."

"Kellie, yeah, I do. You're amazing."

"We haven't known each other that long," I say in my casual voice. "There's no way you love me yet. Like me, sure."

"Way to ruin a moment," he says, but he smiles.

"Sorry, but be serious." I thread my fingers through his, kiss him, rest my head between his shoulder and head. "What time is it? Am I going to get in trouble?"

"No, you're safe." Hopefully he is over his post-sex love-professing. "So was...was that okay?"

"What you said?"

"Obviously, what I said wasn't. No. Before."

"Before was really good," I say, which is absolute truth. It hadn't hurt as much as I'd expected, and Oliver made really cute faces during, and I guess I'd just been ready. I'd been so nervous about all of this, but even afterward when my brain had more time to think, those fears seem to have vanished. I made the choice to be here with Oliver and to be honest with Oliver and to have sex with Oliver. And I know it's cheesy to be..._proud_ of all of that, but I am. Also, as much as anything can, it erases that stupid afternoon in May.

"Yeah, I thought so, too."

We're both smiling, and it's maybe the best moment we've ever had, right then, and I really do think about asking, _Hey, did you murder someone? Hey, are you crazy? Hey, why is Dexter's life devoted to making up for yours?_ But I think about something Adelaide had said to Mitchell during a newspaper lunch when he'd inquired as to what went into the taco filling from that place down the street. _Mitch, don't ask_ *questions you wouldn't like the answer to.*

So instead we order in a pizza, go through his roommate's CDs (just to mock his bad taste, not to steal or anything malicious), and of course eventually have sex again, because it's now an option. And Oliver is nuts to think he loves me, or maybe just in some kind of post-sex haze, but okay, I like him *a lot*. I even tell him that while he's walking me to my car.

"I like you, too, but you know that." He kisses me for maybe the thousandth time tonight. "Talk to you soon."

"I can text you or whatever when I get home. It's not like Mom cares what I do as long as I'm in the front door by one." I sort of hear myself and realize how strange that sentence is to be coming out of my mouth. The fact that I now have a curfew-crazy mother is definitely among the low points of this fall. "Later."

Mom is, of course, up when I get home, deep into a book, but all her attention is on me once I walk in. "Hey, baby."

"Hey, Mom." I hover near the doorway instead of going in because I feel like if she gets close to me, she'll have an idea of what I've been out doing. Not that it isn't okay. I just don't really want to involve my mom in my sex life any more than I already have.

"Kellie, I won't be mad, but were you looking around in your sister's room for anything?" she asks. "I did some laundry earlier and noticed a few of her things were moved."

"Yeah," I say quickly, remembering Sara's request. Wait, why exactly am I protecting her? "No, actually, Sara was here, getting some stuff."

"Oh," she says. "Oh."

That last *oh* breaks my heart a little. "She's being a jerk."

"Try to be understanding. Your sister has a lot to deal with right now." Mom gets up, walks over, and kisses my forehead. "Good night, baby."

"'Night, Mom. You know…" I give her my very practiced casual look. "You don't need to stay up so late waiting for me. I won't break my curfew again."

"It's just part of being a mom," she says, even though this is clearly a very new part for her. "You'll understand someday."

Considering this is all Sara's fault, I hope I won't.

Chelsea texts me the next morning to see if I want to meet up for lunch. I assume it'll be her and Mitchell (so I agree), but when I get to Weber's, it's actually Chelsea, Jessie, and a few other girls from the paper. I start to ask why Adelaide isn't there, but even though I'm maybe closer to Adelaide than any other friend right now, I know exactly why. Adelaide can be crazy annoying.

I know that I'm sitting in a crowd of girls, and technically, they're my friends or at least fellow *Ticknor Voice*-ers, and last night I had sex for the first time and maybe kinda want to talk about it with someone. But I'm not there yet with any of these girls, not even Chelsea who I've been sitting with five days a week for a year now. It's not just that it's private—because of course it is—but also because they all already know I have a college boyfriend, and I've assumed my general attitude has seemed like I've already been there, done that. Literally.

So I don't tell anyone why I keep forgetting to pay attention or why I accidentally grin goofily multiple times or even who I'm texting. Half of my life might have completely been demolished, but at least I'm sitting in a group of girls who don't hate me—or make fun of me for ordering cocoa when everyone else orders coffee—and texting the amazing guy I've had sex with who—too early to say or not—might even love me.

After losing my best friend and being in the midst of losing my sister, I'm trying to dwell on what's still around.

CHAPTER TWENTY-TWO

On Tuesday I assume after newspaper I'm going straight to pick up Finn and then home, but once Mom texts that I don't have to, plans shift. I have coffee with a bunch of the staff and end up walking down to Dr. Jazz with Jessie and Paul to get ice cream. Paul makes another reference to me having a secret tattoo on my butt, and so even if I didn't already think he was into me or whatever, there's now seriously been enough butt talk to confirm that. Afterward, I immediately make a call to Oliver because I feel sort of weird spending so much time in the presence of one dude who thinks I'm that awesome when I am having sex with another one.

I still can't believe I am having sex.

When I finally get to the house, Mom is dashing around upstairs wearing her splurge-of-a-purple-dress. "Why do you look so fancy?"

Mom laughs, but it isn't in her eyes. That's weird; Mom isn't a lady who fake laughs. "Just a dinner I'm going to. Sorry,

Kell-belle, I'd love to ask about school and how everything's going, but I'm really in a hurry. Oh, and Finn's with Linda, you don't have to worry about him. Russell will get him on his way home."

"You texted me that part already," I say. "What dinner?"

"It's nothing." She kisses my forehead. "Just meeting with Sara and your dad and Camille."

Right, like that's nothing. "Are you guys going to talk to Sara about—"

"You know this isn't any of your business, baby."

It's not?

Mom walks to her and Russell's room and looks under the bed. "Where would I have put my brown shoes?"

"The ones with the little buckles? I have them." I run and dig them out of my closet. "Sorry, I should have asked."

"It's fine." She steps into them and surveys herself in the mirror. When I was little, I hadn't realized we looked alike at all. Something about getting older, though, the more I see myself in her, or her in me, or however that works. I guess it's nice then to see how pretty she looks in the purple dress.

"Maybe I should wear boots instead." She steps back out of the shoes. "What about yours, Kell-belle, can I borrow those?"

"Totally," I say and fetch them for her. With the boots in place, I realize you can't really see any of her ink, like she's just any old mom going to any old dinner. "Maybe pull up your hair?"

She shrugs, brushes out her dark blond hair, and secures it into a ponytail. Now, just barely, the four-leafed clover on the back of her neck is visible. She'd gotten it inked not long after Finn was born; every leaf is supposed to be one of us:

Russell, Sara, Finn, and me. Otherwise, Mom actually doesn't have a tattoo symbolizing Finn yet; she says she wants to know more of who he'll grow up to be before making such a permanent mark. (She's turned down all my suggestions, from a zebra to a ninja to the singing fish.) I understand, but hopefully by the time Finn is old enough to get a complex from such a thing, she'll have figured out the right image for him.

"Better?"

"Definitely." I'm still sort of angry, but I hug her anyway. "Have fun."

"Oh, sure." She gives me a tight hug. "Have a good night. Do you have something to eat for dinner? Give me a minute, I'll leave you some money so you can—"

"I'm okay, Mom," I say for whatever reason. "Just go."

She still shoves a few bills into my hand, then kisses my cheek before taking off. Obviously, since I have the house to myself for awhile, I call Oliver, who drives right over. I figure we'll just have sex, but he brings a pizza, since I'd mentioned I hadn't eaten yet. (I make him take half of the money Mom gave me.)

"Everything okay with you?" Oliver asks. Considering I've barely spoken to him, outside of making him take seven dollars, it would have been weird if he didn't ask.

"Just stupid family stuff," I say. "I really don't want to talk about it."

"If you don't want to talk, why'd you want me to come over?"

I try to give him A Look. It must have worked because he laughs.

"Yeah?"

"Oh, yeah." I get up from the table and take his hand to lead him to my room, like suddenly I'm the boss of our sex life. From the way he follows, though, it's safe to assume I am.

"This is a small room," Oliver says when I lock my bedroom door behind us.

"It used to be half of a really big room, but Sara and I didn't want to share." At Sara's name I feel like crying, so I pull Oliver back on the bed with me as a distraction to my brain.

Total success, of course.

Afterward, Oliver gets nervous that Russell or Mom is going to arrive home any moment, so he gets dressed and runs downstairs in a blur. I put on pajamas because they're more comfortable than the jeans and shirt I'd been wearing and chase him down in the driveway.

He hugs me really, really tightly. "You okay?"

"Sure," I say, because as far as he's concerned, I am more than okay. "Go, you probably have homework or something."

"I always have studying, trust me. But if you need anything, let me know." He kisses me before getting into his car, and I watch until he's backed out of the driveway and driven off down the street. Before I've even made it inside, Mom speeds in from the other direction and parks where his car had just been. It probably looks odd that I'm just standing there, barefoot and in my pajamas with messy hair, but it would look even stranger at this point if I dash inside. So I wait.

"Hey, baby." If Mom finds me suspicious in any way, it doesn't matter, because her face is red with mascara streaked down her cheeks in mean, wet lines.

I've never seen Mom look like this.

"Are you okay?" I ask, even though no one's looked like this in the history of being okay.

"Oh, Kell-belle, I'm fine." She gives me a big, big hug, like I'm a little kid, and I kind of scoop myself into it because despite the ten million reasons I shouldn't receive little kid hugs anymore, I really need this one. "Did you eat dinner?"

"Pizza," I say.

"Good girl." She smooths down my hair a little. "Are there leftovers?"

There are actually bizarrely few slices left, assuming I hadn't split the pizza with anyone (How can guys, even skinny guys, eat so much?), but Mom doesn't say anything about that, just takes the box out of the refrigerator and sits down at the table with a slice. I try to think of a good reason the pizza is from the place near Oliver's dorm that definitely doesn't deliver out here, but again, if Mom notices, Mom doesn't care. Maybe we are all lying, like me sitting here watching her eat like someone just let out of a hunger strike when I know she's just come from dinner.

"I'm glad we're here without Russell and Finn," Mom says finally after consuming the two remaining slices. "We need to talk."

"Sara," I say.

"Sara's going to move in with Camille," Mom says in a very normal voice. "For the time being."

"What?" Sure, I'd felt this coming, but I thought it would involve Sara running away and lots of protesting from Mom and Dad. "Seriously?"

"It's what she wants," Mom says, which makes me shake in what I realize is anger. There is a lot I want that I can't just go and do, and I don't believe for one second that once I turn eighteen all the gates will open.

"I can't believe you're just letting her," I say. "We're her family, Camille's—"

"Camille's her mother, too." Mom cries as she says it. This time I don't hug her. "And this is her decision. Not yours, not mine."

"No, it totally *is* your decision, but you're so obsessed with coming off as open-minded and supportive you're letting our family fall apart."

Mom bursts into fresh tears, which should have stopped me, but I'm on a roll. A roll of being a jerk, sure, but it's called a roll for a reason.

"Dad would have done something." Gross, why am I suddenly all pro-Dad? "He's just going along with you because you're so convinced letting us make our own choices is what's best, but sometimes it *isn't*."

"Kellie—"

"I'm really sorry you didn't make enough good choices for yourself and ended up with a job and a husband you didn't want, but that's not going to happen to me, and it wouldn't have happened to Sara." I don't know what I'm even saying, but I do know I mean every awful word of it. "We're not you, okay? And maybe if you'd been more of a normal mom, Sara would still be here."

"Go to your room, Kellie," says this voice behind me. Russell, who must have come in while I was yelling like an asshole at the only person who probably feels worse about all of this than I do. So I march upstairs.

I sit down at my desk and try to just text everyone like it's a normal night, but it isn't a normal night. My family is falling apart—*has* fallen apart—and now some of that is due to me.

After getting dressed, I throw some things into a small suitcase and walk back downstairs, where Mom and Russell are sitting on the living room sofa, her head on his shoulder, her hands in his. She is still crying. My heart and brain ache in a way I didn't know they were even capable of, but that isn't enough to stop me.

"I'm going to Dad's," I say.

"Kellie, baby," Mom says.

"Drive carefully," Russell says. "And call your mom when you get there so she doesn't worry."

"I will." And I know I will, too, even if it makes me so angry that Sara doesn't have to cater to Mom's feelings anymore, ever. "Bye."

I let myself in to Dad's, which I guess I shouldn't have done, because he's sitting on the couch with Jayne, watching TV, being totally normal except in Dad World. "Oh, hey, Kellie, there she is, we have plans tonight?"

"No, I just thought I'd... Sorry I'm interrupting or—"

"It's fine, it's fine." He jumps up and hugs me, a really tight hug from Dad. "You remember my friend Jayne?"

"Hi, Kellie," she says, walking over and shaking my hand. "It's good to see you."

"You, too. I'm sorry I didn't call, and I really just need to sleep, so—"

"Jayne was just leaving," Dad says, which is obviously news to Jayne.

"Dad, she doesn't have to go," I say, and not just because even in my current state, I'm dying of curiosity. His craziness is so unfair to her, which means we have at least that much in common.

"Well," he says, giving a wary glance at Jayne, "all right."

"Are you hungry?" she asks me. "We have leftovers from last night."

I'm suddenly starving, actually, so Jayne ducks into the kitchen even though I insist I can help myself. Dad still stands next to me. "Sorry for—"

"Kiddo, you okay?"

Hello, of course I'm not okay. "Sara's gone. Why aren't you guys freaking out?"

Dad sighs and shakes his head. "You don't get a standard-issue rulebook when you become a parent. You're just trying to do the best thing, and right now this is what Sara wants."

"I want to quit school and travel the world," I say. "Are you going to let me do that?"

"I'm sure you feel like you've lost your sister," Dad says, weirdly enough understanding me for the first time in forever. "But I think everything will be fine."

"Why would Sara come back when she finally gets to leave the freak family behind? It's like her dream come true."

Dad ruffles my hair. "You've got to be wrong about that much, kiddo."

"Here you go, Kellie." Jayne walks back into the room with a plate of some kind of fish with carrots and a little salad (clearly she'd cooked because Dad doesn't even order meals that well-balanced), and the three of us sit down. Them on the couch, me on the floor. "How have you been?"

It's either a really generous or really stupid question considering I am clearly mid-meltdown. "I'm fine. How are you?"

"Great," she says with a big grin. Jayne is sort of average looking, but her smile is really good. Straight white teeth, dimples, the whole nine yards straight out of a toothpaste ad. "Three cats at the shelter went to new homes today."

"Good for them."

"It's wonderful," she says. "How's school? The paper sounds fun."

I nod and take a few bites of what turns out to be salmon. Not bad. "The paper is really fun, yeah. Which I guess is weird."

"Not at all, I was on yearbook in high school, and I loved it."

I nod. "This salmon is really good, did you make it?"

"Well, my friend sent me the recipe," she says. "But I did, and I'm glad you like it. Though Clayton says you and Sara aren't picky like he is."

I can't imagine Dad talking about us beyond things like *Sara does everything right* and *What did I do wrong in a previous life for my genes to produce Kellie?*

"I should probably head out." Jayne rises to her feet and walks to the coat tree to get her blue coat and matching scarf. "I'm trying to line up enough volunteers for an upcoming event, and I won't feel settled until I have more accomplished."

"What kind of volunteers?" I find myself asking.

"We're throwing a fund-raiser for the rescue group," she says. "Do you know anyone who'd like to help?"

"If my friend Adelaide's free, I know she'll help. She's addicted to volunteering. I can ask if you want."

"Kellie, that'd be great."

"Oh, and I guess I can probably help, too, if you need

people, though I'm not very good at much."

Jayne bursts into laughter like I've just made the best joke of all time. "Of course I'd like your help. Clayton, send me Kellie's email address so we can get everything set up, okay?"

"Okay," he agrees like he's just been beamed in from another time period and can't imagine what has led him to this very moment.

I stand up to carry my plate and glass into the kitchen. "I should probably try to sleep."

"Hey, kiddo." Dad walks into the kitchen after me. "That was a nice thing you did. I know Jayne really appreciates it."

I nod and find myself giving him a hug like when I was little, clingy and sad and broken. Sometimes I wonder if he misses those days, too. Yeah, people rarely think fondly of a divorce, but back then he was just *Dad*. He wasn't the guy I'm capable of disappointing just by being me.

By the time I brush my teeth and change into my pajamas, I remember I'm supposed to let Mom know I'm safely here. The thought of talking to her is way too much for me, so I just text. And for maybe the first time in my cell phone–having life, Mom doesn't respond right away with an, *I love you, Kellie baby*.

CHAPTER TWENTY-THREE

I go straight to English lit the next morning, dropping my head to the surface of the desk and praying Jennifer will let it go. For some stupid reason, I haven't counted on the real boss of that classroom demanding otherwise.

"What's with you?" Adelaide sits down in front of me and turns around to tap the top of my head. "Night is for sleep, the day is for knowledge."

"Shut up," I mumble. "My night was not for sleeping."

"Brooks, look alive." She keeps tapping me until I finally sit up. "Much better."

"Seriously, you have no idea how bad my day was."

"Oh," she says. "Are you okay?"

I fold my arms on top of my desk and rest my chin on them. "I am completely the opposite of okay."

"Is it about Oliver?"

"It's about Sara moving out for good."

"Oh!" Her brown eyes are round behind the horn-rimmed

glasses she wears on occasion. "That's *interesting*."

"No, it's not *interesting*, Adelaide, it sucks. My family's falling apart."

"I read an essay the other week about adoptive families versus biological—"

"Do you get this is something I'm actually going through? I don't want to hear about some essay you read."

"Kellie?" Jennifer walks over to my desk, holding out a hall pass. "Get your assignment and notes from me later. You look like you could use a free period."

"Thank you." I grab the pass from her and don't look back. Of course Ticknor cares a lot about their students' mental health—or they want to appear that way at least—so we have a little lounge where you can hang out quietly if you have a pass. There's a rule against sleeping, but it's enough just to curl up on the sofa by the window and try to turn off my brain. By the time first period is over, I feel a little more like I can deal with life, though I change my mind on that when I practically run into Kaitlyn in the hallway.

"What?" I snap.

"Kellie, are you okay?" She touches my shoulder, a move only Former Kaitlyn would have made, not the one standing in front of me. "You look—"

"I'm not, not that it matters." I pull away from her even though that brief touch had felt as if we'd never fought. "I have to get to class."

"What about that?" She points to the pass, still clutched in my hand. "You could get another hour out of that if you wanted."

Kaitlyn uses one of her free periods to work as an aid to the school administration, sort of weird for someone who isn't a goodie-goodie or obsessed with her college application. It is helpful in skirting the rules without getting in trouble, though.

"I could come with you." She pulls a laminated pass out of her purse. Laminated! "If you want."

Yeah, Kaitlyn is practically my enemy now, but I do want.

We get our jackets and walk outside to the courtyard. It's been chilly out, so no one's been using it lately, but it's not so cold that everything has been put away for winter yet, so there are still chairs to sit in.

"What happened?" Kaitlyn asks me. "Is it your boyfriend?"

"Why does everyone think it's him? No. It's Sara."

One thing I have to admit that Kaitlyn is very good at is listening, when she wants to, even now. She sits there quietly while I lay it all out there, from me learning Camille had called Dad in the first place, to last night when I'd found out the horrible news immediately before turning into the biggest jerk in the whole world. Of course by this point in the story I'm crying, but Kaitlyn doesn't look horrified, just wraps her arms around me, a hug like we haven't had in forever. Way longer than we haven't been talking.

"I wish you would have told me sooner," is what she finally says.

"When? When you were yelling at me or ignoring me or—"

"I miss you," she says. "A lot. I just didn't know how to keep being your friend and doing the same stuff all the time when there was all this new stuff, too."

"Everything else that's cooler than me?" I ask but at least in what I mean to be a semi-joking tone.

"Not cooler," she says, which is probably her attempt

at being nice. "Just different. I've known you since we were eight, Kell. I'm not the same as when I was eight. You aren't, either."

"I guess I understand that," I say. "But you weren't really fair to me. It's dumb that just because I'm a nerd about music and I think coffee's gross that I wouldn't have anything left in common with you anymore. There are a lot of ways to grow up."

"Yeah." She nudges my foot with hers. "I guess I see that. We just felt like we were going in different directions. And I didn't know how to keep being your friend if that's what was going on."

It's the kind of thing I want really badly to disagree with, but then I think about secretly applying for newspaper, and in one go I get what she's saying. Even if she was a jerk about it.

Why is this stuff so weird and complicated?

"I *miss* you," she says again. "And I'm sorry stuff's been bad for you. At least you have a boyfriend, though."

Leave it to Kaitlyn to keep priorities straight.

"You should eat lunch with us today. I know you don't think you like Lora and Josie, but they're actually—"

"No, I mean, they're your friends now, so I won't say anything, but I just don't think we'd get along. I probably have newspaper stuff today anyway."

"Your articles are really good, I keep meaning to tell you."

"Aren't you too cool to read the *Voice*?" I smile so she'll know I'm kidding, even if like 5 percent of that isn't a joke. Maybe 15 percent? "Thanks."

"So your boyfriend's *hot*," she says, which I'd had no idea

I'd been desperate to hear, but, *yes*. At one point it would have been as if Oliver hadn't even existed until Kaitlyn had agreed on his level of attractiveness. "Have you guys done it yet?"

"You're not just asking so you can report back to your posse to help them complete some sort of virginity chart of our grade, are you?"

"Kellie, God, you know I'm not." She is awfully huffy for someone who's ignored me for so long. "So you haven't."

"No, we…we have," I say, as it dawns on me that she is still, after everything that has happened, the first one I've told.

I kind of like that.

"Oh," she says, "my God. You have to tell me everything."

"I do not." But I grin at her. "I'll tell you some of it, though."

We sit there until the bell rings, and then she hugs me again as we head in separately. Honestly, I want to cry even more now, because now that I don't hate Kaitlyn, I just have to miss her even more. Maybe we mean everything we said, though. Maybe even without sitting together at lunch and basing our weekend plans around each other, it will be okay to text when we need to, to chat if we're both on our computers, to say hi in the hallways and sit by each other in class. It's hard to wrap my mind around it—having Kaitlyn back but not really all of Kaitlyn. I guess it is a lot better than nothing. I'm pretty sick of nothing.

I go back to Dad's after school (well, and after hanging out with the newspaper staff for a while). He's working from home, which I don't expect, though he doesn't seem shocked to see me. Even more strangely, he asks about school and offers to make me dinner without any prodding about my homework or upcoming tests or college prospects.

"I talked to your mom today," Dad says while I'm plowing into the tortellini that is surprisingly edible. "She told you not to worry about Finn this week, and if you want to stay with me, of course that's fine."

Of course when I'm a royal jerk to Mom, she repays me by being fair and kind and all of that. Way to make me feel worse. Also, maybe that whole time I'd been hating how I felt taken for granted while Sara began her rebellion, I should have just said something instead of expecting Mom to read my mind. Open and honest probably does make a lot of sense, as far as family mantras go.

"Seems like you're a lot of help to Mel," he says, like he's just figured out I'm good for anything besides disappointment. "I'm sure she appreciates it."

"Don't go on Mom Defense," I say.

"Trust me," he says. "I'm not."

"I don't know why you ever married her," I say, only because it's my first real chance to say it to him. I've never gone to Dad's to get away from Mom before last night.

"Kellie..." Dad sighs and rubs his eyes with his hands. "It was a long time ago. We were both pretty different people then."

"Really?" I say. "*You* were different."

Dad sort of shrugs and then takes a few bites of pasta. "I guess I wasn't. Nothing to be ashamed of, is it?"

"I think it's a good thing to figure out who you are and just go with it." I shrug. "I hope I don't have to wait as long as Mom did to know that much."

"There's a lot about your mom that hasn't changed at all,"

he says. "Like you and Sara being her number one priority."

That's true, but I don't want to give him the satisfaction of being right at the moment.

"And why would you say that anyway?" Dad asks. "It's pretty obvious to me who you are."

I'm afraid he'll temper anything nice with also defining me as crappy at school or something, so I just jump up and hug him before carrying my plate and glass to the dishwasher.

I call Adelaide a few minutes later, hoping for advice on theorems as well as my very own family situation drama. Of course she's only good for the first, but it's still good to hear her voice and think about geometry instead of real life. And I know Kaitlyn would be good for both, but despite my determination to try to have her in my life in this new way, I'm not quite ready yet to call her up like things are fine and dandy.

Sitting on my little futon and resting my head against the tastefully painted wall, I realize I'm homesick for my Oprah-approved paint job and impressive collection of Beatles posters. The thing is, though, even if I were ready to make up with Mom, which I most definitively am *not*, it isn't fair to her yet.

If I'd really lived my life to her open and honest mantra, we would have talked sooner, and it wouldn't have built to this head that exploded like a disgusting zit when the Sara stuff happened. Right now Mom and I probably need each other, but here I am in this stupid Asian-influenced room that doesn't feel like mine, and Mom is without both her daughters.

And no matter how far I dig down in me—and it turns out I have way more depth than I realized—I have no idea how I could fix it.

CHAPTER TWENTY-FOUR

After a few days at Dad's, I'm not necessarily any better. My nerves make me feel wound up like one of Finn's toys that marches across a flat surface, my guilt makes me feel, I don't know, Catholic or something, and sadness sort of oozes all around me like I've gone emo. This needs to change; the last thing I want to be is a Catholic emo wind-up toy. I guess I'm less raw, but it's hardly enough to call my state of mind an improvement.

Eventually, my curiosity gets the best of me, and while I'm killing time with the newspaper staff after school, I do a little Googling until I pull up the information I want. (Google, unlike many things in life, rarely lets you down.) I'm terrible with directions, but I pull those up, too, say good-bye to everyone, and am on my way.

Camille's house is a cute, midsized brick two-story in the enviable location of U City, with my sister's car parked out front. I seriously believe that my heart literally aches to see it.

As always, knowing is one thing, seeing another.

I pull in without thinking, and somehow am thinking even less as I park, get out, and walk up to the front door. My finger pokes the doorbell, and I wait. (Obviously, by now, I am absolutely not thinking at all.)

The door opens, and while I'd hoped for Sara, it's Camille standing behind it. Of course she's wearing great jeans and a gray sweater I can tell is expensive, and her hair is brushed back into a Sara-style perfect ponytail.

"Hi," she says. "Can I help you?"

I kind of stare at her, like how dare she forget who I am?

"Oh," she says with a bit of a start. "You're Kellie."

"Yep. Sara's sister," I add for emphasis.

"I didn't realize Sara was expecting you," she says.

Something about how she says it has me clenching my fists. Clearly, I'm supposed to turn around and go. "She's not. Can you let her know I'm here?"

"I know she's in the midst of her calculus—"

"It's important," I say. "It's a family issue."

"Well," she says. "Let me check with her."

She at least has me wait inside the front door and not out in this windy, cold air. Her front room is pretty plain, totally Sara's style, with everything neat and in its place. I would hate a home like this. At least Dad's has calculated personality.

Sara walks down the stairs toward me. "What are you doing here? It's kind of creepy."

"Right, checking in on my only sister who I have hardly seen in forever is so frigging creepy." I'm relieved Camille at least seems to be giving us privacy. "Sara, we really need to talk. Things are falling apart."

She shrugs with her eyes on her feet, not me. "Why is that my fault?"

"I don't know how you could say that. You know we need you, Sara, you're like the only normal person any of us have."

"That's not true," she says.

"Is it because Mom's a freak?" I ask. "And Russell? And Dad's all…Dad?"

Sara doesn't say anything, which feels a lot like *yes*.

"Right now I think this is where I need to be," she says finally.

"Does she know what's going on?" I point upstairs like I actually have any idea where Camille is. "Or care?"

"This isn't about Camille," Sara says. "And I know you refuse to believe me, but it's not about you, either."

"Right," I say. "So who's it about, then?"

She finally looks at me, stares really hard. "God, Kellie. *Me*, maybe?"

Why do I suddenly feel like the role of Kellie is being recast as a villain?

"Nothing's about just yourself," I say. "Everything you do touches everyone else."

"You," she says, "make things…" She holds out her arms, like for a hug, but I know that isn't the point. "So *big*. Sometimes they aren't. Sometimes they're…" She brings her hands in, clasps them together like she's just captured a lightning bug.

"Sometimes they're bigger than you think." I turn and walk outside, surprised but not upset that Sara follows me. "What?"

"I'm asking you to understand," she says. "Even if you

don't think you do. I think you can try."

"Trust me," I say. "I understand why you'd want to leave us. We're weird and useless, and you're everything someone should be. I get that. What I don't get is why you think it's okay."

"Kellie, *shut up*," she says, the knifelike edge back in her voice. I can't believe I'm already used to it, when it didn't even exist before Camille came into our lives. "If you can't even try to understand..."

"I hate how unfair you are."

"I could say the same about you." She turns on her heel, looking colder than the chilly air. "Drive home safely."

I think about not doing so just to spite her, but, really, self? Bad idea. Instead I just get into my car as she walks into the house, and I crumple over my steering wheel in tears. I text Oliver a frantic *can i please come over??* And start to—with my crying now under control—head there, before my phone beeps with *Tonight? Am stuck in meeting for group project.* I deliberate between the rock and a hard place of texting Adelaide (not awkward, not helpful) or Kaitlyn (super awkward, potentially super helpful) and think about seeing what Mitchell or Chelsea is up to. But I know I can't really fully be honest with them about Sara, so I text Dexter instead.

Even though he suggests a half dozen places to meet up, I am not exactly in any shape to hang out in public. So I end up just heading to his house, which is probably actually worse than being tear-stained in public, considering the last time I'd been here had been that day in May. I've stopped dwelling on it, especially now that apparently Oliver and I are going to have sex regularly and it isn't going to make me cry, but it's still a little weird.

"Hey." Dexter opens the front door and steps aside. "You any good at zombie slayage?"

"The situation's never presented itself," I say. "Also I really hope you're talking about a video game."

"Just got it, not having any luck with the zombies. Come on."

I follow him downstairs to the TV room, which seems to be only for him and Oliver given the total dude movie posters. It's not shocking, considering that the McAuleys are definitely better off than either one of my families. They can afford a room just for kids to hang out in. "Is this like your fortress of solitude?"

"More like my bat cave." He settles on the floor and grabs a game controller. "Come on."

"Fine, fine." I sit down next to him and glance his way, thinking I probably should tell him what just happened with Sara, but it's tough forming the actual words. All of it sucks, from Sara being a jerk, to me falling apart in the car like someone in a made for TV movie. I do at least successfully take down a line of zombies, though. Small victories.

"You okay?" I ask like I'm not the one who's clearly been recently crying.

"My girlfriend's still refusing most of my calls," he says. "Not really. You?"

"Not at all," I say. "But aren't you like the most popular guy at Chaminade?"

"And that has to do with what?"

"Just, you know. Is pining over Sara necessary?" Sara is my family, and I have to fix things with her for something bigger than both of us. For Dexter, though, it is totally a choice.

"What're you saying, Kells?" he asks as I accidentally collide zombie-killing gun barrels with his avatar.

"Oops, sorry."

"Get out of my space, woman. And there's girls lined up so I can just forget about Sara? There are dudes besides Ol who want to jump you, so if something happened you'd be over him right away?"

"I guess that wasn't fair of me."

"Not much, nope." Dexter's avatar is killed in battle with the zombie lord, so I do my best to take care of that job on my own. "Also the hot/genius combo thing doesn't come along all the time."

My little avatar is also reduced to a pile of bloody guts, so Dexter restarts the game. "Yeah, Sara's pretty special."

"So things good with Ol?" Dexter asks. "He's cool to you and all?"

"Is there some reason he wouldn't be?"

"Well, Alice," Dexter says like he would have said *blue* if I'd asked what color the sky was. "But he's better now, yeah? I guess I still worry about the guy sometimes."

My heart hammers out a scary rhythm in my throat. "Who's Alice?"

"The girl?" Dexter is still talking like I'd missed out on life lessons like how to breathe and whether or not ice cream is tasty. "You know, the whole reason for the direction of his life."

"Oliver's life is all directed at some girl?" I ask, adding *who isn't me?* only in my head.

"No, just—You know the story, Kells."

"I actually don't." I know enough, though. I know this

has to be what Oliver had done to also change the direction of Dexter's life. Maybe I shouldn't learn this thing.

"Oh." Dexter sets down his controller, meaning zombies quickly devour him. "I kinda think you should know."

I don't like the sound of that at all! People don't say things like *I kinda think you should know that you're actually owed a billion dollars!*

"Ol had this girlfriend his junior year," Dexter says. "Alice. He was really serious about her, but I guess she was just having fun. He falls pretty fast when he's into someone."

I start nodding like *oh my God, yes!* but stop when I realize this is not something to bond over and be excited about.

"Alice was a year older and was getting ready to go off to college in Seattle. Ol *freaked* out, started saying all of this crap to get her to stay, tried to find out if he could follow her to Seattle, just crazy shit. Of course, she breaks up with him, because she's going off to college and doesn't want to deal with a lunatic. One night after she'd left for school, Oliver took a bunch of pills. I found him right away, called 911. They pumped his stomach, and he was fine."

I just sit there and stare at him.

"I'm sure he's cool with stuff now," Dexter says, like that will take away all I've just heard, from the craziness to the wanting to move and the *trying to kill himself.*

"Was it scary?" I ask, even though it's hard imagining Dexter scared of anything. "When you found him?"

"Scariest thing in my whole life." He runs his hands back through his hair. "He's a good guy, Kells. It shouldn't change things, if they're good."

"Mostly they're good," I say.

"Mostly ain't bad," he says and picks up his controller again. "Trust me."

"I'm in high school, though," I say. "Isn't making stuff work for marriage and other crap grown-ups do?"

He looks at me so long the zombies get him again. "I guess I don't expect everyone to be so perfect."

Oliver calls me while I'm driving from the McAuleys' to Dad's, but I just side-button him. He leaves a message about hanging out tonight, but even though it'd been my idea, I delete it and don't call back. It definitely isn't his fault I found out today, but I don't know how to just talk to him like things are normal. I mean, except that they are.

Obviously, I don't say anything to Dad, just finish all of my homework except geometry, which I slog through just enough not to fail. Hopefully. Oliver sends a cute text (*Roommate wants to know why his stuff was moved, I blamed a hot oceanography major*), but I can't make myself respond to that, either.

If I were home, I might talk to Mom about it—not that Mom and I have some great history of boy talk (as much as she'd love that)—because while she's kinder to people than I am, she would also look out for me above anything. There isn't anyone else in my life who can dial up that particular combination. If she were here, she'd know what to say. Too bad she isn't. And worse, that I don't exactly deserve her advice now.

The guilt should have eaten at me the next day, but it just gets easier ignoring him, even after he sends a checking-up-on-me text that isn't even creepy or intense. I really don't like this side of myself. Also, I hate that the one person I'm shutting out is the one person in my life right now who is 100 percent there for me. After Sara had completely shut me out, how can I do it to anyone else? Does the crazy excuse it?

Adelaide and I meet up at The Beanery after school. She's brought all these environmental issues of actual newspapers and magazines for me to look over, like something *Time* did is really going to have an effect on the *Ticknor Voice*. I sweep them into a neat little stack that I can reach but she can't.

"So," I say. "Dexter told me about Oliver."

"And?"

"'And'? It's a big deal."

"What's a big deal?" asks Paul, who out of nowhere sits down at the table next to us.

"This is private," I say and look back to Adelaide, whose eyes are of course on the stupid stack of planet-saving publications. "I'm being serious."

"I don't know what to say," she says. "I don't think it is a big deal. Oliver's a good guy. He dove into boyfriend mode before I could have handled it, but you and I are different people, and you seem to have handled that much fine."

I wad up my napkin in frustration and even think about throwing it at her, which would be pointless but a little satisfying. "I just wish I knew what to do."

"You have to figure that out yourself," Adelaide says. "All I can say is that if you like Oliver, you'd be a jerk to end something just because of that. People have all done crazy things before."

I want to say that I haven't, but I guess that just depends how you define *crazy*.

"It doesn't *define you*," she says, like if she could speak in all-caps, those two words would get that treatment. "I will absolutely lose respect for you if you break up with him over this, Brooks."

"Oh, sure, that makes sense. Oliver and I have nothing to do with you. Like maybe I have enough crazy to deal with right now." I don't want to sit around and hear how I am a bad person about this, when in my head I'm already dealing with what a bad person I am to Mom and Russell and Finn. And of course what a bad person Sara is to all of us. It's way too much. "I think I'm going."

I grab my bag and walk out to my car. There are footsteps behind me the whole time, but I don't bother to look. "What?"

"Hey, Kellie, you okay?"

It isn't Adelaide. It's Paul. His presence makes me feel like some idiot on a dating show forced to pick between her cute, smart college boyfriend who just might be crazy and a saner-seeming high school guy who she knows little about except that he's a responsible member of the *Ticknor Voice* who's stared at her butt on multiple occasions. Door number one or door number two?

"There's just a lot going on," I say.

I should have said I was fine and just gone. I know. If this were actually that dating show, I'd be screaming at my TV by now.

He leans against my car. "Want to go talk?"

No, no, no. "Don't you have something to do?"

"Not really," he says. "If you need someone to listen…"

The voice in the back of my head is still screaming *no*. "I just need to sit down." I unlock my door and get in, and then I hit the button so the passenger door unlocks, too.

Clearly, I've taken leave of any brainpower I once had.

"Adelaide's just stubborn." He sits down in the car. It's always weird seeing someone new in an old setting. "I wouldn't take her that seriously."

"It's not just Adelaide." Not that I want to talk about all that it is. "Are you guys friends?"

He leans over to mess with my iPod resting in the console. Why is this dude in my car? I don't even want him touching my stuff. "Anyone who's taken a class with Adelaide knows that much. I like her, but she's a lot to deal with."

I feel a defense of Adelaide rising in my chest. "She's probably going to run the world someday, so you should stay on her good side. Maybe you should go."

"If you want." Then he leans in and kisses me. I push him back as it happens, but I feel weird that it even got to that. Should I have known that letting him into my car meant getting kissed? No, I'm pretty sure that's not a rule.

"I have a boyfriend," I say. "You know that."

"I saw you guys arguing at the Halloween party," he says. "I thought maybe you didn't anymore."

"You have to go," I tell him.

"Sorry if I—"

"Just go, okay?" I'm not sure if I should be this snappy to him, but I don't want him around, either. "I just—"

"It's cool," he says, like it actually is. "See you at school."

I give him a little wave before peeling out of the parking lot and getting on 44 right away to drive straight to Oliver's dorm. I've ignored him *for days*. And I didn't kiss another guy, I got kissed, but it still doesn't seem like the kind of news to break my silence with.

Oliver opens the door looking all excited to see me, which just makes me feel worse. I'm planning on nicely explaining things have been tough, and I was surprised, not terrified—I promise myself I will not at all use any word like *terrified*—to hear about the Alice situation.

But instead I start crying like that day back in May, like yesterday in my car parked in Camille's driveway, the crazy kind of crying I still can't really accept I'm capable of. Oliver, to his credit, doesn't look disgusted with me, even when a big glob of snot escapes my nose and kind of flings off onto the floor. A guy who doesn't flinch at snot is a good find.

Then it all comes out at once: "Sara moved in with her biological mom, and I said some really crappy things about it to my mom—even if they were true—and Adelaide and I are fighting, and I don't even know why, and I went to Camille's, and Sara acted like leaving us was no big deal, and—"

"Kellie—"

"And Dexter told me what happened with you—with you and some girl named Alice, so—"

"Kellie." He puts his hands on my forearms, sort of like he's steadying me but also clearly to turn off my rambling confessions. "Are you all right?"

"Do I look all right?"

"Upset, yeah, but okay, too."

I'm able to stop crying, so I guess he's right.

"I probably should have told you about what happened with Alice, but it was a while ago and it's not like that's how I am now."

I nod because I want it to be true. I nod because I think about all the changes I've made myself to be a person I'm proud to be—exempting this week of course—and if I could manage to do that at just the start of my junior year, Oliver could come a long way in a couple years.

"I don't mess up like I used to," he continues. "I promise, I—"

"It makes me nervous," I say, which is true and honest and sounds a lot better than *terrified*. "And some things, you know, they made me nervous already."

He runs his hands through his hair, steps back just a little. "Are you breaking up with me?"

"No, I—" I cut myself off because I don't actually know. I wasn't here to break up with him, but now that I am and I think about how there's a dark side to his intensity, I don't know what I want to do. "Another guy kissed me. Do you hate me?"

"Who?" he asks. "Did you kiss him back? Was it mutual?"

"Just this guy from the paper. And it wasn't mutual at all. All him." But I can't stop thinking about how I'd kept thinking in the moments leading up to the kiss that Paul would be an easier boyfriend than Oliver, and I still feel guilty. Nothing about Oliver could necessarily go in the *easy* column but maybe that doesn't matter? He's unafraid of my snot, and he's always been there for me. "Honestly, right now I don't know what I want. Is it okay to think that?"

He takes a really deep breath. "You mean with us."

"I mean with *everything*. If I've lost Sara…" I cover my

face with my hands so he won't notice a few more tears slip out, not that face covering is some subtle move. "I'm sorry, Oliver. I think I should go."

"Yeah," he says. "I think you should, too."

"Okay." I back up to his door. "I'll text you?"

"Are you okay getting home?" he asks.

For now I nod again. It's sweet he wants to make sure of that first. Maybe once you try to kill yourself, you get really sensitive to other people's stuff.

"I'm fine," I say finally. "Well, obviously not fine. But you know."

I wait a moment for him to say something sweet, even something weirdly intense or a little crazy. I wait for him to be *Oliver*. But all he does is reach past me to open the door and nod as I continue backing up, into the hallway.

"Bye," I say.

"Good-bye, Kellie," he says. And I wish hard that it won't be the last thing he ever says to me.

CHAPTER TWENTY-FIVE

At Dad's, I cry a little more, then distract myself with homework and a marathon on Bravo of some real housewives of wherever. Now that I'm at Dad's full-time, he's not working from home as much, so I'm on my own. Normally, here that's preferred, but there's literally no one at all I can talk to right now. The fact that Dad suddenly seems like ideal company probably is a red flag we're headed toward the apocalypse.

My phone buzzes, and I feel the caller has just saved humanity from the end times.

"Hi," Oliver says. "Are you okay?"

"Sure," I say, trying to infuse that syllable with enough sanity to be credible. "And, hi."

"Do you have time to talk?"

"Yeah," I say.

"I know you have a lot going on," he says. "Because of Sara and everything else. I really was going to tell you about Alice eventually. It might have freaked me out, too, if I heard it about someone."

"Maybe it shouldn't," I say. "I don't know if I was fair about that."

"My therapist says maybe I fell for you too fast," he says. "He says maybe I'm going to mess up again, but I think I just like you a lot."

"I like you a lot, too," I say, something I know without uncertainty. "I'm sorry if I overreacted or whatever. Sometimes you freaked me out, though. Before I knew about you and Alice, too, just…getting obsessed with my Facebook, stuff like that. You should just trust who I am."

"I know." He's silent for a bit, so long I almost make one of those lame *Can you hear me now?* jokes. "Maybe we should just take a break or something."

"Does that mean break up?"

"No, you have stuff to deal with that's really important with your family, and you're right that some of the crap I said to you wasn't that cool. I mean, if that's what you want."

"I don't know what I want," I say.

"You don't always have to, Kellie."

I laugh and realize I'm sniffling a little, so the laugh comes out loud and snotty. It's good I already know Oliver can handle that. "I hate it when I don't."

"I get it, but letting go of control can be really helpful sometimes," he says. "So…a break?"

I agree even though I can't believe I'm purposefully putting distance between myself and someone else right now.

"We can still talk, though," he says. "If you need to. Or want to. And I don't care what you put your status as."

"You totally still do." I laugh so he'll know I'm not creeped out by the truth.

"Maybe. I'll try not to. Call me when you want to talk."

"I promise I will," I say.

"I know you will. Good-bye, Kell."

I find Paul first thing the next morning, unfortunately hanging out with Mitchell. "Hey, can we talk?"

"Yeah, sure," Mitch says, before he catches on that I'm not talking to him.

"Later," I tell him, walking off in the opposite direction of my locker.

I turn to face Paul, who's strolling along besides me. "Sorry if I was rude yesterday."

"You're sorry? It was all me." He claps me on the arm, like that isn't weird or anything. "Don't worry about it."

"Sorry if you got your hopes up or whatever," I say.

He laughs in this way I don't really *love*. "Kellie, you're cute, but I'm not in love with you or anything. It's not a big deal. At all."

Yikes, blow to the ego, sort of. "Oh, okay."

"See you in class," he says and strolls away.

I guess a bad part of me did hope Paul was desperately in love with me, because maybe it would prove something, like that I was interesting or super appealing to guys or mature in a way I'd like to be. But I know deep down it wouldn't prove any of that, and also, I'm trying to apply my honesty all around—including with myself. And that also means I don't avoid Adelaide when we walk into Jennifer's classroom at the same time.

"Hi," I say.

"Brooks, what?"

"Was I a jerk yesterday?"

She makes a bunch of huffing sounds.

"I'm sorry. Okay? I just have a lot going on. And you should *know* that." I sit down in my usual spot, and luckily, she takes her usual seat in front of me. "Are you free after school?"

"Not until eight," she says. "Distributing flyers for Growing American Youth before. You can just come over if you want."

It's not the friendliest invitation, but she's stopped huffing, so clearly we're fine. And I pick up coffee for her and cocoa for me that night at the local coffee shop in Dad's neighborhood before driving over to her house, and if there's anything that fixes everything for us, it's our usual beverages.

"So." I take a few sips of my cocoa. It's scary even thinking about saying this. "You got really mad yesterday, the way you thought I was mistreating Oliver or whatever. Like up until now, you've been the first one onboard the Oliver Is Maybe Too Crazy for Me train."

"I never said that. I said I personally wouldn't have been able to stand the way he jumped right into being your boyfriend. His sanity never came up."

"I just mean that you seemed to take it really personally. You can say if it's none of my business, but…" I summon the strength to ask Adelaide of all people a freakishly personal question. "Did something happen?"

"Nothing as dramatic as Oliver's post-Alice episode," she says. "But, sure. I used to cut myself. It wasn't a big deal."

"You don't have to say it wasn't if it was. You don't have

to be so frigging *Adelaide* about everything."

"Look who's talking, jeez, Brooks." She elbows me, hard, before grinning at me. "You sound like my therapist."

"I guess your therapist is pretty cool then."

Her smile fades just a little, and she shows me some faint scars on her arm. "It was a big deal then, but it isn't now. Therapy's a good thing."

"Yes, definitely," I say.

"Your mom said if I get a tattoo here, the scars won't show at all anymore. So next year, as soon as I'm eighteen…"

"You talked about this *with my mom*?"

"It just came up, because I had been thinking about the tattoo for a while. And your mom's easy to talk to, you should know that."

I don't want to sit around and think about how great Mom is, even if it is true. "You can hardly even notice the scars."

"*I* notice them." Her voice falters a little, which is weird. Adelaide doesn't falter. I guess everyone's more than you think they are. "Whatever, it's dumb."

"It's not dumb. I just didn't want you to be self-conscious or something. Mom says tattoos are—ironically—really healing. Also like life-changing, I guess. She wouldn't have figured out she needed more in life if she hadn't gotten her first one." Great, now *I* am saying nice stuff about Mom.

Adelaide sort of bolts toward me, and I worry she's going to knock me down or something. But, no, Adelaide is hugging me.

"It would kill me, Brooks, if you went back to being chummy with Kaitlyn Hamilton. I know it's ridiculous; it isn't as if I ever get possessive about Byron. You should be friends with whoever you want to be, sure, but you're smarter than that."

"I'm not sure I am," I say. "I mean—Kaitlyn's a really big part of my life, well, at least she was. I guess it's good that isn't gone completely. I don't really want to lose people, though, if I don't have to."

"Just because your sister's having some sort of quarter-life crisis, that's no reason to cling to heinousness."

"Kaitlyn can be a good friend," I say. "Sometimes. I don't think that because it's not smart, I think it because it's just true. She's a better listener than you, for sure."

Adelaide narrows her eyes. "Nice."

"It's true," I say. "It's awesome you care about the whole world. But I'm part of the world, you know, and I'm right here."

"Point taken." Adelaide flops onto her bed. "Back in grade school, I used to be really popular. You probably don't believe me, but I was."

"I believe you. Also I remember."

"I've tried really hard to limit my friends to people who won't pull that crap on me anymore," she says. "If I'm wrong about you—"

"You're not wrong about me," I say. "Trust me. I'm a really honest person."

Dad and I go out for Mexican that night, which involves driving across town to the place on South Hampton he's really into, weirdly enough, despite it not being boring or stuffy. I normally don't eat there, because even the beans are cooked in lard, which means it's basically a huge danger zone for Russell. How weird is it that I miss worrying about his stupid eating habits? Not that they are actually stupid, just annoying sometimes.

I'd asked him about it one night, because we were supposed to be this open but respectful family. Okay, at the time I'd just been mad we couldn't go out for burgers at the place Sara and I really liked that doesn't have veggie burgers, but it gave me the excuse to finally bring it up.

"After Chrystina died, I'm not proud, but I did a lot of things that weren't good for me or anyone else," he told me. "Too much drinking. *Way* too much drinking. And the way I treated my ex back then, just terrible. I was in a lot of pain, Kell, but that was no excuse."

I liked that I was just a kid but he still laid it out like that, not trying to make it something it wasn't.

"When I got myself straightened out, I knew I had to give something back, make things right with the world, I guess, some kind of sacrifice for me," he said. "That's what I came up with."

It's totally not fair, but even now sometimes I want to ask Dad if I'd be worth going vegan for.

As I get into bed later, my phone blinks with a text from Oliver making sure I'm doing all right, and I think about how even though maybe we won't ever be together again, he's still looking out for me. I think about Sara, and how — despite what she's done — she probably needs taking care of just as much as I do. So I tap out as innocuous a text as I can manage (*sorry for drama last time we talked...up for real talk soon?*) and send it to her.

She doesn't respond, but I still feel better when I fall asleep.

It's about a week later when Dad knocks on my door (a somewhat big occasion, as we've mostly been keeping to ourselves). I minimize my chat windows with Adelaide, Chelsea, and Jessie, and make this big show of looking over my copy of *Macbeth*.

"You have a minute, kiddo?"

"Sure, what's up?"

"I'm glad you've been spending more time here lately, don't get me wrong, but you think maybe it's time you head back to your mom's?"

"Right now?"

Dad laughs like that's actually funny. He is still pretty weird. "Not this second. Just later this week? Soon? Mel's got to be missing you."

"You don't miss me when I'm not here?"

"It's different, kiddo," he says, which isn't at all what I want him to say. "But you're welcome here, Kellie, you know that."

I'm really happy to hear that, which then makes me really sad. Being wanted at your dad's shouldn't be some cause for celebration.

"What's wrong?" he asks me, and this is probably the first time he seems to have accurately picked up on one of my emotions.

"Nothing," I say, but then I change my mind. Honesty,

self. "I know you wish I was more like Sara and less of a screwup. But I'm just me and I wish you could finally be okay with that."

Dad's eyes go really wide, and I laugh despite that this is kind of a serious moment.

"I don't wish that," he says.

"Dad, come on. You're always saying stuff about how Sara never gets Bs or that I could take things more seriously—"

"Well, you could, kiddo. I can tell how smart and talented you are, and sometimes it's like you go out of your way not to make use of any of that."

I shrug. "I've been trying not to be like that lately. I just wish I didn't have to figure out what to achieve so you'll finally be proud of me."

"Maybe I'm bad at showing it, but of course I'm proud of you, Kellie." He ruffles my hair. "Okay?"

"Proud of me for what?" I laugh so I won't cry. Crying out of happiness always feels so goofy. "Give me a specific example."

"Always trying to take such good care of your whole family," he says. "And you're a very clever writer. Maybe next year for the paper you could—"

"Stop talking," I say because I can tell the nice stuff will be over any minute. "And thank you."

"Have you been thinking about our trip?" Dad nods to the college guide he gave me that, truthfully, I've been looking through more and more lately.

"A little." I haven't highlighted or flagged any pages, but I do have a small list started. "We're definitely going?"

"Sure. Start a list, we'll get a route planned."

I really like the sound of it and that I've already made the right first step, so I promise I will. I also promise I'll at least think about going back to Mom's soon.

The thing is, I want to return with Sara in tow. There isn't any proof my twice-daily text plan is breaking any ground, of course. Still it feels good not to be completely out of contact with my sister—one-sided still counts, doesn't it? And how great will it be to walk back into the little house on Summit Avenue a hero, our prodigal Sara returned to us?

Still, I can't avoid the inevitable forever, and maybe that's how long Sara will be gone. Also I want to work on this part of my rep or whatever I'm comfortable with. And being honest doesn't seem to go with hiding out at Dad's.

Not forever at least.

CHAPTER TWENTY-SIX

It's Thursday of the next week when Adelaide brings fliers about a writing competition to English class and gives me my own copy before handing the others off to Jennifer. My instinct is to shove it into my bag without a second look, until it hits me that would be incredibly stupid. After all, not only do I actually *like* writing now, but people seem to think I'm at least okay at it.

"You really think I should enter?" I ask Adelaide, since I'm still getting used to this whole idea of not sucking at everything useful, not because I'm fishing for compliments or anything. (Okay, I am fishing a little.)

"Hmmm." She seems to consider this. "No, but only because I want less competition."

I could have jumped up and hugged her right there.

So I'm going to say that it's my excuse, or my proof of, well, *something*. Because even though ideas for an essay are flooding my brain, I shove them aside and spend the day writing something else instead. Normally, I just write my

"Ticknor Ticker" columns to crack myself up, but next week's is going to be different, even if at our meeting I said I'd be writing about standardized testing.

When I turn it in to Adelaide, she slips it back to me. I'm expecting a big note like, *WHAT ARE YOU THINKING, BROOKS?* but she just has her standard edit notes for me and a smiley face.

"Kellie!" Jessie flags me down after our last class on Friday, and I realize she's standing with Kaitlyn. "I read your column for Monday."

"Oh, um, cool," I say, even though I'd kind of forgotten that even if you write something super personal, if it's for the paper, other people will read it.

"It's really good; I related to it a lot."

"We're getting coffee," Kaitlyn says. "Do you want to come with us and get your stupid hot cocoa?"

She grins as she says it, so I agree. And we grab Chelsea on our way out, who has typical Mitchell-type complaints, and Kaitlyn tells us how disappointing it was when she finally made out with Garrett because apparently he's not that great of a kisser, and I feel okay admitting to everyone that Oliver and I are on a break. It's not the most personal conversation in the world, but everyone has advice. Maybe at this very moment I don't have anyone I could call at one a.m., but maybe before long I will again.

After school on Monday, I drive up to U City, ignore the car in the driveway, and reread my column and attached Post-

It one more time before sealing the *Ticknor Voice* in an envelope labeled SARA and leaving it in the mailbox.

SARA! We're not allowed to dedicate our columns to people (I asked), but if we could, this one would be for you. Let's talk about everything. Whether or not you want to come back, I think I can ask this much, I hope? So let's meet tomorrow: 4pm at the Old Orchard Starbucks, totally safe, no one we know goes there. Love, your sister, Kellie

THE TICKNOR TICKER
BRAVERY (IT'S NOT FUNNY)
By Kellie Brooks

I always thought I was brave. Being brave seemed the best thing a person could be. You could defeat anything or at least not be afraid of it as it defeated you.

Earlier this year it started hitting me that maybe I wasn't actually that brave, at least not all the time. This seems like a pretty obvious statement, because who's brave all the time? Even lion tamers probably cry over a breakup, and astronauts might get a little freaked out if their best friend wasn't returning their texts. I don't know why I thought I was some magical exception, when in all truth I wouldn't even be comfortable one-on-one with a lion or the depths of space.

This probably seems like a personal topic and not something to be explored in my column, not like a universal issue like why the lunch courtyard still smells a little like poop. But I've been so preoccupied this year trying to be what I thought everyone expected of me that I got tackled by change. And once I started worrying a little less about being brave and more about being honest, everything's been easier.

Change doesn't have to be the end of the world anyway. What if no one had invented the wheel or iPhones or hot cocoa? Those probably all seemed like crazy ideas at the time, but we'd live in a horrible place without that stuff.

So, my advice—not that anyone's specifically asked for it—is to just worry about being you and letting other people be them. Life works a lot better that way.

When I pull into the parking lot at Starbucks the next afternoon, the nearest empty spot is right next to Sara's car, and I feel my heart soar. I wasn't really sure my column would work—and maybe it won't, not completely—but it's a start.

Sara's sitting on one of the plush purple chairs inside, and I force myself not to barrel into her for a hug like Finn would. "Hey."

"Hi, Kellie." She doesn't get up, so I just sit down across from her in the other purple chair.

"Thanks for coming," I say, instead of telling her how

great she looks, because she does, new haircut and highlights or something, like she isn't perfect enough as is. Also she's wearing jeans and a sweater, not her uniform, and it's always sort of special seeing her in anything but.

She opens up her cell and shows me her text message inbox. *KELLIE KELLIE KELLIE DEXTER KELLIE.* "I never realized you're so…"

"Annoying?"

"Tenacious. Let's get cocoa."

"Definitely."

I follow her to order our drinks and then settle back in the purple chair with my hands around the warm cardboard cup. I haven't really thought my plan out past getting her here.

"Sorry about the other week," she says. "We should have just talked then, I know. You just really caught me off guard."

I nod. "Me, too. I mean, if you needed some space to think or whatever, I guess I could have tried to give that to you."

"I know I messed up," she says. "Not with you—not *just* with you."

"Yeah," I say and want to punch myself almost as soon as it's out of my mouth for not just forgiving her and hugging my arms around her and saying something like, *We'll be okay forever and ever from now on.* Honesty, though.

She shrugs, leaning over so her blond hair falls in front of her face like a shampoo commercial. "Camille gets it. You know? I know it's a really clichéd accusation to make, but Mom's never understood me. I know she's proud of me—"

"Mom's not exactly shy about telling us that."

"Well, right. I always feel like I'm a letdown, though.

You're so creative, and Mom's so *interested* in your life. I feel so dull. Dexter seemed like the only exciting thing I've ever done."

We both giggle at how sexual that sounded, like perverted little kids.

"I just always thought it evened out," I say. "*More than* evened out. Considering Dad—"

"I know it seems like that," Sara says. "But it's not like he seems much more interested, as long as I keep up my 4.0 and follow in his footsteps."

"Do you even want to be a lawyer?"

She shakes her head and laughs. I join in. "Dad just expects so much, and Mom expects so little. And then I met Camille and it was as if someone finally saw me as I am."

"I totally get that," I say.

"Really?" She sounds genuine so I don't protest. "I read your column, but still, someone like you—"

"Someone like *me*? What does that even mean? I'm frigging *nobody*."

"Right, yeah, you're just really funny and interesting, and you always have people to hang out with, and…" She pauses and blinks a few times, and it really takes me this long to realize that Sara is crying. "Anyone can make people proud the way I do. You have so much more going for you. It makes me crazy you act like that isn't true."

"We should just stick together," I say. "Our powers combined can rule the world."

Sara laughs again, which is much better to hear. "I like the way you think." She bows her head down for a few moments, but I know her well enough to give her the time to get her thoughts together. "This might sound kind of strange, but I just needed to keep Camille all to myself. I didn't want her getting your or Mom's version of me, definitely not *Dad's*. With Camille everything felt pretty limitless, which I don't think I've ever had. I could be whoever I wanted to be, which, honestly, was just myself."

"I never used to realize people needed fresh starts when they were in high school," I say. "Like it feels like it's this big thing I'm on newspaper and trying to be…"

"More?" Sara asks gently.

"More. *Exactly.*"

We exchange smiles.

I pause before I say the next thing, because it is really nosy and I'm not even sure I want the answer, especially after having this amazing little connected mind-meld thing. "So is Camille, like, your mom now?"

Sara shakes her head for a long time. "Camille's important to me, and always will be part of my life. But Mom's my mom."

"So then you'll come back home?"

"I don't think it's that easy, Kell," she says. "I've hurt Mom a lot. I can't just walk in and have things be fine now."

"No, but…" I rack my brain for ways to end the sentence. I guess the truth will have to do. "I hurt Mom a lot, too."

"Right," she says. "As if that's even possible with you two."

So I tell her. I repeat the terrible things I said, and I tell her how Mom cried and I did nothing. And I even tell her about that disappointed look on Russell's face, even though it hurts my stomach just to think about it.

But then I keep going. I guess I'm getting better at thinking on the fly, because all of a sudden I see so clearly this plan that is going to fix everything. So—making up big chunks of it as I go—I lay it all out for her. I know from her raised eyebrows she is dubious, but I've found I'm really good at winning people over through sheer enthusiasm. How else would my little brother be so okay with eating vegan cheese?

"I don't know," is all she says at the end of it.

"You can't hide out forever," I say. "And I can't, either."

She is silent as she sips her drink. I feel her slipping away from me again.

"Sara, this is our *family*. It's the most important thing in our lives."

"I just…" It feels like such a revelation seeing Sara unsure of anything, but maybe I've just never allowed myself to before. "I don't know."

"You *do* know," I say, even though who knows if that is true or not! I am on a mission. "Sara, we cannot be people who sit back and just let stuff happen. We have to be more than that. *Right*? We have to fix this."

"Oh, fine," she says. "I don't see you letting up anytime soon."

I leap to my feet and do a victory dance, not caring that the place isn't exactly empty. Not only is Sara coming back, but it's definitely safe to assume I'll never be considered useless again (except with math). "Let's go do it."

"Yeah, you'll need my research skills. Come on, if you're quiet, we can go use the college library."

I call the shop while we walk over. I assume Jimmy will probably answer, but it's a relief when he actually does. Through very little effort, I find out Mom is working late and Russell is already off. So after our few minutes of research

(Sara really does have mad skills), Sara and I drive home, like it's a normal day, even though of course she'll have to drive me back to my car later.

"So." She takes an opportunity to glance at me as she merges onto Big Bend Boulevard. "How's everything with Oliver?"

"We're actually on a break." Ooh, I am using TV relationship lingo for real. "I sort of messed up with him, too. But there's also him being kind of...intense."

"Yeah, I don't know how much you know, but...that's why I was initially wary about you going out with him. It was never that you weren't good enough."

Maybe she'd been butting in, but I do like that she was looking out for me.

"So, I know it's not really my business, but...I totally get why you felt like you needed space from everyone, but Dexter—"

"It's just never really been easy being with him," she says. "I'm this total nerd who just cares about school, and for some reason this hot, popular guy *likes* me. And I've always tried to ignore how it shouldn't work at all, but the more I was feeling truly accepted as I was, the less I could stand the thought of trying to be cool enough for him."

"You are an idiot," I say, but nicely. "Dexter is frigging crazy about you. Yeah, you're a school nerd, but he is, too, sort of, and you guys like all the same stuff, and he thinks you're gorgeous, and he is going totally insane over the way you're treating him."

She laughs. "I should have talked to you about him sooner."

"Yeah, you should have! And you're calling him later. I

will dial your phone myself if I have to."

"I promise," she says, pulling into our driveway. "You don't need to go that far."

"Can I ask...have you guys done it?"

"You can ask, sure," she says. "But no. I've been so stressed about school and college applications. We've agreed to wait until we get our acceptance letters."

I can't help it. I laugh really loudly. "That's the nerdiest sex plan ever."

"I didn't say it wasn't." She grins at me. "What about you?"

"Yeah, that happened. Before the break. Yes, I was careful, yes, he was nice, yes, it was great." I never expected to experience anything big before Sara, but it doesn't feel like some life contest. It just feels like how we've always talked, and I'm so glad one less topic is off the table now. "I kind of wish it wasn't over. Does that seem crazy? Even with knowing about the whole Alice thing and all?"

"It doesn't sound crazy at all," she says. "Dexter says he's better. And your judgment's good, Kell. If that's what you want, it can't be too crazy."

Coming home has never felt so scary and awesome simultaneously. Everything looks exactly the same—I've only been gone a few weeks, what did I expect?—and it smells the same, too. That sounds weird, but houses definitely have scents, and the house on Summit Avenue smells like Mom's giant collection of vanilla candles at all times. Even though she isn't there, it makes me miss her just a little less.

This is how it goes: we say sorry, Russell has practically forgiven us before we even speak. There is more hugging— especially enthusiastic from Finn. I make some dumb joke about how you *can* come home again, and not only does Russell laugh but Sara does, too. I let Sara lay out the plan and watch Russell's face slowly light up like sunrise after too long a night.

Sara and I go back to Dad's afterward, all part of the plan. Dad is—not surprisingly—very low-key about my sister's return, which just feels like the universe clicking back into place. I, on the other hand, want to make a really big deal, shout it out like Finn had, leap around and praise the heavens. Someone like Sara, though, wouldn't love that, so instead I give her little smiles whenever I can, and at the end of the night, I give in and hug her. The good news is that she hugs back really tightly.

"Don't ever leave again," I say.

"I have college next year," she says. But her arms stay wound around me. "By then I'm sure you'll be dying for me to go."

"Probably." I grin at her again before taking off to my room. I text everyone while working on my homework, but not about anything big or important, just the regular stuff. As always, being alone with my phone can be dangerous, and tonight's no exception. I scroll down to Oliver and click to text him. *i miss u. can we talk soon?*

He doesn't respond immediately, which I take as a good sign that he's working on his intensity. But my phone lights up my nightstand once I've turned the lights off to sleep, and his response is exactly what I was hoping for. *Of course. Call me when you can.*

Sara and I walk into The Family Ink at four. Russell just grins at us, but Mom leaps up from her station, her eyes wide and a smile threatening to break loose from her lips. "Girls!"

"Hi, Mom," Sara says, and Mom's grins breaks out full force. Right away I know everything will be fine.

"Sara." She hugs her for a really long time. "You look beautiful, sweetheart. Your hair's amazing."

"Think you can copy it next time?" she asks. "The salon's really overpriced."

"Definitely," Mom says, but I hope Sara gets less sentimental by the time that rolls around, because Mom can definitely not handle those perfect blond highlights, no matter what she thinks of her skills. "Kell-belle."

In a weird way I'm pretty sure I've let her down more, but still she hugs me for just as long. "I'm really sorry, Mom."

"Oh, baby, I know." She pats my head like I'm a dog or something. "It's okay if we don't always get along, you know. My mom and I fought all the time when I was your age."

"That's not me, though," I say, which is kind of silly because even though things are fine, it isn't like I'm suddenly never going to argue with Mom again. It feels good to say, though, and from Mom's expression it probably feels good to hear.

"Girls, I'm really sorry, but I've actually got two back-to-back appointments starting any minute. After that I'm probably free so—"

"We know," Sara says.

"We're your back-to-back appointments!" I shout, even though I promised Sara she could say this part. Sometimes I worry my emotional age isn't that far ahead of Finn's.

"Excuse me?"

"You heard 'em." Russell carries over the design we'd requested. "Here you go, Mel."

"But!" Mom stares at us, her blue eyes wide. It's such a Finn expression I giggle. "Is this a joke?"

"We really want to do this," Sara says. "We did some research on family coats of arms. And we gave Russell the Brooks and Stone ones, and he combined them so—"

"Stone," Mom says. "Our name, really? Not—"

"We thought about your maiden name," I say. "But Stone's the name you picked, and it's Russell's name, and Finn's name, too. So—"

Mom bursts into crazy tears, and I throw my arms around her to calm her down. (Of course she just cries more.) "You two are serious about this?"

"Like the plague." I worry the design will get crushed in the mayhem, so I hand it off to Sara. "So come on. You're eating into our appointment time."

She laughs as she wipes away her tears. "You're not even eighteen, young lady."

"Russell'll sign for me. Come on."

"Who's going first?"

"Kellie." Sara shoves me toward Mom. "Right?"

"I guess I have to." Up until now I haven't really fully considered I'll be actually getting a tattoo today. I've only seen a million, but this is going to be mine, and therefore is going to hurt *me*.

"Where are you getting it?" Mom asks, and I also realize I haven't considered that much yet, either. But my bicep seems a good choice. Lots of people can see it, but I can keep it hidden when I need to, and also it isn't one of those stereotypical girl places to get inked. I'm not starting off with that.

Mom rolls up my sleeve, cleans off my skin, and presses on the transfer design, just like I've seen her do a million other times for a million other people. She tells me to walk to the full-length mirror so I can decide if I like the placement or not (I do, and Sara and Russell approve, too). The Brooks coat of arms is topped with a little lion, while the Stone one has a lamb, so it is totally like destiny knew we'd do this one day and got Mom and Russell together accordingly. Russell designed the animals to face each other, which is like the cutest thing ever obviously, but he did it in a way where it doesn't look cutesy. Within the shield part, he combined the funky little turrets of the Brooks shield (Sara promises me it doesn't necessarily mean we were historically warmongers or something awful) with the eagle and flowers of the Stone one without making it look crowded or messy or ill-planned.

It is seriously good we're family because there's no way Sara and I could afford artists of Mom's and Russell's caliber otherwise.

"This is so funny." Mom lines up little tubs to hold the different color inks, securing them in place on the Saran-Wrapped counter with Vaseline. "I guess I thought I'd give you a tattoo someday, but never so soon."

"You have to tell me exactly how much it hurts," Sara says to me.

"I don't think it works that way," I say.

"The pain's part of the process," Mom says. "Don't you want to feel like you earned it?"

I don't know about that, but all of a sudden the tattoo machine is buzzing, and Mom is moving it in my direction.

It's a lot louder when it's coming right at you.

"I'm just going to do a tiny bit," Mom says. "So you'll be prepared. Okay?"

I nod.

"Breathe out, Kell-belle."

I do, and the tattoo machine is on my skin for just a second. It is sort of like a very direct bee sting, maybe not even that bad, though one you can't slap away. "I thought it'd be a lot worse."

"It isn't that bad," she says. "Also, you're a tough one."

"Also, that's not really a painful place to get one," Russell calls, but I decide to ignore him and dwell on being tough instead. I watch my reflection in the mirror as Mom slowly does the outline.

"This is such a milestone," Mom says. "My first tattoo changed my life."

"How did you know?" I ask, because even though I've heard the bluebird story a million times, until now I've never really thought about what led up to it, only what came after.

"It's hard to explain. I just *did*. All of mine, I knew. Even my tree, which took the most planning—" She gestures like I won't know what she's talking about, when the magnolia tree, inked by Russell, growing up the length of her inner left forearm isn't exactly easy to miss. Russell sports a matching one inked by Mom, as they'd gotten them in between their wedding and honeymoon. "I just knew this is what I wanted. I'm definitely more me than without."

I try to imagine Mom without her ink, and my mind grinds to a stop. "Well, *yeah*."

The outline's finished, so she switches off to coloring in the tattoo. The shading hurts way less than the outline—it's a fatter needle—and it goes just as fast as I've seen hundreds of times for other people.

"Okay, baby, I think we're finished." Mom wipes the tattoo a few times, cleaning off the excess ink and blood. I can see in the lighter spots that it's still bleeding, but not really that much. And who can't feel like a bad-ass with a still-bleeding tattoo? "Go look in the mirror. Sara, I'm getting a soda, and then you're all mine."

I walk over to the mirror, examining my newly inked arm. "It looks good, right?"

"It does," Sara says. "Russell, you did a really good job with the design."

"Thanks." He nods toward Mom in the back room. "This is a really good thing you girls are doing."

"We just wanted cool tattoos," I say, which makes him laugh.

"Right." He looks from Sara to me. "Good to have you both back."

Mom rushes out with a Diet Coke and her camera. "Russell, take a picture of Kellie's arm for me, would you?"

"Of course." Russell takes the camera from Mom and zooms in on my tattoo. "You know they're addictive, right?"

"All the customers say so. I don't know what I'll want as badly as this one, though."

"You did start off pretty big," he says, while Mom is getting to work placing the design on Sara's ankle. I knew she'd go with one of those girl spots. I guess for Sara it is still pretty bad-ass. "Good to see her like this, isn't it?"

"Both of them," I say. "Seriously, Russell, I'm sorry I was such a jerk."

"We're all jerks sometimes," he says. "Don't make it

more than it is. I gave my parents way more hell. Crossing my fingers Finn's like you two and not me."

"Me, too." I laugh and walk over to Mom's station where Sara is grimacing as Mom inks the outline. "It didn't hurt that much."

"Ankles are worse, Kell-belle," Mom says. "Be nice."

"Are you free after this, Mom?" Sara asks. "We could get dinner."

"Kellie would have more of an idea than I do. Do you know what a great job she does helping us run the shop?"

"I'm not surprised," Sara says as I walk over to check Mom's schedule. The spot is wide open so I ink in, *Dinner with my newly tattooed daughters!* "Kellie's really good at keeping everything together."

ACKNOWLEDGMENTS

Thank you to my agent, Kate Schafer Testerman, for signing me many billions of years ago based off of this book and believing in it for the same reasons I did.

Thank you to my editor Stacy Cantor Abrams for helping me whip this sucker into shape. The heavy lifting and the tears were worth it! Lots of thanks to Alycia Tornetta for being truly one of the most helpful people I've ever worked with.

I am sure I never would have completed this book without the help and encouragement of friend, critique partner, and generally cool person Meghan Deans. So, you know, thank you for that.

Thanks to all the early readers and supporters. *Ink* was technically my first book, regardless of publication schedule, and letting others into my fictional world was a new and scary thing for me. So thank you to Andrea Robinson-DiNardo, Liz Kies, and Lindsay Ribar. And thank you to critique partners who helped more recently: Sarah Skilton, Christie Baugher,

Maurene Goo, Brandy Colbert.

A huge thanks goes to Kevin Fanning for (correctly) correcting me on Kellie's favorite album by The Beatles. Thanks to Scott Singer, who has a PhD in physics, for telling me what a person might do with a PhD in physics. Thanks to my St. Louis crew for help with the research that was hard to do from long-distance: Jessica Hutchins, Stephanie Myles, David Sullins.

Thanks to my incredibly talented cover photographer and designer Jessie Weinberg, and to model Kristen Williams. Thanks also to Mike Erwin for designing the cover's tattoo.

Thank you to every tattoo artist who's inked me.

And, lastly, thanks to my parents for their constant support, for playing the oldies station so much in the car when I was little, and for having (almost) as cool a family business while I was in high school as The Family Ink.

Get tangled in our Entangled Teen titles

The Summer I Became a Nerd by **Leah Rae Miller**

On the outside, seventeen-year-old Madelyne Summers looks like your typical blond cheerleader. But inside, Maddie spends more time agonizing over what will happen in the next issue of her favorite comic book than planning pep rallies. When she slips up and the adorkable guy behind the local comic shop's counter uncovers her secret, she's busted. The more she denies who she really is, the deeper her lies become…and the more she risks losing Logan forever.

Allure by **Lea Nolan**

Emma Guthrie races to learn the hoodoo magic needed to break The Beaumont Curse before her marked boyfriend Cooper's sixteenth birthday. But deep in the South Carolina Lowcountry, dark, mysterious forces encroach, conspiring to separate Emma and Cooper forever. When Cooper starts to change, turning cold and indifferent, Emma discovers that both his heart and body are marked for possession by competing but equally powerful adversaries. A magical adventure where first loves, ancient curses, and magic collide.

Relic by **Renee Collins**

In Maggie's world, the bones of long-extinct magical creatures such as dragons and sirens are mined and traded for their residual magical elements, and harnessing these relics' powers allows the user to wield fire, turn invisible, or heal even the worst of injuries. Working in a local saloon, Maggie befriends the spirited showgirl Adelaide and falls for the roguish cowboy Landon. But when the mysterious fires reappear in their neighboring towns, Maggie must discover who is channeling relic magic for evil before it's too late.

Get tangled in our Entangled Teen titles

Olivia Twisted by Vivi Barnes

Olivia's natural ability with computers catches the eye of Z, a mysterious guy at her new school. Soon, Z has brought Liv into his team of hacker elite—follow his lead, and Olivia might even be able to escape from her oppressive foster parents. As Olivia and Z grow closer, though, so does the watchful eye of Bill Sykes, Z's boss. And he's got bigger plans for Liv...

Hover by Melissa West

On Earth, seventeen-year-old Ari Alexander was taught to never peek, but if she hopes to survive life on her new planet, Loge, her eyes must never shut. Because Zeus will do anything to save the Ancients from their dying planet, and he has a plan.

Out of Play by Nyrae Dawn and Jolene Perry

Rock star drummer Bishop Riley doesn't have a drug problem. But after downing a few too many pills, Bishop will have to detox while under house arrest in Seldon, Alaska. Hockey player Penny Jones can't imagine a life outside of Seldon. Penny's not interested in dealing with Bishop's crappy attitude, and Bishop's too busy sneaking pills to care. Until he begins to see what he's been missing. If Bishop wants a chance with the fiery girl next door, he'll have to admit he has a problem and kick it.